IRON-BOUND FLAMES

THE RAEK RIDERS SERIES

Iron-Bound Flames

A Warrior at Heart

As Easy as Falling

A Flight of Fancy

The Middle of the End

IRON-BOUND FLAMES

THE RAEK RIDERS SERIES
BOOK 1

MELANIE K. MOSCHELLA

For Louisa, my everything.

NOTE TO READER

Dear Reader,

This series addresses serious, potentially upsetting topics. For a full list of sensitive subject matter, please visit my website: melaniekmoschella.com and select the Content Warnings page. I hope you will join my characters in finding the strength they need to overcome their struggles. However, if you feel any of these topics might be detrimental to your well-being, I encourage you to pass on my books and find your reading bliss elsewhere.

With love,
Melanie

IRON-BOUND FLAMES

Arborea
The Penchin Sea
The Cerun Sea
Terratelle
Altus
Harringbay
Cesor
Disputed Boundary
Terratelen Troops
Aegorn Troops
Aegorn
Sangea
Forest of Noavan
Riders Peninsula
Levisade Estate
Riders Holt
Levisade

PROLOGUE

Meera awoke to the shouts and stomping feet of the other palace staff. She sat up in bed and rubbed her eyes to clear them before realizing she couldn't see; it was still full dark. Heart racing, she leapt up to pull open the shutters of her small window and collided with her roommate, Teardra, who had also risen hastily from bed. Teardra shoved her aside, flew blindly to the door, pulled it open, and went running down the hall in her nightdress, barefooted.

The dim light from the torches in the hall illuminated the room enough for Meera to pull on her boots and cover her immodest slip with a blanket before joining the stampede. Panicked staff in varying stages of undress jostled through corridors, eddying her with them in a bumping, rocking tide. She breathed heavily, her heart pounding as she stumbled down the hall and descended the narrow, winding staircase. She was swept away by the rampant panic despite having no notion of its cause.

Was there a fire? An attack? Why were they fleeing, and would she get out in time? Then she heard it—the sound that had raised her fellow runners from their beds: a horrible, hair-raising shriek. It was an unfamiliar and frightening sound, and as she and the other staff rushed toward the outer doors, the shriek rose again— this time louder. It was then she realized they were running *toward* something, not away.

She and—it felt like—all the other palace inhabitants, staff and nobles alike, poured into the front courtyard. The moon was a fingernail sliver, providing very little light, and Meera could only see those closest to her. They were all awake and alert, if disheveled from their haste. Heads swiveled, and wide eyes groped the night air, searching in the dim light for the source of the noise. Some were scared and huddled close to friends and family, appearing to shrink against the unexpected and unknown. Others craned their necks, growing larger in their excitement—fueled by the deviation from their usual routines.

Meera tried to step to the side and find space for herself but was jostled and pressed forward in the heaving crowd. Stumbling along, she focused on keeping her feet under her so as not to fall and be trampled. She tugged her blanket tighter around her shoulders in the chill of the night, but when the cry came again, her chill moved bone-deep, contracting her core like freezing water. The piercing wail echoed in her body, rattling through her frigid insides and lodging tightly in her chest. The crowd froze with her.

"It's a raek! They caught a raek!" someone yelled. Sure enough, over the heads of the others, Meera could see a writhing black shape being dragged through the palace gates into the courtyard. In its hulking presence, the uniformed men trying to maneuver the struggling animal looked more like toy soldiers than flesh and blood. The only known creature that size was a raek, though she had never thought to see one in her life. The scholar's daughter in her craned her neck in fascination even as the rest of her recoiled from the savage scene.

A cheer rose in the crowd. Servants and nobles alike lauded the accomplishment of the returning soldiers, striking their hands together in a strangely violent expression of joy—celebrating the men's success in capturing what they believed to be a monstrous beast. She didn't join them; she felt more like crying than clapping —like the animal's anguish and agony were her own.

The raek was tied with ropes and being dragged along by at least thirty soldiers. A cart in front of it held a crate, and when it passed before a group of torch-wielders, she could see the figure of a man hunched at the bottom; the soldiers had two captives. Meera had seen enough. She tried to turn, to leave, but was herself caught, unable to direct her movements in the throng.

The still-growing crowd quickly impeded the procession's progress, and the shout of "Back inside! Get back inside!" sparked a slow herd movement through palace doors. But Meera's relief at the shout was quickly replaced by a growing, unutterable panic as bodies continued to surround and suffocate her with no end in sight. She held in her own wail as it strained to escape her mouth and rend the night air alongside the raek's, not wanting to cause a scene and embarrass herself.

The shuffling of the others shepherded her inside where the stone walls and low ceilings of the servant's hallways only increased her sense of confinement. She was crated on all sides by people and palace, moving forward in an agonizing trickle. She clasped her arms even tighter across her chest to make herself smaller—to make herself disappear. The staleness of the indoors and thick stench of breath and bodies made her lift her face and gasp for fresher air.

When the opportunity for escape arose, she flung herself into a side hall that led away from the servant's quarters, and she breathed and breathed. Still, the jumbled frenzy of the herd's excitement rang out around her even as the masses of people passed her by. Everyone was eager to share what they had seen of the fabled creature outside. She heard shouts of demonic horns and a pronged tail, red eyes, and some even swore they saw it breathe fire. Meera had seen none of those things—only a large, mistreated animal. She tried to tune out the uproar and steady herself.

She waited until the shuffling of feet and ringing of voices died out. She waited in silence, unnoticed. She breathed again and again until the crowd thinned and dispersed, then she emerged to walk back to her room, alone. Teardra was already snoring when she returned.

1

Meera stood over the kitchen basin, scouring the large stew pot for what felt like the hundredth time that day. Her hands were raw from the near-scorching water and lye soap, steam billowed into her face, and she could feel little hairs lifting away from her scalp to frame her in a halo of frizz. A loose curl swung down from its haphazard bun and stuck to the sweat on her forehead. Wiping it away with the back of her hand, she paused to straighten her aching back.

Standing and stretching, she groaned, knowing no one would hear her over the din of shouting and clanking metal. It had been half a year since she'd started working in the palace's kitchen, and she had just started to feel like her body was acclimating to the job's physical demands when the bustle of the exceptional week had seen fit to prove her wrong. The raek's arrival had caused an unexpected uptick in kitchen work with the coming of soldiers, curious nobles, and messengers from all over Terratelle, and she could feel the added work in her screaming arm muscles, pounding feet, and spasming back.

Meera was accustomed to spending her days at home, pouring over books and manuscripts by her father's side—a far cry from the demands of kitchen work. She smiled, remembering how she had had to remind her passionate but forgetful father to eat, bathe, and go outdoors when he had obsessed about his research. Then her wistful smile evaporated from her face with the steam rising around her and the realization that there was no one to care for her father now—wherever he was. Moisture clouded her eyes, and she brushed at them self-consciously as if brushing away sweat.

Gripping the stone sink basin and scrunching her eyes shut, she tried to conjure an image of her father's face—his crinkly eyes under wire-framed glasses and hair slightly darker than her own. She wished she had a likeness of him, but he had always said portraits were for people important enough to be in books, and the two of them didn't *make the bacon, they just ate it.* Then he would laugh. Meera chuckled quietly to herself, thinking how now she was quite literally the one *making the bacon* some mornings.

Her laughter was cut short, however, when one of the other kitchen maids passed behind her and rammed a sharp elbow into her side. She winced but didn't bother to look up or acknowledge the offense; she merely sighed and wondered whether she should have ever come to the palace. After her father had gone, she'd stayed at home waiting—waiting for news, for his return, for anything to shake her from her crippling worry and isolation ... until she hadn't been able to wait anymore—until her hope hadn't been enough to sustain her, and her books hadn't been enough company. Then she had left, seeking distraction, occupation, and mostly, a cure for her loneliness.

A neighbor had introduced her to the palace's housekeeper, who had introduced her to Cook. Meera had not been a likely candidate for kitchen work, having never worked let alone performed hard physical labor, but Cook had taken her in regardless. "Oi, Meera! Get that pot ready! A crowd's formin'," Cook called, startling her. Cook wore plain shirts, trousers, and aprons and had a mouse-brown ponytail at the nape of their neck. Cook had a few errant chin whiskers but otherwise no beard, and if Cook's gender had ever been known by the other staff, it had long since been forgotten. All referred to Cook as—"Cook," and since they reigned over the kitchen as if born to it and made the finest food anyone had ever tasted, no one asked questions.

Meera heaved the great big dripping cast iron pot out of the water, gave it a perfunctory once-over with a clean bit of cloth, then passed it over to a younger, pock-faced girl called Hilly to put on the fire. Hilly didn't look at her or thank her. Meera didn't expect her to, but the slight still stung her throat. Being from the merchant class made her stand out among the serving class, and while she didn't care about such distinctions herself, her fellow staff did. In their eyes, she spoke too well, knew too much, and bore none of the scars or signs of diseases and malnutrition that often plagued the poor in Altus. She stood out, and like a chicken with a limp, the other staff had honed in on her and endeavored to peck her into the dust.

The women, particularly, had been cruel—tripping her, mocking her, and giving her tedious but ultimately pointless tasks on *Cook's orders*. Meera had endured quietly, reminding herself that her father, surely, faced much worse hardships, and over time, her tormentors had lost interest in her. Now the other staff, like Hilly, mostly ignored her and occasionally knocked her supplies to the floor. The past few days, especially, hadn't left any of the servants time for errant cruelty. With a sigh, Meera supposed she would have left the palace already if being there was worse than being at home by herself—surrounded as she was by the constant chatter of other people, she was at least less alone if not less lonely.

Taking up a position at the long wooden table in the center of the kitchen where most of the food was prepared, she began peeling a towering heap of red potatoes. There were other tables in the kitchen, but those were for the servants to sit and have their meals—and gossip. That said, most of the tables were presently occupied by soldiers. There were also several boys—pages sent to the palace to glean news—as well as a couple of bold city folk hanging around for the same.

Meera focused hard on the small, curved knife in her hand rather than the people before her, not wanting another nick from clumsiness. It was difficult for her to even hold the lumpy potatoes steady since her weary hands shook, but as she labored, a satisfying collection of reddish shavings grew before her. Once she'd piled a decent-sized mound of naked potatoes to the side, she allowed herself a break and glanced around. Old Mrs. Henderby was folding laundry at one of the busy kitchen tables, and Meera caught her eye and smiled at her. The wrinkled laundress returned her smile with one missing several teeth. Some were kind to her, Meera reminded herself; Mrs. Henderby always appreciated when she helped her carry and fold linens in her spare time.

Taking a resolute breath, she bent her head and resumed chipping away at her potato heap, but just as she brought her blade to a spud, a man roared, "I say they kill the beast!" Meera's knife slipped, nearly stabbing her hand, and she looked up along with everyone else. The man who had shouted wore the red and black uniform of a career soldier; his clean tunic shone with the silver stitches of Terratelle's bear emblem, complete with the sword in the bear's paws that marked him as a member of the Royal Army. "I was in the unit what took 'im, and I says do away wit' the demon!" he added, swelling proudly for his audience.

The man sat at a crowded table and was met with some murmurs of agreement, though quiet ones compared to his boisterous outburst. Mostly, the others looked eager for news but unwilling to risk an opinion. Meera squinted and eyed the soldier critically; his clean appearance and rounded gut betrayed that the man's most recent post was an easy one, likely close to home, and she didn't believe for an instant that he'd been a part of the unit that had captured the raek and the man that everyone assumed was its rider.

The soldiers that had returned with the raek had shown obvious signs of hard living and recent conflict. They had been ragged, thin, dirty, and occasionally injured. Meera hadn't liked to think that her father might be in similar shape or worse ... It was on behalf of the returning soldiers that the king had declared a feast every night that week, keeping her and the other kitchen staff inordinately busy, so while many of the palace's inhabitants had since gone out to the back grounds behind the gardens to catch a glimpse of the raek, Meera had been too preoccupied with her work. She also wasn't sure she wanted to see how the animal was being treated—or mistreated, more like. She'd heard many descriptions of a giant, fire-breathing demon creature with foot-long fangs and a wicked grin, but she assumed people were exaggerating.

For several moments, she watched the frantic gossipers at the tables before her while they thrust and parried bits of information they'd heard about the raek and the war. The one soldier continued to be the loudest among them, reminding her of the criers she'd seen in Altus, hired by the king to spew about how raeken were dumb, bloodthirsty creatures that took pleasure in eating humans and burning villages in an effort to drive enlistment for the war with Aegorn. The criers always proclaimed the war to be a necessary in order to protect the innocent of Terratelle against evil—evil like raeken.

Meera found the man before her just as distasteful and wrinkled her nose at him. Then she tried to temper her judgment, reminding herself that she knew more than others—about most things but primarily about raeken. Her father had a small collection of scrolls and leaflets about Aegorn, specifically the creatures called raeken and the people called knell who rode them. Such manuscripts were banned, but he had found them in the library and smuggled them home, refusing to destroy texts for any reason. Meera had often read them, fascinated by the notion of magic. It was treason, she knew, for them to possess the texts and for her to read them, but she had found the fanciful stories irresistible.

One of her favorites was an epic about a warrior raek rider named Kallan, who had rescued the captured Queen Thea from pirates. She could clearly imagine Kallan's raek—the long, serpentine creature with wings that the scroll depicted in a faded, patchy green. Meera didn't know if her father's manuscripts were factual, but the raeken were unanimously portrayed as intelligent and honorable beasts. She, therefore, felt inclined to believe the best about the creatures and struggled to believe all that was said about the one held captive behind the palace.

However, the imprisoned raek had killed two soldiers on the previous two days when they had attempted to feed it, and while Meera didn't know the details of the incidents, the soldier's deaths were certainly fact and not legend. She hadn't yet heard that day whether a third attempt had been made and whether it had been successful or not—whether the person assigned to feed the rack had survived. She didn't understand why anyone needed to approach the raek to feed it, but she assumed it was necessary or the king would not be sacrificing soldiers to the task —would he?

Shaking her head to dispel her thoughts, she put her mind to her own task; she was almost finished peeling. She hoped this would be the last batch of stew for the day and that she could eat a large helping of it before crawling into her bed and resting her aching body. She squirmed her hips side to side to try to loosen the angry tension in her low back, but just then, the captain of the palace guard entered the kitchen, followed by a group of washerwomen, serving boys, and other palace staff, all looking intrigued but wary. The captain was a stony-faced man, and a pale scar angled down on his brown cheek lent itself to the impression that he was always frowning.

The small procession caught Meera's attention enough to divert her from her last few potatoes, and she put her knife down, waiting. Slowly, without being asked, the other kitchen staff also paused in their chores and stood as if at attention. The gossipers at the tables gaped in eager anticipation of news, and in a matter of seconds, the din of the kitchen fell away completely, supplanted by silence. "Listen up!" began the captain unnecessarily. "As I'm sure you're all well aware, the palace now houses a raek on the back grounds. I've orders from the king to select a person—any person—from the palace staff to uh ... take over maintenance of the animal."

The staff all looked around, confused. Maintenance of the raek? As in approaching it to feed it like the two soldiers that had died in the last two days? "Our king has decided that the soldiers in his army have more pressing matters to attend to than that of uh ... animal husbandry," the captain continued haltingly. There were a few guffaws and giggles at *animal husbandry*, but most were looking nervous, realizing what the captain was getting at. A rush of hushed whispers broke out all around Meera, though no one spoke to her. She merely shifted from aching foot to aching foot, hoping the meeting would end quickly so that she could finish her work and get off her feet.

The captain cleared his throat to regain everyone's attention: "Echem—I do not relish the task of choosing one of our own for such a ... challenging position, and so I am speaking with all palace staff today in the hopes of finding a volunteer. Should a volunteer not be found, I will uh, select whoever seems most ... appropriately qualified." Looking down at the floor, he clenched his jaw, clearly not relishing the task before him. The captain cut a striking figure in his black guard uniform with his long, sculpted beard, and Meera thought he must have been handsome when he was younger. Then, as she observed him, it dawned on her that he was essentially there to choose a sacrifice, and she chewed the inside of her cheek at the thought of someone being forced into the raek's enclosure.

She presumed the fact that the captain was standing in the kitchen addressing a group consisting mainly of women, young boys, and elderly meant that none of the palace guards had volunteered. If not even the youngest, most brash of the palace guards had seen fit to prove their bravery against the raek, she doubted the captain would find a willing person among the remainder of the staff. At least, she fervently hoped that none of the very young staff members would be so foolish ...

Still, even as she feared for her fellow staff, she longed for the captured animal outside to be well cared for. Meera hated to see any animal mistreated, and the intermittent shrieks of pain and— what she imagined to be—desperation that she had heard from the raek over the last few days had tightened the muscles in her chest and tugged at her sympathies. She pitied both the caged beast and the captive audience before her.

Looking around, she wondered who, then, would be chosen. If

the king didn't see fit to waste more precious soldiers on the raek, she assumed the captain wouldn't be willing to sacrifice his own strong, capable men. So, who would it be? The oldest staff member? Someone whose work seemed the least important? Meera knew whoever was chosen would have no choice; this was the king's will and refusing would be tantamount to treason. She could sense growing anxiety in the group around her, and the noise in the kitchen rose. "Echem—" the captain cleared his throat once more. "Is there a—uh ... volunteer?" he asked, gazing over the heads of the crowd like he didn't really expect an answer.

Silence fell once more. No one moved—no one breathed, it felt like—as if any form of movement could be misconstrued as volunteering. Meera saw fear in many of the familiar faces around her. Old Mrs. Henderby's hands shook in her lap where she sat next to a basket of towels that still needed folding. A bead of sweat worked its way down the neck of a stable hand whose name she did not recall, but who she had seen care lovingly for the palace's horses.

Meera shifted her weight on her feet once more, this time from nerves. Then she sighed; she hoped whoever was chosen would be able to safely approach and feed the raek. She also hoped they would care for its wounds and prevent any more cruelty from befalling the poor creature ... As if hooked on a fishing line, her right hand rose slowly into the air. It was the only movement in the kitchen, and all eyes turned to her.

Suddenly, her stomach flopped. Had she just volunteered? Her thumb hovered by her temple, and she thought about using her hand to adjust her hair but dumbly couldn't make herself move— she just stood there with it raised, pledging herself to a deadly task. For a moment, nothing happened, and she held her breath while the captain stared at her blankly. His eyebrows rose, spasmed briefly as if surprised by their own display of surprise, and settled back into position. Then he quickly strode around the table toward her, probably so as not to leave her any time to think or change her mind.

Reeling in her right hand, she clutched it with her left to prevent it from further action and resumed breathing in short, shallow pulls. Then she peered around at her fellow staff members, whose shocked faces mirrored her own. When the captain reached her, he took her elbow firmly, and steered her toward the outside door. "Come with me, Miss."

2

O nce outside, the captain released her arm and took off down the path leading away from the palace, and Meera half ran to keep up with his long strides and brisk pace. It wasn't especially cold outside, but the air was thick with dampness. After a long day in the heat of the kitchen, she quickly became chilled and clutched at her arms. Scurrying after the captain, she hurried down the path and through the gardens. Then, veering left, she looked out over a field of grass that sloped down to the canal. From her vantage point, she could see the raek but not clearly—the moisture in the air fogged her view. She could just make out its curled shape through the mist and in the shadow of the walls.

The canal running parallel to the back of the palace was lined with stones. A docking beach had been carved from the hillside to allow boats to be pulled ashore, and tall stone walls framed the beach on either side, holding the soil in place to prevent the hill-sides from eroding. Iron hooks were built into the walls to tie off boats, however, currently bolted to the hooks were long iron chains attached to manacles on each of the raek's legs. The dark, snake-like coils of the chains were just visible on the sand.

The captain leaned forward like he wanted to run straight down the slope through the long grass, but he restrained himself, turning instead to the road that meandered down the hill in a switchback. As he rushed to the canal below, Meera followed, keeping her eyes down to avoid tripping. Her heart was hammering—not entirely from the exertion—and her head was stumbling, trying to catch up to the decision her hand had made in the kitchen minutes before. Had she really just volunteered herself to feed a dangerous animal? The previous two attempts had ended in death—had she volunteered to die?

Meera panted in panic. Would her father return from the war to find that she had been killed by a raek? That she had died volunteering unnecessarily for something ridiculous while performing a job at the palace that she didn't even need? Perhaps her judgment wasn't as sound as she had previously thought ... Perhaps she should have married—marrying likely wouldn't have ended with her being publicly disemboweled by a large, exotic animal and dying alone on the ground.

Halfway down the hill, she finally found her voice: "Sir, how close do I need to get? Can the food not be thrown to the creature?" Her words came out soft and quavering, and for a moment, she thought maybe the stern-faced man hadn't heard her through the dense fog.

The captain didn't turn or slow, but after a hesitation, he replied, "No. It wears an iron muzzle to keep it from opening its jaws enough to breathe fire. The food must be put through the gaps in the iron and into its mouth."

Meera blanched, picturing her hand going into the mouth of a giant, fanged animal. She didn't bother asking any more questions; she had volunteered, and now she must live with the consequences—she only hoped she did *live* with the consequences and not die from them. As they rounded the last turn, she could see the raek clearly at last. It was a long, serpentine creature with wings and four legs sporting clawed feet. And it was enormous—standing about twice as high as she did. What Meera could see of its head was scaly; a bulky iron muzzle obscured everything below its eyes, but beyond its scaly head, the creature was feathered! She hadn't expected that—it wasn't discernible in the illustrations she'd seen; she had thought raeken were large, winged lizards of a sort, but the raek, while reptilian, also appeared avian, with feathers covering all but its head and lower legs and a tuft of them at the end of its long tail.

Even more striking than the raek's size was its color: a bright shade of cobalt blue with teal undertones and both lighter and darker blue stripes on the tips of its wings. The stripes brought a certain scroll to mind for Meera, and she thought she remembered that male raeken have stripes or other patterning to distinguish them from females. Supposing the raek was male, she found it mildly comforting to think of the animal as a "he" instead of an "it," as if having a gender made the raek more animal and less monster. Of course, gender or no gender, the raek was what he was, and she could only hope he wouldn't eat her.

Meera observed the raek anxiously as they approached the beach. He stood with his tail-end to the canal and his head toward them, cocked to the side and hanging low from the weight of the iron muzzle. He was perfectly still as he watched them from one eye, and his left wing dangled awkwardly at his side, arrows protruding from it. Beholding his many wounds, Meera's pity for the creature reared up within her as did her bitter anger toward the men responsible. But then she tried to repress those feelings, reminding herself that she didn't know the full circumstances of the raek's capture. Perhaps he had attacked the soldiers, and they had defended themselves—she just didn't know; the stories circulating through the palace were too varied to be reliable sources of information.

Glancing up, she found that there were soldiers with spears stationed atop the high walls on either side of the raek. The spears, however, looked like sticks compared to the size of the animal, and she doubted they had enough length to reach him let alone do any damage from the top of the enormous walls. Then her eyes traveled down, and she noticed that in front of the raek was a curved demarcation line in the sand. For a long moment, Meera stared at it in confusion, then she realized that the line illustrated the raek's range of motion; the sand on the beach was darker from being clawed and churned. Deep gashes in the ground were visual reminders of the raek's deadly claws—as were, of course, the bodies. Two dead men in soldiers' uniforms lay on the beach just within the line.

Meera stared transfixed at the bodies and almost walked into the captain when he stopped about fifty feet away from the raek. Blinking, she tore her gaze from the gruesome scene to gape at the tall young man the captain had paused in front of. The man—boy more like, Meera thought—wore a palace guard's uniform, black with the silver outline of Terratelle's bear emblem, but he didn't wear the sword that usually went with the uniform. That combined with his age made Meera assume he was some sort of trainee. "Linus, Miss ..." the captain started to say to the young guard before looking at Meera searchingly.

"M-Meera Hailship," she stuttered.

"Miss ..." The captain coughed into his hand. "Yes, well—give her the supplies, Linus."

"But, Sir!" the young man replied, his red-rimmed eyes widening on his pimply face. "She's ..." *A girl*, Meera finished for him in her head. She might have rolled her eyes except that at that moment she would've gladly gotten out of her foolish position on account of being a girl. In fact, if she were at all practiced in what one might consider "girly behaviors," she might have simpered and batted her eyelashes at the two guards to evoke their supposedly innate masculine chivalry. As it were, she just stood there helplessly, eyes blinking normally.

"Let's just get this over and done with," the captain said with a sigh, averting his eyes to the horizon. His words were harsh, but his tone sounded more dour than stern. Meera wondered if the captain had hastened to the canal not to prevent her from changing her mind but to prevent his own resolve from faltering. She supposed he must also obey the king or commit treason—whether or not he found his job distasteful.

Linus stepped aside to reveal a wooden cart laden with a bucket under a folded piece of canvas. Then he dipped stork-like over the cart, pulled out a pair of long metal tongs, and waved them around, saying, "Miss, these here are for you to get the food into the beast's mouth if ..." Trailing off uncertainly, he dropped the tongs back into the cart. Then he stepped aside to allow her to access it. *If you live that long*, she finished for him again. She was beginning to tremble and not from her chill.

Meera looked at the captain, expecting there to be more—assurances that he and the present soldiers would do everything they could to protect her, gratitude for her voluntary service to the king ... nothing. The captain continued gazing toward the horizon, lips pressed together in a white line. Meera drew in a shaky breath and moved to the cart. Bending down to extract the handle from the dirt, she pulled it slowly over the bumpy ground, keeping her eyes cast down and to the side in order to watch the front wheels and her feet maneuver around rocks and tufts of grass. She told herself all she had to do at that moment was walk and pull the cart, and she focused entirely on her movements, trying not to think about what came next. Even so, her legs wobbled almost as much as the cart did.

She stopped dead just as she reached the first claw marks gouged into the sand and looked up. The raek hadn't moved and was a lunge and a slash away from her—watching. The bodies were close now, and the fetid stench of decomposition and body fluids filled her nose and mouth, gagging her. Her stomach heaved, but she managed to press the feeling down, swallowing her revulsion. First, she breathed through her mouth to avoid the smell, then she covered it with a hand when she noticed the clouds of flies swarming around the bodies.

The dead soldiers were strewn to either side of her: one had been thrown against a wall, his head visibly bashed in, and the other was gutted, his stomach ripped open with a mess of old blood and decaying intestines littered around him. The flies were busy with that one. Meera had never seen such carnage, and nothing she had ever read had prepared her for the smell, the sight of the bloated faces and rotting gore, and the sound of the flies exulting in their prize; it was physically overwhelming.

Legs suddenly weak and bloodless, she gripped the cart handle for support, unsure she could take a step over the claw marks even if she wanted to. Then she started sweating despite the damp chill of the air, and her dress clung to her skin, the rough fibers of the inexpensive cotton uniform chafing her. Swaying slightly, she looked up at the raek—anything was better than looking at the bodies. The animal's one visible eye was a lighter shade of blue than the surrounding scales, and he stared back at her, unblinking.

Meera shook, but her eyes remained steady. She held the hulking creature's gaze and willed herself to think, to try some-thing—anything—to save herself. She couldn't take back her hand in the air, but she didn't want to die for a foolish, baseless decision. She didn't want to die at all! Panic gripped her, and she gasped for breath, trying to think of some way out of the situation ... But she couldn't think; her mind was frustratingly and uncharacteristically blank. Tearing her gaze from the raek, she chanced a look back toward the captain and Linus. The captain regarded the horizon as if studying a painting at a museum, but Linus watched, eyes still wide but their redness no longer visible.

The men were only a short distance behind her—maybe forty feet—but that distance stretched like an ocean, and Meera was shark-bait. Suddenly, her knees buckled, and she gripped the cart handle harder to hold herself upright. First, her mind had failed and now her body. Taking a deep breath, she tried to calm herself —to find herself again. What if she couldn't do it? Or, what if she just didn't do it—didn't move? How long would she have to stand there before the captain would come and shove her over the ominous dark line in the sand?

She didn't like that image—the indignity of it—and her pride jolted her mind back from its lifeless state. With another deep breath, she thought about her father's scrolls and all she had ever read about raeken. By all accounts, they were intelligent animals —noble, even. A niggling thought inched across her mind that perhaps only the raeken whose deeds earned them places in legends were noble, and the rest were monsters ... But she stomped on the thought; she needed all the hope she could muster if she was going to survive. Once more, she willed herself to do something—anything.

Feeling ridiculous and glad she was out of earshot of the captain and Linus, Meera lowered her hand from her mouth and called, "My name is Meera Hailship. I have a father, who loves me, who I hope to see again someday ... I have read that raeken are intelligent and noble creatures, and I would like to make a bargain with you." She stumbled over the words and hadn't projected them as well as she would have hoped, but the raek should have heard her. Whether he had understood her was another matter.

Fidgeting with her hands, she watched him carefully. He didn't move. Meera's mouth was growing dry from breathing through it, and she couldn't remember the last time she'd had a drink of water. She tried to swallow, but her parched throat merely contracted painfully and didn't provide her any relief. A fly buzzed in front of her face, and she swatted at it jerkily, defending herself from any trace of the death and rot she knew was strewn to either side of her. Obstinately, she focused on the raek instead of the bodies, and pitching her voice forward once more, she rasped, "I promise to feed you, care for your wounds, and always tell you the truth if you promise not to harm me in any way ..." Then, after a brief pause to think if she'd missed anything, she asked, "Do you agree to this bargain?"

For a long moment, she stared hard at the animal, willing it to reply while simultaneously wondering if she could outrun the captain and flee into Altus. Then the raek raised his head ever so slightly and blinked. Was the blink for her? Was it just a blink? She didn't know, but she hoped ... Clutching the cart handle, she hesitated, then slid her right foot slowly and shakily onto the slashing line in the dirt. Pausing to judge the raek's reaction, she felt like a marionette with unsteady strings; her stillness was not still but tremulous and twitchy. Her heart slammed against her chest, reverberating into her arms and throat. Her chest *hurt*. She hadn't known fear could actually hurt. Staring at the raek, her eyes went in and out of focus with her quaking. It—he, she reminded herself—didn't move.

She slid her left foot forward onto the line. Pause. Not wanting to make too much noise, she hadn't pulled the cart with her, and her torso leaned back awkwardly with her feet out in front of her so that she could grip the handle. As if the raek wasn't already fully aware of her presence, she thought, feeling foolish. Teetering precariously in her slanted position, she was forced to jerk the cart toward her retroactively to avoid stumbling backward or losing her grip on the handle.

The cart rattled and creaked up to her ankles, but the raek didn't react to the noise. Meera continued to struggle to balance and glanced at her feet, wondering if she had placed them wrong. She had barely taken two steps, but they'd been the most difficult two steps since her very first—she couldn't remember ever focusing so entirely on standing, and the more she tried to focus, the less steady she felt. The raek maintained his stillness; his clawed feet did not shift the thick iron chains trailing away from them.

Tremulously, Meera chanced another slow shuffle forward. She was past the furthest claw mark now, inside the raek's space. The beach was large enough for several boats to dock at once, and yet it didn't feel large enough for both raek and woman. Regardless, she continued her slow forward shuffle, panting through her mouth and gripping the cart in her hand with more strength than she felt in both of her legs. As she inched forward, she left ragged trails in the sand behind her.

The raek didn't move, but the closer Meera got, the more he loomed over her. Once she was only a handful of shuffles away from the raek's head, she had to look up to keep her gaze fixed on his, and when she was little more than a body's length away, she stopped. She had crossed onto the beach and was still alive! Had the raek really blinked in agreement to her bargain? He must have, she told herself, only half-believing it.

Close up, the details of the creature's vibrant feathers and scales were mesmerizing, but Meera's eyes kept darting to his claws and muzzled head, checking them for movement. She was loath to look away from the towering animal, but she couldn't leave until she had actually fed him. Turning quickly—before she could lose her resolve—she pulled the heavy canvas cover off the bucket in her cart. Peering inside, she found a pile of live mice swarming within, crawling over one another. Her stomach churned at the site, and she felt like her own abdomen was full of the writhing rodents. She whipped her head back toward the raek. He hadn't moved, and his large, blue orb of an eye was still focused on her.

With effort, Meera drew her lips back in a feigned smile and reached into the cart for the tongs. She narrated as she went so as not to startle the raek: "I'm reaching to get a pair of tongs, so I can transfer the food through the iron bars of that muzzle. You're having mice. I'm sure it's not what you usually eat, but they're at least fresh, and you must be hungry!" Her voice sounded strangely high and upbeat like a caricature of a serving girl. Meera had noticed how the server's voices changed when they were speaking to each other versus when they spoke to palace guests, but she wasn't used to putting on such performances and had never heard herself sound so forced.

Drawing the cart the last few steps alongside the raek's head, she reached a trembling hand into the bucket and groped for a squirming mouse with her tongs. She felt a pang for the little mouse but would rather it die than she. The raek's muzzle was constructed of thick iron with slits along the sides. Chains going between his eyes and around his neck held it in place. She could see that the weight of the cruel device caused its blunt edge to cut into the raek's face between his eyes and snout, and she winced at the sight of the raw, red flesh.

Lifting the mouse, she maneuvered it through the bars, knocking her metal tongs into them and cringing at the noise. The raek parted his lips, revealing gleaming, sharp teeth with trails of saliva clinging from top to bottom. He could open his mouth only far enough to fit the tongs and mouse before hitting the edges of the muzzle. Meera dropped the piteously squealing rodent between his white teeth, and he clamped his mouth shut, cutting off the smaller creature's cries and swallowing. She'd done it, she thought; she'd fed him! She felt a brief wave of relief at accomplishing her task before looking down at the full, swarming bucket and realizing she was far from done. She continued to feed the raek, mouse by mouse, until the bucket was empty, and her arms ached and trembled.

Suddenly, the raek moved, making Meera jump and drop her tongs. He raised his head and lifted his body from the ground, and her heart renewed its violent pounding. She had fed him, and now he would do away with her, she thought in panic. She tried to move—to run—but her legs didn't budge. She only managed a pathetic, solitary step back, then she blinked and realized that the raek was turning away from her, not attacking; she was safe. She clutched her arms to comfort herself and watched as the raek dragged his chains through the sand and pivoted, crisscrossing them, before bending his neck to drink from the canal. From her new vantage point, she could see more arrows stuck in the animal's body as well as the mud caking the long feathers on his tufted tail.

As her heart calmed once more, she watched the raek with interest. He at least had plenty of fresh water, so she wouldn't need to bring him any. Peering around, she judged from the cleanliness of the area—bodies aside—that the raek also eliminated in the water, so she would not need to clean up giant raek-sized turds. Because this was her job now, she realized; she had survived and would need to continue feeding and caring for the raek. The task before her was still frightening and daunting, but she had at least survived this first challenge. Sighing, Meera let her relief seep through her quivering body like soothing water.

Now what? There wasn't anything she could do about the raek's injuries without supplies, and the sun was about to go down … "I'll return tomorrow with more food and supplies to treat your injuries," she promised, and she backed awkwardly away from the animal, turning and dragging the cart with her as she retreated across the furthest line in the sand and blew out a breath of even deeper relief. She was safe and done for the day, and as her fear lifted and floated away, she felt a sweeping wave of giddiness.

Meera grinned and looked up to find that the captain and young guard had drifted closer to the beach. The captain stood loose-armed and slack-jawed in open disbelief, but when he noticed her attention, he quickly reassumed his usual neutral demeanor. He could at least smile at her, she thought—or slap her on the back and congratulate her for not dying. Unlike the captain's carefully blank face, Linus's was ruddy and wet with tears, his eyes fixed on something. Confused, Meera's smile faltered, and she followed the young guard's gaze to the body by the wall before promptly averting her eyes from the dead man slumped against it. Had Linus known the man? She empathized with the grief he must feel; it would be horrible to see a loved one so destroyed—it was horrible enough seeing a stranger turned from man to carnage.

Heaving a great sigh, Meera realized she was the only one who could safely enter the raek's space, so she was the only one who could collect the bodies of the fallen soldiers. She wasn't done for the day, after all, and her stomach lurched at the thought of what she now had to do. Resigned, she took a hesitant step back over the line in the sand, holding her breath and watching the raek closely. He had turned back around and observed her once more, but he didn't move at her approach. Meera wasn't entirely convinced he had truly agreed to their bargain and not just blinked a fly out of his eye at a convenient moment. But the animal had tolerated her before, and she hoped he would tolerate her again.

With stronger steps than her first foray onto the beach and more confidence than she felt, she walked to the cleaner of the two bodies—Linus's apparent loved one—against the right wall. Dragging the cart along with her, she moved the bucket off it. Then she unfolded the bucket's canvas cover and laid it over the cart, positioning them next to the body. For a minute, she just stood there, breathing through her exceedingly dry mouth and wondering how to move the body onto the cart.

The dead man in question was not very large and was propped against the wall as if sitting. Holding her breath and trying not to look at the details of the body, Meera grasped his uniformed shoulders and heaved. She had thought to pull the torso over the cart but hadn't realize how stiff the body had become. Instead, the whole corpse jerked forward and away from the wall. The man's seated position didn't change, but the movement dislodged a loud burst of gas from his decomposing intestines. The sound shocked Meera, and she inhaled reflexively, immediately gagging and retching. This time she couldn't tamper down the reflex, and the meager contents of her stomach spilled onto the ground at her feet. Shaking and swallowing the bile in her mouth, she stepped back to consider what to do next.

The raek was watching her, the captain and Linus too, and the soldiers on the wall, she assumed, though she couldn't make out their dark faces against the light of the sky. Meera didn't want to fail—not in general and not in front of so many onlookers. She had volunteered to do a dangerous job, and against all odds, she had done it. She refused to now appear weak. In a swelling of pride, she squared her shoulders and got to work.

First, she moved the canvas off the cart and onto the ground next to the body, as close to the side of the man's legs as she could get it. Then she went to his other side and pushed, tipping him onto the canvas. Crouching down, she shoved and slid him to the center of the sturdy fabric. All the while, she studiously avoided looking at the man's wrecked head. Gripping two corners of her makeshift sled, she leaned all of her weight back in short, staccato movements to drag the man off the beach. She stepped and heaved over and over, slowly hauling the canvas back and across the furthest slash in the dirt.

Meera stopped only to catch her breath, but suddenly, Linus and some soldiers from the wall were there, lifting the body from the canvas and carrying it further away. She wondered when the soldiers had made their way down and around from the wall top. She also vaguely registered Linus sobbing and saying something to either her or the body, but she didn't process what it was—her mind was spinning. But she couldn't stop to think—she couldn't stop what she was doing and lose her momentum.

Taking the canvas, she turned and went for the second body, marching confidently across the claw marks in the sand and starting to blur them with her repeated trips on and off the beach. The second corpse lay prostrate on the ground, abdomen gaping and writhing with flies. Meera tried not to look and breathed through the tiniest sliver of parted lips. This time, she gripped the man's ankles and dragged him onto the tarp. As she yanked the body, organs and intestines tore free where they stuck to the dried blood on the ground. A cloud of buzzing flies erupted all around her, and the air was so thick with their disjointed movements that she felt the need to breathe through her nose or risk letting their corpse-tainted bodies into her mouth. She retched several times at the smell, but her stomach was too empty to vomit. Flies landed and rose all over her hair and body, leaving her feeling spoiled and foul, but she kept working.

Once the man was on the tarp, Meera collected the scattered

remnants of him with the metal tongs she had used to feed the raek, holding the slippery bits of intestine as far away from her as she could. Her arm shook from exhaustion, and she dropped one of the smaller organs several times before finally getting it onto the tarp. Once done, she tossed the tongs next to the man's body and heaved him to more awaiting soldiers. Then she crossed the line onto the beach yet again to retrieve the cart, too bone-weary to pay the raek any attention whatsoever. Their bargain had held that day, and she could only hope it would continue to hold. Turning her back on the creature, she left his beach for the last time that night.

The captain silently took the cart and walked Meera back uphill to the palace and the kitchen door. She was so shaky from spent terror, she barely managed the trip; the fear and stubborn pride that had been propelling her body deserted her, and she felt close to collapsing. Dehydrated, hungry, and exhausted, she stumbled into the kitchen to find it uncharacteristically empty, except for Cook and old Mrs. Henderby. Holding her filthy hands out and away from her body, Meera gazed imploringly at the two people before her. Cook and Mrs. Henderby bustled her to the sink basin to scrub her soiled hands, and when she saw that they also had a tub waiting for her, boiling water over the fire to fill it, as well as food and drink laid out on a table, she was overcome with emotion.

Shaking and gasping, tears and snot ran down her face and into her mouth. Her thoughts were mostly jumbled and incoherent except for the gratitude she felt to be cared for in a world in which she felt so terribly alone. Relinquishing control to her caretakers, Meera let them wash her before rousing herself enough to dress and feed herself. When she eventually climbed the stairs to her bedroom, she didn't so much as look at Teardra who was readying herself for bed; she collapsed on top of her blankets, expecting her exhaustion to overtake her instantly. However, she instead closed her eyes and repeatedly pictured the bloated faces of the men she'd dragged off the beach. It took her a long time to finally sleep, and when she did, she dreamt of an iron muzzle being chained to her face and flies entering her mouth.

3

The next day, the morning bell roused Meera. It chimed to announce that it was time for the palace's staff to get up and attend to their respective duties, coinciding with the earliest light of dawn. Meera would have liked to sleep in after her ordeal the previous day, but she'd given up that privilege when she'd taken her position at the palace. Once again, she wondered whether she had been making the right decisions for herself or whether her judgment had left with her father. Then she took a deep breath; she was alive and unharmed, the raek had not killed her, and strangely, knowing she had to get up and care for him gave her a sense of purpose.

The small room she shared with Teardra consisted of two narrow beds, each accompanied by a side table, with a slit of a window in between that her roommate always insisted on keeping shuttered. In the dim light filtering through the shutters, Meera opened her trunk and pulled out her second dove grey uniform dress since the first had gone down the laundry chute the night before. As she dressed, she noted that despite the increase in her physical activity since working at the palace, her full figure hadn't changed much—a testament to Cook's cooking, she thought.

She wasn't what her father would call *boastfully portly*—as it was the habit of some of the wealthy in Altus to eat to excess in order to physically display their wealth—but she wasn't especially slender either. The uniform dress she pulled on had been altered from previously belonging to someone else, and was, therefore, slightly too short for her; Meera was taller than the other women who worked in the kitchens. From what she could tell, she was actually an average height and assumed the height discrepancy between herself and the other kitchen workers was owing to the poor nourishment of the lower class. She frowned at the strip of ankle showing over her leather boots; it was one more small thing that separated her from the women she worked with and contributed to her isolation.

Meera kept a mirror propped on her side table. It was finer than anything the other women could afford, and she was surprised no one had snuck in to break or steal it yet considering how she had been treated early on. Crouching down, she studied her reflection. She felt odd after the previous day, but she looked the same, if a little puffy around her eyes from crying. Her skin was a light golden brown—a mixture of her father's bronze complexion and her mother's light beige. Her eyes were almond-shaped—brown like most Terratellens. In general, Meera thought she was average looking: she had brown eyes, brown hair, and a round face, but she wasn't displeased with herself. Her father had always said she resembled her mother who she had lost as a small child, and she found the thought gratifying. Gathering her curly hair on top of her head, she jabbed pins in it until she was reasonably satisfied with the shape.

Just as Teardra was starting to drag herself from her bed, Meera hastened to the door. By unspoken consent, they tried never to be moving about the room at the same time. If one of them was up, the other would generally feign sleep to avoid any interaction whatsoever. Meera had tried to be friendly with Teardra at first but had been met with irritation and disdain and had quickly given up on having a relationship with the dour woman.

When she left, she used a chamber pot in a room at the end of the hall dedicated to their use then made her way down the narrow spiral stairs toward the kitchen. While she seemed to have gotten up and out of her room before most, there were always people in the kitchen. Cook, she was convinced, didn't sleep. Meera entered the warm, well-lit space to find Cook laying out a spread of bread, cheese, and hard-boiled eggs for the kitchen staff to eat before they made everyone else's breakfasts, and she started to walk over to eat and thank Cook for their kindness the previous night.

More people than usual crowded the tables in the kitchen—even considering how busy the palace had been since the raek's arrival—and Hilly was standing and talking to a group at one of the tables. Before Meera made it two steps toward her food, Hilly pointed to her and exclaimed, "That's her!" with a satisfied smirk. A hushed conversation ensued with many glances her way, and the excitement quickly spread to the other tables. Meera froze in confusion before processing that her actions the previous day had not gone unnoticed among the palace staff. Hilly was speaking animatedly, holding court in front of the onlookers, and Meera could only imagine what nonsense the younger girl was spewing about her.

Sighing, she rolled her eyes at her own naivety; she should have known people would be interested in her and supposed the tale of her volunteering would have spread throughout the palace by now. There had been a crowd in the kitchen at the time, and at least twenty soldiers on the wall had seen her feed the raek and survive. After months of ignoring bullying to finally become a background figure in the kitchen, Meera had inadvertently drawn all eyes back to her. Turning around, she resolved not to acknowledge her observers. Cook handed her a very full plate of food, jostling her out of her reverie. "Cook, thank you for everything last night. I ..." she started to say.

"Whatcha go 'n' do that for anyways?" Cook asked with a penetrating stare and a frown.

"Oh, I ... don't really know. I ... like animals, I suppose, and I didn't want someone else to be forced to do it," Meera replied sheepishly. She wished she had a better answer—one that made her sound less like a moron with a death wish. She couldn't admit to what she knew about raeken from her father's scrolls, although she didn't think it made her decision any sounder regardless. Quickly, she averted her eyes to the floor, not wanting to pile Cook's obvious judgment on top of her own.

"Too terrible for some'n else to go in the demon's nest but not too terrible for you?" Cook asked. They didn't mince words—only food. Meera glanced back up at Cook's face, and with one brow cocked and their lips pressed tightly together, she knew they disapproved of her actions if not thought her completely insane. "I took you on in my kitchen when the others thought me foolish. I 'spect you to live long enough to prove 'em wrong," Cook added.

Meera laughed. "I'll do my best," she assured them. Then she took her food to one of the few empty tables, just for the seats around her to fill in moments later by curious staff members, most of whom she didn't even recognize. She did know Stan, one of the older, more experienced stable hands, who sat across from her. "I'm glad yer alright, Elmira," he said earnestly but with an undeniable spark of intrigue in his eyes.

"Thanks, Stan," she replied, never sure how to correct people when they got her name wrong and reluctant to further the conversation in general.

"So, what happened? Why'd ya do it? Is it true ya just walked in and fed the thing, 'n' it didn't even try to get ya?" Stan asked, voice rising. He was leaning toward her eagerly, practically breathing on her plate of food, and Meera shrunk back reflexively.

A few others added questions of their own, but her flustered mind could only concentrate on Stan's face right in front of her face. Her mouth opened and shut—twice—but nothing coherent came out. She was going to have to come up with some decent short statements to fend off people's curiosity, she realized. However, in that moment running away wouldn't be construed as treason, so she scooped up her plate, mumbled that she needed to speak to Cook about something, and moved back behind the relative safety of the kitchen worktable.

Cook barked a sharp laugh at her reappearance. "Guess you didna do it for the attention."

Meera gave them an apologetic smile and dug into her food. Then, halfway through her plate, she realized there *was* perhaps something she needed to discuss with them. "Cook, I want to see to the raek's wounds today. Could I take some things from the kitchen?" she asked. While caring for the raek was a palace duty, it wasn't a kitchen duty, and Meera wasn't sure where she should be getting her supplies or who she should be reporting to—the captain perhaps? She supposed no one had bothered to think through her position since no one had expected her to survive the first day.

"What sorta things?" Cook asked, hands busy with food prep.

"I'll need a step ladder and some vinegar to wash the wounds, and I'd like an apron to wear to preserve my dress. I can probably take clean scrap linen from the maid's closet for dressings ..." Meera said. Her eyes rose to the ceiling as she thought if there was anything else she would need. She didn't know much about wound care.

Cook bustled into the large kitchen pantry and returned with a folding step ladder and a cask of vinegar. They put the items down then held up a finger and went back into the pantry, this time returning with a small crock. "Vinegar to wash 'em then honey to keep 'em from festering," they said, handing Meera the crock of honey. Honey was a precious commodity; Cook's kindness and generosity shone through once more, but Meera didn't say anything, knowing it would likely make them uncomfortable. "You might need to find somethin' to sew the wounds shut. Normal needle won't get through hide that thick," Cook added.

Sew the wounds shut? Meera cringed—she hadn't thought of that. "Thank you, I'll find something. I'll come back to help in the kitchen later when I'm done, too," she promised.

Cook barked another poignant laugh, and Meera thought they might be right; she had no notion of how long it might take to treat the raek's wounds, assuming she could do much for him at all. It took her two trips to get her supplies out the door, but she at least had the foresight to pack water and food. Then she set herself up on a crude bench outside the kitchen and waited for someone to come with the cart. She was pretty sure the captain had told her it would be brought to her, although her mind had been muddled on their walk back the night before. She didn't know when someone might come, but she didn't mind the excuse to sit alone in the fresh air. It was still cool and damp, but there was a mildly warm breeze beckoning in the peak of spring.

Maybe an hour later, the young guard, Linus, walked around the corner from the gardens, cart in tow. Meera smiled and waved to him as he approached. "Good morning, Linus," she called, standing from the bench.

"Good morning, Miss," he replied, brushing hair from his face.

He had honey-brown hair that looked like it had been cut short sometime recently—likely due to fever—and hadn't yet grown long enough to be tied back. The shaggy hair added to his youthful awkwardness, and his cheeks were flushed red from exertion; he was pale by Terratellen standards.

"Please, call me Meera. Did you draw the short straw again?" she asked good naturedly, thinking that he likely always got the least desirable palace guard assignments due to his age.

Surprising her, Linus dropped to one knee and pulled a flower out from behind his back. "Miss—Meera, I must thank you for the service you rendered my family yesterday. You see, my brother ... The soldier whose body you recovered from the wall? He ... was my brother." Clearing his throat, he continued, "Thanks to you, my family can now bury him with the dignity he deserves. I have spoken with the captain, and he has consented to me assisting you with your duties in any way I can—though he has expressly forbidden me from entering the beast's space. Otherwise, I am at your service." He rose from his kneeling position and stood very straight, clearly trying to look dignified.

The boy spoke well compared to most of the palace staff, Meera thought, blinking at him. Then, awkwardly, she reached out and took the flower he offered her. She didn't know what it was called—she was never especially interested in the names of plants—but it was pretty, with white petals and a yellow center. Unsure of what else to do with it, she pushed the stem into the mess of curls on the top of her head and replied, "Thank you, Linus. I will appreciate your help. The flower is lovely, too, but I hope the head gardener didn't see you pick it; he'll want your hand!" Pausing, she saw he wasn't in the mood for joking, and she hastily added, "I'm so very sorry for the loss of your brother. What was his name?"

"Sam," he said quietly. "He was my big brother, and when I'm a year older, I'll join the army like he did." Linus was sixteen, then —four years younger than her. The royal army had some requirements, one being that the men must be at least seventeen to enlist. It still seemed so young to Meera to be fighting and dying, and she was momentarily speechless, wondering why Linus would want to enlist after seeing what had happened to his brother. Then she involuntarily pictured the soldier's bloated face and caved in head, wondering what Sam had looked like before death's disfigurement. "We're burying him tonight," Linus added when she was silent.

"I might take a while today," she finally replied. "I'm going to treat the raek's wounds as best I can, and I'm not sure how long it will take. Please leave if you need to for the burial! I can manage on my own ... Although, if you know where I can find an especially large and sturdy needle and thread, that would be very helpful," she added, once again running through the mental list of what she could do for the raek's injuries.

She was moving her ladder into the cart behind Linus as she spoke and therefore didn't notice when his demeanor changed. When he didn't answer right away, she glanced up at his face and was shocked at what she saw: anger, hate maybe—Meera thought if murder wore an expression, this would be it. Startled, she took two steps back. "Linus?"

"You're going to treat its wounds? That ... that thing—that monster?!" he shouted. Meera gaped at him, but before she could answer, he went on: "Didn't you see? Didn't you see what it did to my *brother?*" His voice cracked on *brother*, reminding her that he was both young and experiencing grief. Then he turned away from her, and she could hear him sniffing in his tears.

"Linus, of course you're angry and upset, but think: the raek is just an animal ... If a horse had trampled your brother in fear, would you want it tortured and neglected?" she asked. Knowing what she did about the intelligence of raeken, Meera wasn't sure her argument was a good one, but she kept that to herself. She also wasn't sure why she kept feeling the need to care for and defend the creature. She *had* seen what he'd done to those soldiers. But regardless of her doubts, she continued: "Besides, the king wants the raek cared for, and that is my job to do to the best of my ability. I understand if it isn't a job you can set yourself to."

Her second argument worked even better than she might have imagined. Linus was a loyal palace guard who aspired to fight in the king's Royal Army, after all. "You're right!" he said, nodding vigorously. "It is for the king to decide what is best, not the likes of me. I am equal to any task my king sets me!" And with that, he grabbed the cart handle and took off down the path, forcing Meera to trot after him.

After several minutes of fast-paced walking and silence, however, he deflated somewhat. Meera asked where his family lived in Altus and what kind of ceremony they would hold for his brother and coaxed him into amiable conversation. When she got Linus talking, he raved about his mother's cooking and admitted that his younger sister Kathleen's obsession with dolls gave him nightmares. They talked and laughed through the garden and down the hill, and Meera genuinely enjoyed herself; it felt nice to have someone to talk to—someone who didn't think her speech was too fine and wasn't jealous of her quality boots.

Reaching the canal, she was relieved to see that the rain from the previous night had mostly cleaned away any gore left on the beach. The raek seemed to have spread sand over the worst areas too, and the flies had left for dung-filled pastures. Only a faint smell lingered, and sniffing, she realized that the raek itself didn't actually have a strong odor despite his size. The animal in question had been lying down with his heavy, muzzled head resting on the ground when they descended the hill, but he stood as they drew closer and observed them through one piercing blue eye.

"Linus, do you think you could go back to the palace and try to find the large needle and thread that I mentioned earlier?" Meera asked. She needed the items, but she also didn't relish the idea of him standing and watching her attempts at raek healing. It was bad enough knowing the soldiers on the wall were likely observing her from a distance.

"You don't want me to stay ... in case you need me?" he asked. He looked apprehensive and was clearly imagining the raek attacking her.

"I'll be just fine on my own. Besides—" Meera gestured to the soldiers standing dutifully at the top of the wall. They didn't give her any peace of mind whatsoever, but she thought Linus might find their presence reassuring.

"I guess you're right," he replied. He looked as if he would turn to go but instead, he asked, "Why didn't it hurt you? I mean, I don't get it ... It didn't even move ..." There was an almost accusatory note to his voice that Meera tried not to find offensive; he was only upset that she had survived, and his brother hadn't.

"I suppose kitchen maids are less threatening than soldiers," she said with a small smile and a shrug, hoping to diffuse the young man yet again. She wouldn't tell anyone of the bargain she had made with the raek.

Linus managed a smile in return, dimpling his right cheek. "That must be it," he replied, and he turned and ran up the hill with coltish energy.

Meera sighed and couldn't believe it was still only the start of what would surely be a long day. She wished she had stayed in bed a little longer. Then, with another deep breath, she steadied her resolve and decided to plunge ahead, not leaving herself time for fear or doubt. Grabbing the cart's handle, she pulled it across the dirt, over the scratches, and right up along-side the raek. Her heart accelerated but not in the painful, violent way it had the day before. "Good morning! Smells like you're getting fish today," she said in her overly cheery serving girl's voice.

The raek blinked, and Meera proceeded with the long process of slipping fish through his iron slits. When the bucket was empty, the raek turned to drink from the canal as before, dragging and crisscrossing the chains from his ankle manacles. His initial movement unnerved her but didn't startle her as badly as the last time. She could do this, she thought; the raek had not shown any inclination of aggression toward her, and she was coping with her task heartily.

It was a bright, clear morning, so Meera could get a better look at the raek today: his royal blue feathers were brilliant in the sunlight if a bit dirty, his left wing still dangled at his side due to the arrows protruding from it, and she could see many more arrows and wounds on his body. Without the use of his muzzled mouth, he clearly hadn't been able to attend to his wounds or groom himself in any way. Furthermore, his scaly snout was bloody and raw from the heavy iron muzzle, and his ankles were cut where he'd strained against his manacles.

"I've brought some things with me to clean out your wounds. Will you allow me to attend to them?" Meera asked. The raek turned back toward her and blinked what she assumed was a yes, so she put on her apron and pulled out the ladder, vinegar, honey, and clean linens. "I suppose I should start by removing the arrows that are still stuck ..." she said uncertainly, positioning the ladder to start at his shoulder. Even though the raek couldn't respond, talking to him made her feel more comfortable. The enormous animal crouched down and rested his head once more on the ground to prevent the muzzle from cutting further into his flesh, and Meera thought his posture was a clear display of trust—helping her relax.

Removing the arrows and spearheads from the raek turned out to be a grisly task. She started with an arrow lodged in his shoulder and soon realized that she would have to be quick and brutal. When she first grasped the wood shaft to see if it could be slowly wiggled free, the raek shuddered and emitted a low groaning noise. Deciding to just rip it out, she grabbed the shaft and jerked at it, making the raek cry out but failing to free the arrow. His cry pierced her gut, and she scrunched her face in empathy.

"I'm sorry!" she called, her hands shaking. She didn't like the idea of pulling something out of another creature's body to begin with, and the raek's agonized noises upset her. She had to do it, though. Gritting her teeth, she gripped the arrow once more and tugged, putting all of her strength and weight into the movement. With a horrible ripping sensation, the weapon tore free. The raek screeched in pain, and the force of Meera's effort propelled her backward. She lost her footing on the ladder and fell, landing hard on her backside just as a spray of blood gushed from the wound and showered her in warm droplets.

For a moment, she just sat on the ground, shocked and trying to assess whether she was hurt. Then, deciding she was unharmed, she shot to her feet and hurried for some linens to staunch the bleeding. Climbing the ladder, she pressed the cloth to the wound. It soaked through quickly, but the blood slowed from a spurt to a seep. The sight of the deep wound and the tangy smell of blood made Meera queasy, and she hoped she wouldn't vomit on the beach again.

Continuing to apply pressure and waiting for the bleeding to stop, she looked at the raek's feathered shoulders and back and wondered where his rider usually sat and whether he used any sort of saddle. She thought his shoulder ridge looked comfortable enough, but she had never even ridden a horse—what did she know of raek riding? Once the bleeding slowed considerably, she poured some vinegar into the wound and left a fresh cloth over it, deciding to move on for the moment as there wasn't anything else she could do without a needle.

The first arrow turned out to be the worst. It had a large, notched arrowhead which was why it had been so difficult to remove and had caused so much damage. Most of the arrows had simpler arrowheads without notches or were made from sharpened sticks without metal heads at all, making them easier—though still upsetting—to yank out. When Meera got to the raek's wing, she pulled the arrows through instead ripping them backward, and after that, she found a deep wound on his back right haunch that was old but still oozing blood. She struggled to get a good look at the wound because of the raek's dense coating of feathers, so she probed two fingers inside, grimacing at the hot, meaty feeling of the flesh under her fingertips. Sure enough, there was something metal stuck in there.

A spearhead must have broken loose from its haft, she thought. It was a slippery, horrible business, but after a long effort, she managed to grip the base of the spearhead and pull it free. The raek shuddered considerably but no longer shrieked in pain, and by the time Linus returned, Meera was standing in front of a disturbingly large pile of arrows and spears. Transferring the pile into the empty fish bucket, she went to scrub her hands and arms in the canal as best she could, but when she wiped them on her skirt, they were still red with blood—the rest of her sprayed and smeared with it as well.

It wasn't yet noon, but it was turning into a warm day. Meera drank some of the water she had brought with her before scampering off the beach to meet Linus, who took in her appearance with round, button eyes. "Well?" she asked, "Did you find anything suitable?"

"I got a needle and thread from the Palace Upholsteress," he announced proudly, brandishing said needle. "They're made for thicker fabrics for furniture and the like."

"Palace Upholsteress?" Meera asked with a laugh. "There really is a position for everything here. Well, I suppose I'm proof of that!" she added, laughing some more. She was in a good mood; she suspected the hardest part of her day was over and felt pleased that she had succeeded in her task thus far. She was filthy and her hands still shook, but she was proud of herself. Taking the needle Linus offered her, she studied it and supposed it looked large and sturdy enough. "Thank you, Linus. Why don't you return home now and spend the day with your family? I can get the cart up the hill when I'm finished. Where should I return it?" she asked.

Linus didn't need persuading. Despite his family living right in Altus, Meera didn't think he made it home to see them very often. "Leave the cart with the butcher!" he replied, already turning away. "I'll see you in the morning—same time. Good luck!"

Meera waved as he sprinted once more up the hill. She didn't think she would need luck; she was feeling very safe in the vicinity of the raek at this point. Despite her clumsy ministrations —tearing arrows from his body, and obviously causing him pain —he had shown no inclination toward harming or even threatening her. She felt a little less foolish for volunteering, although she didn't relish the thought of the additional questions she would undoubtedly receive in the kitchen when she returned.

Thinking about the kitchen made her realize how hungry she was, so she walked back to the cart and sat on the edge of it, pulling out the food she had packed. Then she ate, doing her best to only touch the food by the wrappings since her hands—and nails, especially—were still bloodied. As she chewed, she looked at the raek, and the raek looked at her, his muzzled head still resting on the ground. "Am I correct in thinking you're male?" she asked around a mouthful of food.

The raek blinked, which at this point, she took to mean *yes*.

"Do you have a name?"

The raek blinked.

Swallowing and thinking she said, "I suppose I can't ask what it is ... Can I choose a name to call you?"

The raek considered a moment, then blinked.

"How about Lapis like lapis lazuli?" she asked, looking up at the sky, which normally seemed vibrant but appeared oddly pale and dull after staring at the raek.

No blink: his eye remained fixed on her.

"Hmmm, something more mundane? Rupert?" she asked teasingly.

No blink and a snort.

Meera drummed the fingers of her free hand against the cart. "How about Cerun, like the Cerun Sea?" she asked. "My father brought me there once when I was little. It was so vast and so many shades of blue all at once. He said our ancestors had voyaged across the Cerun Sea, and that's how we got our last name—Hailship. He also said adventure had been thoroughly bred out of us since then," she said, explaining: "He's a scholar, you see."

The raek considered, then blinked.

"Cerun it is!" Meera cried. She smiled broadly, but her smile faded almost instantly; this was not a pet, she reminded herself. "You know, I want to like you, but you killed Linus's brother— Linus who was just here. You killed his brother against that wall. He was so young ..." She trailed off, not sure what she was trying to say or what she could possibly gain from saying it.

The raek blinked. It was an acknowledgement of a sort, if not an explanation or apology.

For the next few hours, Meera climbed up and down the ladder, washing Cerun's wounds with vinegar, applying honey to them, and sewing the largest ones shut with large, clumsy stitches. She had never had much patience for sewing but knew enough to get the job done. She also did the best she could for the lacerations under the raek's manacles and muzzle, but the iron would just keep biting into them. Some of the time she worked, she talked to Cerun, and other times, she was silent or hummed. The raek stayed perfectly still throughout. However, as she was packing to go, he touched her arm very gently with the end of his muzzle and rumbled what she assumed was a *thank you*.

It was late afternoon by the time Meera trudged with the cart to the top of the hill. She was breathing hard and longed to lie down, but she knew she would need another bath before she could rest. Meandering slightly, she made her way to the butcher's hut; she knew vaguely where it was, though she hadn't been there before. The kitchens were almost centered in the palace garden with the stables on one far end, nearest the town, and the butcher's hut on the other end, on the outskirts of the forest. Meera found the butcher outside cleaning a deer carcass, and he glanced up when she approached, grinning. "Girl, you's more bloody than I am! You must be the raek girl," he said.

"I am. My name's Meera," she replied, wondering if the moniker *raek girl* would stick with her at the palace and possibly further into her life.

"Glad to meet you. You go ahead 'n' leave the cart. I'll take care of it," he said, then he looked at her again and laughed suddenly, making her jump. "Lil' thing like you sent in there with a raek—a raek! I wouldn't go in there 'less it were to clean the carcass!" he shouted, laughing even louder.

Meera had the feeling he was talking more to himself than to her, so she pulled the cart up by the hut door, left it, and sidled back around the man to go. The cart only contained the bucket and tongs now; she had decided to leave the ladder and what was left of the vinegar and honey by the canal, thinking she would need them again. Hurrying toward the kitchen, she avoided people as much as possible, earning shocked stares with her bloodied visage when she couldn't. She reached the kitchen with a sigh, thinking she'd reached sanctuary, but it was bustling with people, and they all went silent and gawked at the sight of her.

Cook grabbed her arm roughly and flung her toward the stair-case, simultaneously ordering the young kitchen maid, Hilly, to help her get a bath ready. Meera was five steps up when Cook called after, "And Meera, don't you come back down! Can't have every idle loaf in the palace comin' down here to see 'n' speak to you!" With that, Cook slammed the door.

Meera took another bath and ate in her room, which wasn't normally allowed in an effort to reduce vermin. Hilly didn't speak to her as she helped draw the bath and bring her food—clearly put-out at serving a fellow kitchen maid, especially Meera. The younger girl sulked the entire time, but to her credit, she did as Cook had bid her. Meera thanked her for her help and slumped in relief when she left. Then, without the need or desire to do anything else that day, she went to bed early with the shutters open to the fresh air—until Teardra returned and shut them, that is.

4

———————

Meera settled into a routine after that day: she would rise early to get food from the kitchen before others were up so that Cook couldn't accuse her of encouraging idleness and gossip, she would eat her breakfast while she waited for Linus on the bench outside, and when he brought the cart, they would walk down the hill together and talk. Meera had tried several times to release Linus from his task as she could easily retrieve the cart herself, but he always waved away the suggestion. And while she didn't want to be a bother to him, she was glad of his company and came to consider him a friend.

As the days passed, she noticed a budding change in Linus; he gradually grew less burdened by his brother's death and seemed to find something else to focus on. Unfortunately, that which he'd found to focus on happened to be her. It was like he woke up one day and noticed she was a woman; he began blushing and stammering in her presence and brought her a new flower each morning, which she then felt obliged to wear in her hair as she had the first time. Meera tried not to encourage Linus's attentions, but he was undeterred. Unwilling to lose his friendship, she determinedly ignored the awkwardness and hoped he would get past his crush with time. Still, despite the uncomfortable moments when he complimented her appearance or became agitated by her concern for the raek, their walks together were her favorite part of the day.

Once they reached the canal, Linus would return to his duties and she would attend to her own: feeding Cerun, checking his wounds, cleaning his feathers, and providing him with conversation and company. After that, Meera was essentially free to do as she pleased since Cook still didn't want her drawing a crowd to the kitchen—she had become notorious, and serving staff, palace guards, soldiers, and townspeople alike peppered her with questions whenever they got the chance.

It was now only the upper-class she could count on to ignore her presence: nobles and royals. She wasn't sure if they were unaware of who she was or simply considered it beneath them to look at her, let alone acknowledge her. Either way, she took to dressing in her own dresses rather than her kitchen uniform and exploring the palace, often positioning herself in common areas frequented by nobles and alternating between reading books and observing people.

SEVERAL WEEKS PASSED in her new normal, and on one such routine day, Meera sat on a bench in the gardens, partially obscured by bushes and underneath a shade tree. From there, she read a book and watched while the royal family hosted a garden party. She enjoyed seeing the women in their bright floral gowns and found the social etiquette of the upper-class intriguing. As she observed the well-dressed party guests eat and mingle, she noticed the king, King Bartrothomeer Altusroll, who famously hated being called by his full name and preferred King Bartro. Meera thought from watching him at a distance that the less formal name suited his demeanor, though she couldn't place in what way. Then, to amuse herself, she tried to recall the names of the king's many children, but she couldn't remember them all. She thought there were seven, currently, as they hadn't all survived childhood.

The king's eldest son and heir, she knew, was Prince Otto, who oversaw the war effort near the border. She had never actually seen Prince Otto, but the king's second son, Prince Phineas, lived at the palace and was a common sight. He was difficult to overlook with his golden hair—a rarity in Terratelle. The king had a brownish complexion—somewhat lighter than Meera's—but the queen was extremely fair, hailing from Arborea, a land to the north. Most Arboreans were pale white with blonde hair, and there seemed to be enough Arborean blood mixed into the royal line for several of the current princes and princesses to have light hair—though Prince Phineas's gleaming gold was by far the stand-out.

Meera cringed inwardly as she watched the golden-haired prince at the garden party; he had a notorious reputation among the palace staff. Prince Phineas was young, handsome, and charming, but his notoriety among the staff was for being cruel and having a penchant for violence. Meera tried to close her ears to such stories as they were horrible and frightening, but she had heard enough during her six months in the palace to feel extremely wary of the prince.

From her hidden bench in the gardens, she felt quite safe watching his golden head bob among the party guests, but she frowned, seeing that the young ladies in attendance flocked to his side and sought to earn his attention whenever possible.

Suddenly, the party seemed much more interesting than the book in her hands, and she let it fall closed. She attuned herself to the rituals of the upper class, watching the ladies gather around the prince and king and do their best curtsies. Meera had always known about curtsying, of course, but growing up she had not had much cause to curtsy herself or to observe others at the practice.

In that moment, she found the convention fascinating, and she crossed her ankles and leaned back against the bench to get comfortable. As she watched, it occurred to her that despite the different colors and styles donned by the ladies and the many ways in which they wore their hair, it was a woman's curtsy that made the first impression of her character. Meera was accustomed to the shallow, bouncy curtsy that was the mark of a servant and seemed to say nothing more about a woman than: *I am at your service.* However, observing the ladies at the garden party, she realized that there were far more intricacies in the curtsy than she had ever considered.

First, she noticed that some ladies grasped their skirts, while others didn't. Of the ladies who grasped their skirts, some artfully spread them out—an unnecessary gesture that drew attention to the fineness of their clothes. She thought these women looked boastful, akin to birds displaying their plumage. Other ladies, she saw, gripped their skirts in fists, appearing both nervous and inelegant in her opinion. In either case, she decided that women who held their skirts had an aura of desperation, to please or to garner attention. She might have imagined it, but she thought the prince seemed less interested in these ladies and turned away more quickly.

As she continued her observations, she saw that of the ladies who didn't hold their skirts, there were those who let their arms dangle loosely by their sides and those that extended them gracefully like a dancer. The arm-danglers were usually older women, she noted—likely married or otherwise secure in their status. They appeared confident, if somewhat unconcerned with the opinions of others, whereas the ladies who gracefully extended their arms down, spreading their fingers slightly, appeared the most elegant, exuding confidence and grace. Her own fingers spread and contracted on the book in her lap, attempting to mimic the beauty she beheld.

Continuing to watch and mentally categorizing what she saw, Meera determined that the last but decidedly most important aspect of curtsying was speed. The ladies who rushed their dip appeared frenzied and uncomfortable in their own bodies, as if they didn't value themselves enough to take up any of the prince's time, she thought—although, if they were simply trying to get away from him, she couldn't blame them. Still, she believed the ladies who took more time in their curtsies appeared bold, making them the most beautiful and eye-catching regardless of their physical attributes. As the ladies dipped unhurriedly, they held the prince's eye contact and his attention, only releasing it at the very bottom of their bends for a quick nod of respect as if to say, *I respect you, but I do not bend and scrape at your knees.*

At the end of her reverie, Meera sighed. The party introductions had all been made, and the prince had two of his preferred ladies cornered at the edge of the party, whispering into their ears as they giggled and blushed. Suddenly, she no longer felt like watching the scene and got up to go with a sour pit in her stomach. One of the bold, beautiful women she had just observed may end up married to Prince Phineas, she thought, and the thought sickened her. While she tried not to hear the details of the stories about the prince, she knew their essence and would not wish his attention on anyone.

Crossing through the gardens and into the palace, she sought some means of occupation or distraction; she had been struggling to find ways to bide her afternoons and had been exploring more and more of the palace. There were vast amounts of artwork to look at if one happened to have the time, and she did—without friends or family, the kitchen to work in, or hobbies other than reading, she had an abundance of time for idling in front of paintings and sculptures. Now, she meandered the newly familiar halls until she came across a painting of a horse and stopped to examine it.

As she stood and considered the colors and brushstrokes used to portray the—admittedly very bland—brown warhorse in front of her, Meera couldn't help but overhear a conversation between two guards. She was hidden from view by a large bust of a former king, and the guards seemed to assume they were alone. "They have us standin' here like statues all hours of the day when we could be out catchin' raeken and earnin' glory," whined a nasally voice. Meera perked up at the mention of raeken but remained quiet and concealed where she was.

"I can't complain," replied a deeper voice sedately. "I've got a full stomach and no one's trying to hack my head off." The second guard spoke more quietly than the first and without the passion of a debate. He sounded like he was trying to end the conversation before it started.

"Aren't you bored standin' like this?" asked the first guard, scuffing his boot against the floor like a bull deciding whether or not to charge.

"There're worse things than boredom, kid," the quiet guard answered, once more attempting to shut down the other man's complaints. Meera could only barely make out his words, but the irritation in his tone was unmistakable.

"I'd at least like to be in the dungeon, helping to rough up that

Aegorn bastard!" insisted the younger guard, undeterred and riling himself up without any help from his companion.

Meera froze, hoping they would say more. She had heard plenty of speculation about the man who had arrived with Cerun but nothing she had yet deemed reliable; the information was always relayed second or third hand and had always struck her as mere rumor. Everyone assumed the prisoner was the raek's rider, but beyond that, she didn't know where he was being kept or whether he was still in the palace at all. Admittedly, she hadn't given the man much thought, and she chastised herself for not taking more interest in Cerun's rider. Was he really in the dungeon?

"That's not the duty of a palace guard," the calmer guard said, interrupting her thoughts. He was beginning to sound steely with disapproval.

"Bet I could get him talkin' though!" the first guard cried, his nasally voice growing louder with excitement. "You know they've been workin' on him almost a month, and he hasn't said a word! Bet I could beat it out of him!" Meera's stomach dropped at that, imagining Cerun's rider being tortured. The thought of anyone being tortured in the palace while she wandered around idly gawping at paintings was difficult to swallow. Why hadn't she given the man more thought? She felt disgusted with herself—both for not thinking about the prisoner and for not realizing that he would be tortured. She should have guessed it, she realized bitterly, hating the obtuse feeling of missing something obvious.

"Hush! You'll be the one getting a beating if the captain hears you, boy," the previously quiet guard threatened, finally raising his voice in annoyance.

After the guards stopped talking, Meera waited several moments with a hand pressed into her stressed stomach, then she walked away down the hallway, slinking along the wall so they wouldn't see her. Scurrying toward her room, she continued to obsess about Cerun's rider and what might be happening to him. Was he really in the dungeon being tortured? She fervently hoped not even if reason along with a niggling in her gut told her he probably was. After all, the man's raek may have been thus far left whole and unbothered on the king's orders, but the raek couldn't speak—she presumed the man *could* speak, which drastically lowered his chances of being likewise imprisoned but unharmed.

If they were torturing the prisoner, did that mean he wouldn't be released? She doubted a tortured prisoner would be ransomed back to Aegorn; she assumed they would want their rider unharmed if they were exchanging something for him. What about Cerun? Would he spend the rest of his existence muzzled and chained down? Meera had been so focused on healing the raek and making him comfortable that she hadn't given much thought to his future before, and the bitterness in her gut blossomed into full-fledged shame.

MEERA'S SHAME lingered into the next morning, and after she fed Cerun, she told him what she had overheard about his rider. She wasn't sure why she shared the information with the raek, but she thought he had a right to know. Afterward, she watched him closely for any movements that might give her insight into his emotions—that is, assuming raeken experienced emotions the way humans did. She supposed high intelligence didn't necessarily mean they could *feel* as she might expect them to.

Cerun merely blinked his large blue eyes in answer to her statement. He didn't keen or fidget or otherwise display any indication of grief or surprise. Meera wasn't sure why, but she felt certain Cerun was capable of strong emotion even if he wasn't showing it; she had felt it in his cries the night he and his rider were dragged through the gates. Suddenly, she considered the possibility that she was wrong about the man being his rider. "Cerun, is the prisoner your rider?" she asked, feeling self-centered again for never asking before.

He blinked.

"Is he ... important to you?" she asked quietly, bunching her dress in her hands as she stood next to the cart with its empty bucket.

He blinked again, this time holding his eyes shut for longer—she assumed to express just how important the man was to him.

Meera sighed and reached out to scratch the raek behind his jaw in a hopeless approximation of comfort. "I'm very sorry that you have to go through this," she said uselessly. As she stroked his feathers, she mulled over his situation and how she could possibly help him. However, while she felt a great deal of sympathy for Cerun, she thought it was possible she was being naive; she didn't really know the raek and had never met his rider, after all. Maybe she shouldn't empathize with them—maybe they didn't deserve it. They were enemies of her country, her countrymen, her father even ...

Gnawing the inside of her cheek, she considered that while raeken may be more intelligent than Terratellens realize, that didn't mean the stories of them burning and ravaging villages weren't also true. Cerun was gentle with her but had brutally killed the two soldiers before her. At the thought of their bodies, Meera shuddered; she still avoided walking on the areas of the ground where they had lain and often struggled to fall asleep at night, picturing their bloated, staring faces and the writhing flies on their open flesh.

Shaking her head to dispel her heavy thoughts, she urged herself to focus on the present; she was removing Cerun's stitches that day. She had promised to care for the raek, and that's what she would do, she thought, shoving her moral concerns aside for the moment. Cerun's various injuries had closed and healed, but they hadn't done so nicely. As she checked each one, she saw that most of them were puckered and gnarly. They had been days old —if not a week or more—when she had first cleaned and stitched them, and she was not an expert with a needle.

Meera did her best removing the stitches all over his large body and was relieved that his many wounds, at least, hadn't festered and no longer required her attention. However, the cuts under the edges of his manacles and muzzle were another matter. While she cleaned them daily, spread honey over them, and used cloth as a buffer between the iron and the raek's raw flesh wherever possible, the wounds remained open and oozing. The ankle gashes, she thought, might gradually heal if Cerun stayed very still, but the cut on the raek's face was unlikely to heal at all.

The heavy iron muzzle put so much weight on Cerun's snout that just lifting his head to eat and drink reopened the injury daily. The edge of the muzzle was sharp—sharp enough to cut into the tough, scaly skin of the raek's face, and Meera wondered at the unnecessary cruelty of not rounding or smoothing the muzzle's edges. She hoped the offense was done out of stupidity and not malice, but she heard the way people spoke about raeken and doubted many would care about pain inflicted on one unnecessarily.

Once again, she wished she knew who she was supposed to report to in her position as *raek girl* and whether she should ask to have the muzzle removed. She didn't fear Cerun, and no one else ever approached him ... The soldiers on the walls had even been dwindling. Glancing up, she saw that there were only two men on the right-side wall that day, none on the left. She supposed the king felt confident that the raek could not escape. People would still come by occasionally to gawk at him or throw rocks, but no one ever got close. Meera resolved to speak to the captain of the guard about the muzzle for lack of any better ideas. Then she said her goodbyes to Cerun, giving him last reassuring scratches on his neck before trudging up the hill.

On her walk, she considered again whether she should care so deeply for the raek—whether he deserved it. But how could she ever know? He couldn't even speak to tell her of his past ... Then again, how could she know whether anyone was truly good without all the details of their lives? Meera had always felt certain of her own goodness—she tried to be good, at least—but she supposed she had never needed to make a difficult decision before. Sure, she had volunteered to care for Cerun, but she wasn't sure that could be called a decision when it had been more of an impulse. She supposed her impulse had come from goodness ... maybe.

Her father was definitely a good man, she thought. Although, her father was now fighting in the war, and she didn't know what manner of things he would be forced to do in the name of that war. He was forced, though; he was conscripted to fight against his will. That made a difference, didn't it? If he killed because an authority told him to, it wasn't a testament to his own character, was it? She could argue a case for either side ...

What if the war itself was immoral? How could she know whether the war was immoral or not when no one seemed to know why it had started? Terratelle had been fighting Aegorn for over seventy years, but why? It was branded as a war against evil, but the actual catalyst for the fighting was not well-documented nor was it publicly discussed. Meera's head was spinning; people and wars maybe weren't as black and white as they had always seemed in her books. She just had a feeling about Cerun—a feeling that he was good—and she was going to have to trust that feeling.

She returned the cart to the butcher, who was shirtless and singing a bawdy song while stringing up a pig. Wheeling around him, she left quietly to avoid an uncomfortable encounter. Then, after a quick trip to her room to grab a book, she ate her lunch in the kitchen. Cook still insisted she not work in the kitchen anymore since she had her new duties, but most of the initial curiosity about her from the other staff had faded. After weeks of answering questions about the raek as vaguely as possible, most people ascribed her volunteering to stupidity and her survival to dumb luck. This irritated Meera, but it was safer for her—if people knew she had read about raeken, she would be punished for breaking the law, and if people wrongly suspected her of magical ability, she would be hanged.

Spring was in full bloom, so Meera walked through the gardens and sat on a shaded bench near the stables. There, she read and watched people and horses come and go. She had always wanted to learn to ride a horse but hadn't had the opportunity. She and her father used to walk in and out of town and had rented carriages for long journeys, not that they had taken many—just the one trip to the Cerun Sea, really. Meera like bringing the horses fruit from the kitchen and patting their noses, but lately it seemed they could smell the raek on her and shied from the unfamiliarity of the scent. Now she enjoyed their gentility from a distance.

The afternoon was passing pleasantly on her shaded bench when a man bustled up to the stable, spoke to one of the hands out front, and was pointed in her direction. The man then marched straight for her. Startled, Meera considered running away but didn't think quickly enough to decide anything before the man was right in front of her, breathing heavily. The emblem on his shirt marked him as one of the king's servants, depicting Bartro's personal sigil: a fish leaping into a bear's mouth. He was fussily dressed for a servant, though, and appeared to be wearing some sort of paste to cover old pockmarks on his cheeks. Sweating in the heat, the paste ran down his neck into his ruffled collar. "Meera Hailship?" he wheezed, perching his hands on his narrow hips.

"Yes …" she replied, preemptively dreading whatever the man wanted from her.

"Finally!" he exclaimed, placing one of his slim hands over his heart. "Goodness, you were a hard woman to find. You're coming with me—the king has been waiting! Hurry, hurry, my dear!" The fussy man then made sweeping motions with his hands as if to gather her to himself, his fingers twiddling in the air.

Meera gaped at him but didn't move from her seat on the bench. "The king?" She asked. "He wants to see me?"

"Yes, yes!" the man replied, nodding vigorously into his frilly collar. "The king requested I bring you to him, and—goodness, that must have been two hours ago at least! I have been all over the palace and grounds sniffing you out. Now, hurry, hurry!" His arms moved in larger sweeping motions, and his legs joined in with impatient little stomps in the dirt.

Meera was momentarily distracted by the fussy man's garishly impractical heeled shoes before snapping back to attention and asking, "But … why?"

"Why?" squeaked the man. "Come, come! I do not question my king!"

Standing and feeling dazed, she closed the book she had been reading. Then she followed. The man's frenetic energy was contagious; the peace she had felt on her shady bench quickly melted away on their brisk walk, and her heart beat in time to his heeled shoes. However, the man eventually slowed when they entered the high-ceilinged, stone-walled interior of the palace—presumably, racing through the halls would be beneath his dignity. Meera's body calmed somewhat with their pace, and her mind was able to catch up with the situation. Suddenly registering that she was about to meet the king, she tried to smooth her flyaway hairs up toward her bun and looked down at herself to appraise her appearance.

All of her clothes from home were well-made but erred on the side of practical rather than fashionable, and her current dress was no different. It was a light sage green without frills or embroidery and in a simple cut, but she had at least managed not to stain it taking out Cerun's stitches earlier. The heat and her nerves were making her sweat, but she didn't think the sweat was showing through the light dress—yet. Wiping one of her hands across her brow, she patted uselessly at the curly bun on top of her head, adjusting the pink flower tucked into it that Linus had given her that morning. In her other hand, she still clutched her book; she had considered leaving it on the bench, but it was a fine, leather-bound edition that she didn't want to lose or damage.

She was going to meet the king! She repeated the fact inwardly over and over to let it sink in. King Bartro wanted to speak with her. It just seemed ridiculous! Who was she to meet a king? She supposed she *was* the raek girl ... Everyone had been curious about her, the girl who had tamed the demon monster. Meera's new infamy felt so strange after years of living on the fringe of society, and given a choice, she would prefer to return to moving unnoticed through her life. But she didn't have a choice.

As she continued to tail the fussy man, she began to fret about how she would behave in front of the king—how she should present herself. She knew who she was when she was alone, when she was with her father, when she was with Cerun, even, but who was she going to be in front of the king? How could she be herself when meeting a king didn't feel like something she would do? She had never even been to a party or a ball—anywhere a public-facing persona would be required. She wanted to be true to who she was but didn't know how that translated into speaking with a king ... Should she be Meera the quiet booklover, Meera the bold raek girl, Meera the subservient kitchen maid?

When they finally stopped at a door, the fussy man knocked, and another king's servant answered. The answering servant informed Meera's guide that the king was having lunch with his family in their private dining chamber. He didn't mention how long the fussy man had taken in his task, but Meera thought he was sneering when he shut the door in their faces. For a moment, the fussy man looked uncertain of what to do, then, hands flying, he exclaimed, "Oh bother! Come, come!" and they were off again.

Meera followed the man down a flight of stairs to a hallway she had never visited, lined with portraits of former kings and queens. Two guards stood a little way down, marking the door where the royal family ate their lunch, and they approached the guards. Lifting his chin, the fussy man said, "Please inform the king that Meera Hailship has been located and ask if he would like her to wait in a drawing room for his convenience." The guard opened the door, waited for silence within, and did as he was bid.

Meanwhile, Meera craned her neck and strained her ears for a response, hoping to hear a dismissal—that the king had already forgotten his passing curiosity in the raek girl. Then King Bartro's clear, commanding voice found her in the hallway, and Meera's stomach dropped: "No, bring her in. I'll meet her now."

5

———————

efore Meera could process what was happening or object in any way, the fussy man put his hand on her low back and propelled her through the open door, shutting it swiftly behind her. Shocked, she stood in what was apparently the royal family's private dining room; it was an interior room without windows but was well-lit by wall sconces on red-papered walls, and a glittering chandelier over a long, ornate wooden table. The king, queen, and six of their seven children sat along the table, and as silence descended, all heads turned to scrutinize Meera. She was a trembling fawn surrounded by a pack of wolves—except strangely, it was she who had the high ground with the royals seated before her.

After a brief hesitation, she gathered herself and approached the king where he sat at the head of the table. It was relatively cool in the room—the stone of the palace maintained the cold of night well into the day this time of year—but her hands were sweating regardless. Gripping her leather-bound book tighter so as not to drop it, she glanced at the king as she walked the length of the table toward him. King Bartro was a handsome man of middle age with shoulder-length brown hair and a close-cropped beard. Regarding him in close proximity for the first time, Meera noted that his blue-green eyes stood out against his light brown skin. Like his son's golden hair, the king's eye color was a rarity in Terratelle—a land of mostly brown-eyed people—telling a story of centuries of marriages with foreign royals.

While his posture and facial expressions had a practiced ease about them, a fire danced and sparked in the king's eyes. Meera met his flickering gaze and found herself caught by it. She hadn't formulated any real plan of how to conduct herself in the presence of royals and felt frozen with panic. In her peripheral vision, she noticed Prince Phineas's golden hair, and the garden party at which she had observed the prince and his gaggle of curtsying ladies flooded her anxious mind.

Without time to consider, Meera reached the king, and instead of bobbing a servant's curtsy, she extended her arms as gracefully as she could to her sides, tucked her chin, and with a straight back, dipped as slowly as she could while remaining steady and maintaining her eye-contact. At the very bottom of her dip, she lowered her eyes respectfully before rising and being once more burned by King Bartro's penetrating gaze. The room was so silent, she could hear her own heart's timekeeping like the irritatingly persistent tick of a clock, and she wished that time would run out —that she would be excused from this encounter. "Good afternoon, Your Majesty," she said softly into the quiet.

King Bartro's cheeks twitched into a lopsided smile, and he tented his fingers on the table, pushing back his half-eaten plate of food. "The famous Meera Hailship," he said, taking a long pause. "I have heard a great deal about you of late. I confess, I was curious to meet you at once, but I thought it best to let things ... play out on their own a little longer." Meera wasn't sure what he meant by letting *things play out* unless he meant waiting to see if she would survive the raek for long.

Regardless of what the king meant, she was struggling to deduce exactly what he wanted from her in that moment and remained as still as she could, waiting for him to continue. It was not strictly appropriate for her to speak to the king unless he bid her to or asked her a direct question—which he had not. However, after it seemed he wouldn't continue, Meera couldn't bear the silence any longer. "It is certainly an honor to meet you, Your Majesty, and I apologize if my arrival has interrupted your meal," she replied, eyes darting around the table to behold said meal. Finding the royals staring at her with varying degrees of interest and irritation, she swallowed and fixed her gaze on the king once more.

"My, you're awfully well-spoken for a kitchen maid," he remarked, leaning back in his chair slightly and cocking his head. "And what is that you have?" he asked, gesturing to the book still gripped in her hand. King Bartro's natural confidence and coy, teasing tone of voice made Meera appreciate his personal sigil more than ever; he drew to mind the grinning bear ready to catch the unwitting fish, and she could only hope she wasn't the fish leaping into his open mouth.

Reflexively, she clutched her book in front of her stomach and responded, "It is a novel about a sea voyage to look for treasure that goes horribly amiss, Your Majesty."

"One of mine?" he asked. By that, she presumed he meant: did she take it from the palace library?

Meera wasn't sure if palace staff were permitted use of the library as she didn't know any other staff members who read for pleasure—most couldn't read at all. "No, Your Majesty. It's one of my father's," she answered, still holding tightly to the book against her abdomen like a shield from his piercing gaze.

"Your father's? It is of fine make. Let me see," King Bartro said with easy command. He extended a hand, and she placed the book into it. No one else at the table spoke, and she didn't think many of them were eating either. The room was perfectly silent except for the youngest prince, a boy of five, eating merrily and humming to himself. Meera felt like an unwilling actor in a performance she hadn't known would take place, and she endeavored to stand even straighter. "This is fine leather, indeed, and not a book I'm familiar with. What is your father's profession?" the king queried, continuing to hold her book between them as if ransoming it for information.

"He's a scholar at the Altus Grand Library, Your Majesty. Although, he is currently serving in the army," she replied, swallowing.

"The Royal Army?" he asked, immediately noting her omission of detail.

"The Civilian Army, Your Majesty," she replied, keeping her chin raised. The Royal Army was a well-trained contingency of young nobles and career soldiers, whereas the Civilian Army consisted of untrained men conscripted to add more bodies to the fight when needed. There was a distinct sense of pride and accomplishment in the former that was lacking in the latter.

"Ah, and you, finding yourself without a provider, needed to seek employment in the palace kitchens?" he asked, giving her a knowing look as well as handing Meera her book back like he had sussed out everything there was to know about her and no longer needed his hostage.

Meera bristled at the notion that her father had left her uncared for when he had saved enough to ensure she would always be comfortable. She also noted with disgust that the king was aware that the Civilian Army didn't pay enough to support a man's family and didn't seem bothered by it. "Your Majesty, my plight was not one of empty pockets but of empty hands. I preferred not to be idle, so I sought honest work to fill my hands and time," she replied, trying for a neutral tone. Her nerves and irritation mixed within her, however, and her voice trembled slightly with emotion. Suddenly, she felt like she might cry any second and did her best to press back her tears.

"So, you came to work in my kitchens for sheer lack of anything better to do ... What a pitiable life you must have led to make kitchen grunt work sound appealing! What I can't seem to wrap my mind around, Miss Hailship, is why you volunteered to care for my new prize beast, and for that matter, how you have survived it," he said, leaning forward slightly as if poising himself to make a kill. But despite his threatening posture and biting words, his tone remained lofty and amused.

"I have had varied reports about you and your activity," he continued, holding her with his shifting blue-green eyes. "Most think you a dolt of a girl, merely seeking attention for herself. My captain of the guard, on the other hand, insists that neither your manner of volunteering nor your actions in the vicinity of the beast have been attention-seeking. He also insists you are of sound mind." The king paused and sipped wine from his glass, making Meera swallow involuntarily. Releasing his glass, he went on: "My cook reports that you are a good worker, but your privileged life has perhaps curtailed your fear of negative consequences, making you reckless."

That stung Meera. While she couldn't imagine Cook using any of those words exactly, she felt deeply hurt that they had said any approximation of that. Tears threatened her eyes in earnest now, but she refused to let them fall. "Others have reported that you not only feed the raek, but you have also taken it upon yourself to treat its wounds—that you removed arrows from its body, causing it immense pain and still it did not strike you down. That you speak to the beast, though none have heard what you say. That you have been seen *petting* the evil creature." At that, the king's look of amusement turned briefly to one of distaste. "What am I to think of all this?" he asked finally.

While his words were phrased like a rhetorical question, the king stopped speaking there. Meera waited, not wanting to interrupt him or speak out of turn, but the silence dragged on until she felt she must fill it. She had entered the room feeling nervous, but now she felt downright terrified; if this one man—her king—wasn't pleased, he could do anything to her—anything at all—and she shuddered at the possibilities. "Your Majesty, I can assure you that I have never sought attention or notoriety for myself. The honor of being brought before you and your family far exceeds any expectation I had for serving you in your palace," she began, knowing she was groveling and not enjoying the taste of it on her tongue. Meera had noticed that the king liked to refer to everything as *his*, so she did her best to play to his ego.

She continued: "I can also assure you that my motives were not grounded in foolishness or recklessness but in soft-heartedness. I have always loved animals and wanted to see the raek well cared for—though, I'll admit, I did not fully think through my decision when I volunteered and was very lucky to emerge from the beach unharmed. I believe he ..." She realized immediately that revealing knowledge of the raek's gender was a mistake but could only keep going. "... found me much less threatening than the soldiers that had entered before me and had surely also grown quite hungry by then. Beyond that, I can only say that daily exposure has created a familiarity between the raek and me ... I do hope I have performed my duties to Your Majesty's satisfaction," she finished breathlessly, standing her ground. She had managed to hold back her tears and keep her voice from quavering throughout her speech. She even held

King Bartro's gaze and contrived to keep a small smile plastered on her face.

There was an interminable minute in which no one spoke, and Meera resisted the urge to stammer more explanations into the silence. Fleetingly, she wondered if the king had interrogated Cerun's rider himself. If so, she felt a deep respect for the mysterious man for managing to hold his tongue—assuming what she had overheard was true. Suddenly, King Bartro sat back in his chair, tented his fingers once more, and grinned at her, displaying his straight white teeth. "Miss Hailship, you are dismissed. Please report to me tomorrow after your morning duties."

That was it? Meera managed another curtsy, quicker and cruder than the first one, and made for the exit. Fumbling with the knob at first, she got the door open, sidled out, and shut it behind her, releasing her held breath. She felt like a rabbit that had slipped a hound and shook like one too. The fussy man was gone, so she picked a direction at random and made off down the hallway, unsure of which way they had come or how to get back to the gardens. Eventually, she found her way and walked to the kitchen, and once there, she drank several glasses of cold water as if washing away her nerve-wracking experience. Afterward she felt steadier, but when Cook asked if she was alright, her chest clenched. Avoiding the question and the person, Meera fled to her dark, quiet room where, curled up on her bed, she let her tears fall at last. The stress of being brought before the king seemed to wrench loose all of the pent emotions within her.

Meeting King Bartro had been frightening, but Meera sobbed and clutched her arms around herself from sheer loneliness. She had been lonely for as long as she could remember, really. She loved her father and enjoyed his company, but the love of one man had never filled the missing gap of friends her own age or her mother. Her mother's loss was one she had borne for years—

one she could live with—but when her father had been conscripted, she'd been completely alone. Coming to the palace had been a distraction, and for a time, being surrounded by people had made her feel slightly better ... Until it hadn't.

Until the sight of two maids whispering and giggling together had made her chest feel tight. Until watching nobles eat and dance together had made her feel like a statue forced to watch and never partake. Until hearing that Cook considered her too privileged to have common sense had made her feel like she had lost her one true ally. Meera cried all of her loneliness and hopelessness out into her pillow until her nose was clogged with snot, and she started to think rationally again. Then she got back up. What else could she do? Taking deep breaths, she reminded herself that she had a friend in Linus—though it was limited by his crush on her. She reminded herself that her father could still return home —that all hope wasn't lost. She reminded herself that Cerun needed her, and having that purpose helped ground her.

Grabbing a sweater before leaving her room, she packed herself dinner in the kitchen and left through the back door. Now that the sun was lower in the sky, it was extremely pleasant outside, and the fresh air calmed her. After meandering through the gardens awhile, she chose a spot by a fishpond to eat and attempted to process her meeting with the king. Why did he want to see her again the next day? When had she become a person notable enough to be called in front of the king at all, let alone two days in a row? Had she done something wrong? She had read illegal manuscripts before coming to the palace, but she didn't think she'd done anything illegal since ...

Should she have groveled and apologized more? Meera knew she could be prideful, and she hoped her pride had not doomed her in some way. No, she thought; she hadn't done anything wrong. The king must want more information about the raek—

his *prize*, he had called Cerun. She wondered once more what Cerun's future would hold and whether she could say anything to the king to win him his freedom. She doubted it. The king would not release his prize.

Meera sighed, stood, and without conscious thought, found herself moving downhill to the canal. There were no soldiers on the wall now, and she went to Cerun, unobserved by spying eyes. While she didn't speak to the raek of her day, being in his presence soothed her loneliness. She scratched and petted him until the sun sank beneath the horizon, and his large, warm body comforted her. While his inability to speak usually saddened Meera, in that moment, she found it ideal; she could look into his large, intelligent eyes and at least pretend to see compassion and love within them, if only because he could not tell her otherwise. Eventually, the air cooled considerably, and she donned her sweater and started the trek uphill to make it back to the kitchen before darkness could fall in earnest.

6

The next morning, Meera awoke feeling anxious to meet the king again but determined. If caring for Cerun was to be her purpose, she resolved to petition King Bartro for better treatment. His calm authority had frightened her, but his sharp mind and penetrating gaze had also intrigued her. She thought there was at least a small possibility that he would take her suggestions into consideration. As she sat on her usual bench to await Linus, her eagerness to see him and tell him about the king made her legs jiggle in anticipation. Linus greeted her with a smile and a white flower, which she automatically tucked into her bun, and when they began their walk, Meera launched into her story.

Linus's enthusiasm did not disappoint; "You spoke directly to the king? I can't believe it! Did you mention me at all? That I've been helping you and the like? If not, you should! Maybe don't though ... doesn't sound like he was entirely pleased ... And in front of the entire royal family and everything! Wow! That must have been terrifying!" he babbled excitedly. Meera laughed and was about to answer, but Linus kept going: "I mean, I saw you the first time you went in with the raek, so I know you don't scare easy, but still ... even the captain looks shaken after he reports to the king sometimes! He's a good and fair ruler, of course, but a king needs to be a little scary to maintain power. And he wants to see you again today? What for, do you think?"

Linus finally paused to breathe, allowing her to answer him. "I don't know. I suspect he wants to know more details about the raek and the care I've been giving him. I might try to get his muzzle removed if the king seems amenable ..." she said, trailing off and hoping she hadn't triggered one of Linus's moods.

"Remove its muzzle? What if that's all that's keeping it from roasting you, melting its chains, and raising the whole palace to the ground?" he asked levelly. He gave her a skeptical but tolerant look, swiping his hair from his face with his free hand while he dragged the cart behind him. Despite Linus's hatred of the raek for killing his brother, he accepted that Meera cared for the creature—usually. At least, she had argued enough times that a spooked animal could kill without being evil for Linus to understand her point of view—even if he still didn't agree with her.

"*Could* he melt his chains?" Meera asked. She hadn't considered the possibility and didn't know anything about metal or blacksmithing.

"Don't know," Linus replied, scratching at a pimple on his chin. "A regular fire isn't hot enough to melt iron—you need a bellows to blow air in and make it hotter." Meera wondered whether raek fire was hotter than a regular wood-burning fire or not. She was trying to recall if there might be mention of it in her father's manuscripts at home, when Linus kept talking, distracting her: "Hey, why do you think it's male, anyway? My mother always says it's the she-devil that has the sharpest bite."

"I'd like to meet your mother!" she replied, laughing. But she immediately regretted it when Linus's face lit up. She didn't want to mislead him in his affections.

"You should! You should come home with me one day and meet my whole family. I'm sure they'll love you!" he beamed.

"Maybe one day ... but today I have a king to meet," she joked, hoping to change the subject. Thankfully, it worked, and Linus went on another tangent about what Meera should and shouldn't say when she met the king again. They eventually got sidetracked, and their conversation ebbed and flowed easily for the rest of their walk. Meera cherished Linus's company and scolded herself inwardly for often discounting his friendship. He may be young and prone to sulking, but he was kind and enthusiastic. She was not entirely alone.

When he dropped her and the cart off at the canal, she noticed that there still weren't any soldiers on the wall and supposed the military presence had been officially deemed unnecessary. That, or their continued presence had been a ruse to keep an eye on her; the king had clearly spoken to the soldiers about her activity. Suddenly, Meera wondered why Linus hadn't been interviewed about her. Perhaps he had—perhaps he had been reporting on her the whole time, his friendship a ruse ... No, she thought; now she was truly being paranoid. She trusted Linus. The king must speak to the captain with the assumption that any important information from the palace guards would be relayed through him.

Why was she so scared anyway? She wasn't a traitor. She had read some illegal texts, sure, but she was only using that information to perform her duties with the raek and serve her king. She cared for Cerun, but she didn't think that counted as treason. She wanted to help him and hoped that he would be freed, but she wasn't planning to act against the king's wishes ... For now, she supposed, but what if Cerun was never freed—was chained up indefinitely or tortured? Her gut told her not to let those things happen, but she didn't know what she would actually *do* or what the *right* thing to do would be.

Dismissing the questions floating around her mind, she tried focus on the task before her, feeding Cerun through the slits in his bars. On a whim, she asked, "Can raek fire melt iron?"

Cerun rumbled a deep noise in his throat, which she took as a *no*, and they both continued the process of feeding and eating because any time the raek spent with his head off of the ground allowed his muzzle to cut into his flesh.

"I've been called in front of the king today," Meera said in a would-be casual voice. This was new territory between her and Cerun. She talked to him often but usually about mundane things —neutral topics. The king and the war were not neutral topics. However, despite her trepidation, Cerun didn't react except to cock his head slightly in question. "I met him briefly yesterday. He mostly questioned me about my life and motivations. I'm not sure why he requested to see me again today, but I want to ask him if your muzzle can be removed—if it seems appropriate to ask, that is. If your fire could melt your chains, then surely there would be no chance of having it removed, but if raek fire is not known to melt iron, then perhaps there is a small chance ..." she explained. Then she suddenly felt heartsick—like she was offering the possibility of a scrap of sunshine to someone who would be blind for life regardless.

How long would she spend her life caring for Cerun while he suffered and withered? After only a few weeks, he was already looking thin and haggard from being endlessly chained down. She did her best to keep him clean, but his feathers were growing dull and falling out. Meera decided right then that keeping anyone, human or beast, in a constant state of confinement wasn't right no matter what they had done. But she didn't know what the alternative should be ... What if they'd done something truly horrific? Should they be killed? She thought that would be simpler and cleaner than the constant torment of confinement, but who could decide whether something was worth the punishment of death?

Didn't both opposing lands at war always view their enemy's killing as villainous and their own killing as heroic? She wondered again what the war between Terratelle and Aegorn was *really* about. Then she wondered whether it even mattered. Shaking her head, she put her questions aside once more. All she could do that day was try to make Cerun's life more comfortable. She *would* ask the king about the muzzle, she resolved—no matter how awkward it might be. Feeling more determined than ever, she headed up the hill.

When she approached the king's study, two palace guards stood at the door, and she stated her name for them. One of the guards entered the room to announce her presence, and she smoothed the lilac fabric of her dress. It was one of the nicer ones she owned which, admittedly, didn't make it especially fine. She liked the color, though, and thought the cinched waist of the bodice was especially flattering on her figure. The guard returned quickly and held the door ajar for her. Meera entered the room and had to pause a moment to let her eyes adjust to the bright light within.

The study had large windows paned with glass all along the back wall, making it much brighter than the hallway. To her left was an ornately carved desk and to her right a sitting area with biscuits and tea set upon a table. King Bartro was behind his desk with a stack of letters in front of him, and when she entered, he rose and made his way around the desk to stand in front of her, a smile on his face and candlelight flickering in his blue-green eyes despite the distinct lack of candles in the room.

Meera curtsied the dignified, slow curtsy that she had inadvertently claimed as her own the day before. "Your Majesty," she said, as she straightened and met his eyes once more.

"Miss Hailship, what a pleasure it is to see you again. Won't you come and sit with me?" he asked, gesturing to the sitting area. "Help yourself to some refreshments." Moving over to the area himself, he claimed a seat.

Meera was shocked to be asked to sit in the king's presence, but she certainly wasn't going to refuse him. A king's suggestion was a command, after all. "If it pleases, Your Majesty," she said as she perched on the edge of the settee opposite him. Glancing at the embroidered ivy on the plush green seat cushion, she was reminded of Linus saying the palace had an upholsteress whose sole responsibility was maintaining the upholstery of the palace's many sofas and chairs. The thought made nervous laughter bubble up from her stomach, but she pushed it down, causing her diaphragm to do a strange little jump.

Plastering a smile on her face, she sat still and straight and waited, hoping her heart's fluttering wasn't visible in her throat. The king observed her silently for a stretch of long moments, then he rose unexpectedly and moved leisurely around the table, sitting next to her on the settee and leaning all the way back into the cushions. Other than turning her body to continue facing him as he settled next to her, Meera didn't move. The king was in such close proximity, she noticed he smelled like cedar, which she imagined might be from a fine cedarwood chest in which his clothes were kept.

Sitting stiff and uncertain, she forced herself to meet his direct gaze and waited for him to speak. He didn't speak. He reached a hand out toward her, and she stopped breathing. His hand raised to her hair, his belled sleeve brushing her cheek. Then he lowered it with a smile and leaned in toward her. Meera could feel his warm breath on her neck, and her gooseflesh rose to greet it, her pulse quickening. In a low, conspiratorial voice, the king murmured, "You seem to enjoy wearing my flowers in your hair. My gardeners wouldn't take kindly to it, but I won't tell them."

Her eyes widened at his statement as well as his closeness. His lips were only a hair's breadth from her ear and neck. Without conscious thought, she leaned in toward the warm, cedarwood-smelling man ever so slightly, her body reacting to him in unexpected ways—ways she felt too ashamed to acknowledge. Her response to the king surprised and confused her, rendering her speechless and immobile. Then, as quickly as he'd claimed her space, he released it, reclining against the cushions of the settee and crossing an ankle over the opposite knee, eyes dancing. Meera nearly sagged in relief, but she didn't want to show how rattled she was.

Hands surprisingly steady, she reached forward and poured two cups of tea, handing one to the king and sipping from the other. She endeavored to sit against the back cushion of the settee and look at ease while her mind raced, wondering what had just passed between them. The king was a handsome man, but on their meeting the day before she had found him frightening. Setting her tea in her lap, she looked into King Bartro's eyes, expecting him to tell her why she was there.

The king held her gaze and his silence. Meera knew should wait for him to speak as protocol demanded, but she felt the need to fill the quiet and struggled not to squirm under his silent scrutiny. That was his game, she realized, to make her speak without permitting her to speak—to wait for the fish to jump willingly into his awaiting maw. Oh well, she thought; who was she to try to win a game against a king? If he wanted to feel powerful, she would make him feel powerful. She wanted something from him, after all: she was there for Cerun. "Your Majesty, may I ask why you called me here today?" she asked. She decided to entirely ignore his remark about her flowers; she didn't want Linus to get in trouble—or get noticed by the king at all for that matter. It was too late for her ...

"Miss Hailship, you have captured my interest," he replied, his tone more businesslike than before. "You volunteered for something unsurvivable and survived—that in itself was noteworthy. In fact, every person high-born and low in the palace took note and took an interest in you. And yet—when I sent my man to find you yesterday, it took him nearly three hours to locate you! Dodgers is a fatuous man, but he does his job well. Despite your notoriety, you managed to move about the grounds without anyone noticing you. He reported that he could not find one person who could remember seeing you the entire day until he went to the stable where you were in full view."

The king paused to sip his tea, eyes burning into her the whole time. "Miss Hailship, you have proven yourself brave, you have proven yourself discreet, and yesterday, when we spoke, I found you sharp-witted. I can make use of a woman of your particular talents. I can always use more eyes and ears in the palace. What say you to that?" he asked.

Meera hadn't known what to expect from the king, but it certainly wasn't that. He hadn't called her there about the raek at all. He had noticed her—a king of all people had noticed her when, as he had pointed out, she generally went entirely unnoticed. She wouldn't have thought she'd be the type of person to be overwhelmed and flattered by the attention of someone above her standing, and yet ... she had been so alone, so unseen by the other inhabitants of the palace. To have the king himself—an intelligent, striking king at that—notice her stroked her pride in a way she hadn't known she'd craved.

However, while she was deeply flattered, she was also

concerned to know what being the king's eyes and ears might mean—not that she thought her feelings about the situation mattered; she was already well aware that a request from the king was not really a request. "Your Majesty, you honor me with your notice. I am, of course, willing to assist you in any way," she replied, then amended: "Provided I can ... maintain my dignity." Despite her unexpected physical response to the king, she didn't wish to commit to *any* service to him. "May I ask exactly what Your Majesty has in mind?" she inquired with obvious trepidation.

King Bartro smiled with the blatant satisfaction of a cat in sunlight. "Don't fret, Miss Hailship. I have every intention of leaving your dignity *intact*, though your handling of large beasts *is* impressive." Meera nearly choked on her tea. She didn't hear bawdy comments often, but the king's wasn't exactly subtle. Staring down at her lap, she could feel blood pooling in her cheeks and wondered whether it was visible under her light brown skin. If the king noticed her discomfort, he didn't let on, continuing smoothly: "As the weather warms, many of my nobler subjects will come to the palace for feasts and entertainment. I like to be kept aware of their loyalties and personal affairs."

So, he wanted her to spy for him around the palace. She could do that, she thought. She spent much of her time observing people already. She would need to learn the identities of the nobles and get close enough to hear them at times ... Pausing in her calculations, Meera gave a brief thought to what her father would think of her spying for the king. But he wasn't there. He wasn't there, and she was, and that was the whole reason she'd sought diversion at the palace in the first place. Pushing away thoughts of her father, she plunged ahead and asked, "Is there anyone, in particular, Your Majesty would like me to keep an eye on?"

The king's eyes sparked, igniting something in Meera—a new excitement. She wasn't just a scholar's daughter or a kitchen maid; she was a spy for the king. "In the hallway with the bust of King Federo, there is a table containing a small urn with a flower on it. Are you familiar with the hallway?" he asked.

"Yes, Your Majesty," she replied, breathless with her new sense of intrigue. It had been that same bust that had allowed her to overhear the two guards discussing the raek's rider.

"Good. I will leave names in the urn for you. You will write out your reports and likewise leave them in the urn. Do not visit the spot too frequently, however, and do not seek me out in person unless I request it. Do you understand?" he asked brusquely, setting his tea on the table and uncrossing his legs.

"Yes, Your Majesty. I understand," she replied, also setting down her cup.

With a nod, he rose and walked to his desk area. She rose as well, as was required by etiquette. Pulling something from a drawer, he returned to her, holding out an intricately carved wooden fountain pen. "Use this when you write. It is faster and more discreet than a quill. I assume you have paper," he said.

Meera took the pen. It really was beautiful. She considered refusing the gift but could tell by the king's clipped tone that she was to take it and do as she was told. Vaguely, she wondered whether he found his subject's constant bowing, scraping, and polite refusals irritating. He struck her as a man inclined toward efficiency—when he wasn't being playful and flirtatious, a mood he seemed to flicker in and out of without warning. She fingered the pen thoughtfully. Her father had several fountain pens, but they were inexpensive models and wrote unreliably, often spilling large pools of ink. He had never been willing to spend the money on a good one. "Thank you, Your Majesty," she said simply.

The king stepped back and eyed her. "There will be a raise in your earnings as well. I will attribute it to the danger of your duties with the raek. I look forward to working with you, Miss Hailship. A king needs a variety of weapons in his arsenal, and I do not as yet have one as sharp yet unassuming as you." And with that, he moved toward the door to open it for her.

Meera swelled with importance, though she wasn't sure how she felt about being called a *weapon*. Then she hesitated because the king's mention of the raek reminded her of her determination to ask about Cerun's muzzle. He was about to open the door, so it was now or never. "Your Majesty, there is one more thing ..." she said, nervously fingering the skirt of her lilac dress.

King Bartro turned to her, raising his eyebrows, and all lingering amusement died quickly from his eyes, revealing a swaying predator lurking within their depths. Meera's mouth went suddenly dry as if she hadn't had the cup of tea only moments before, but she rallied and continued with what small confidence she could muster, gripping her new pen in her fist. "I do not presume to know what Your Majesty's plans are for the raek. However, I feel I must inform you that the condition of ... your prize is deteriorating. If Your Majesty saw fit, I believe removing the iron muzzle would do a great deal to restore the raek's appearance and vigor and preserve his ... value," she said, looking unwaveringly into the king's shifting gaze.

"You want me to remove the beast's muzzle?" he asked darkly.

"Your Majesty, I admit I have a soft heart where animals are concerned, but regardless of my feelings, should Your Majesty wish to preserve his prize, I believe the removal of the muzzle would be prudent. It has caused a constant, open sore on the beast's face that I cannot heal. Without the muzzle, the raek would also be capable of eating more heartily and grooming itself, which would improve its overall appearance. As Your Majesty said, the palace will soon see many visitors. I would think Your

Majesty would want to show his prize to its fullest potential," she replied, heart thumping wildly and breathless from the amount of "Your Majesties" she felt she had to use for decorum's sake.

The king rubbed his jawline under his short beard. "I suppose the more pitiful the creature looks, the less impressive a victory it will seem. I will think on this suggestion, Miss Hailship. However —" he paused, fixing his mercurial gaze on her once more, "— know that you are playing with fire," he warned. Then he pulled open the door, and Meera curtsied and hurried through it, hearing it click shut behind her.

The dim hallway was just as much a shock as the brightly lit room had been, and she stood blinking for a long moment. Recovering herself, she walked to the nearest door to the garden and subsequently to the kitchen. The whole way, she wondered what the king had meant when he'd said she was playing with fire. Did he mean that her suggestion was inappropriate? That her tenderness for the raek would not be tolerated? Or, did he perhaps mean literally that if he allowed the muzzle to be removed, she could be endangered by fire? Meera puzzled over it but didn't draw any conclusions. She didn't draw any conclusions about the king's intended meaning, that is, but one conclusion she was sure of: engaging with the king was, in itself, playing with fire.

7

———

The next morning, Meera went down to the kitchen at her usual time, but instead of retrieving food and going right outside as had become her habit, she loitered at the table, hoping to engage Cook in conversation. While she still felt a little hurt by what Cook had said about her, she couldn't blame them after spending more time with King Bartro; he was not the kind of man whose questions could be evaded. He had asked Cook for a report about her, and they had given one. Meera also realized that part of the reason she had felt so hurt by Cook's opinion of her was that she saw some truth in it; she *had* grown up privileged, and she *had* been behaving recklessly. She couldn't fault Cook for having an opinion about her, and they had always treated her well. Pushing her eggs and potato hash aside for the moment, she stared at Cook's back. "Good morning," she said tentatively.

Cook turned, slowly, and regarded her with a level gaze. "Talkin' to me today, are you? You must be needin' somethin'. Out with it," they said, their arms crossed in a defensive position.

Meera sighed. Cook was a straightforward person, so she would be straightforward in return. "Cook, I'm sorry ... The king told me what you said to him about me, and I was hurt by it, at first. But I'm not anymore, and I don't wish to avoid you any longer. You've always been so kind to me ..." she said, trailing off because she didn't want to discomfit Cook with too much sentimentality.

Cook smiled and clapped Meera roughly on the shoulder, saying, "There's some good cheese pasties in the oven if you wait a bit." And that was that. All was forgiven and forgotten with Cook.

Meera waited for the pasties and took two, one for Linus. As she left, she wondered why she couldn't approach life like Cook—why she agonized over everything people said and did and held onto hurt feelings for so long. She longed for Cook's self-assuredness, but she didn't even know who she was anymore; she didn't recognize this woman who volunteered for dangerous tasks and willingly agreed to spy for the king. Part of her was excited by her new life, but it felt at odds with who she had always been—who her father had raised her to be. And now she dreaded seeing Linus—usually her favorite part of the day—because she was going to have to lie to him.

When Linus arrived in the soft light of the new morning, he was bright-eyed and eager to hear about her meeting with the king, but Meera couldn't look at his face and fixed her gaze instead on the cobbled path before her feet. She had been so glad to talk to him about the king the day before, and his enthusiasm and empathy had helped settle her nerves. But now she would have to lie to him—her only friend. She didn't want to, but she couldn't tell him about being asked to spy for the king; he was counting on her to be discreet. She decided to tell Linus every detail except for the king's request from her, and as they walked along their usual paths, she told him about the king's study, the tea, the flower incident, and how she had tried to persuade him to remove the raek's muzzle. She didn't share how close the king had gotten to her or her confusion about that closeness, and she didn't disclose her new position as the king's proclaimed *weapon*.

Again, Meera wondered who this woman was who met with kings, lied to a friend, and allowed herself to be used as a *weapon*. But whatever the king called her, she only wanted to care for Cerun—her intentions were pure, and that was what mattered, right? Still, she felt uneasy and wondered what her father would think. He would always say, "explanation is the lesser man to action." If she felt the need to explain her reasoning to herself, maybe she *was* making poor decisions. Then she started—it had been three months since she had heard from her father. Her stomach dropped at the thought, but she comforted herself by thinking that no news wasn't exactly bad news. He could still return soon. Then she would leave her palace life and return home to be scolded for her foolishness.

Linus had listened quietly through Meera's story, but when she trailed off, he jabbed a finger toward her. "Is one of those for me?"

"Hmm?" she asked, before looking down at her hand and remembering Cook's pasties. She handed him one, wondering if he had been listening at all or just waiting to ask for his share of the food.

Linus took a big bite of his cheese pasty and panted open-mouthed to dispense some of the heat from the fresh baked good. "Hot!" he shouted unnecessarily, "but so good!" When he swallowed his bite, he glanced at her sheepishly. "I'm sorry if my flowers have gotten you in trouble, Meera. I never thought ..."

"Don't worry about it!" she said, brightly. "I don't think the king actually minded." She cursed herself. Of course, the one part of her encounter she could share with Linus had made him feel guilty. She was already wearing the yellow flower he'd given her that day. The ritual had embarrassed her at first, but now she enjoyed the routine of it—the comforting expectation that at least one nice thing would happen to her every day. She had even started pressing some of the flowers into her books to save as keepsakes.

Linus didn't stay concerned for long. It was an especially clear, beautiful day, and the weather seemed to bolster his spirits. "I wonder if he'll do it," he mused, "... take off the muzzle, I mean. But if he did, would you be needed to feed it anymore?"

"Maybe not," Meera replied, gazing up at the sky. She hadn't considered that, but she wanted what was best for Cerun regardless and would gladly go back to her work in the kitchen and visit him in her spare time. Then she pondered something else: "Won't the palace eventually need the canal beach for loading and receiving shipments of goods?"

"Nah," Linus said, shoving more pasty into his mouth and talking around it. "They've just been using the next beach down. It's a little further but not much. As long as the walls and chains hold, I doubt they'll move the beast. The dungeons weren't designed for a creature that large."

Meera had just taken a bite of her own pasty, and the rich, buttery flavor turned to mud in her mouth at the thought of Cerun being shut in a dungeon. She didn't want him to be chained next to the canal indefinitely, but it was better than being in a dungeon ... He, at least, had fresh air and running water. Then she spared a thought for his rider, which she—admittedly— didn't do often. She couldn't imagine what he must be experiencing. Looking down at her pasty, she suddenly didn't feel right eating the delicious, decadent food when the prisoner was likely hungry and suffering, and she handed it to Linus, who happily crammed half of it into his mouth at once. "Do you think they're still trying to torture information out of the prisoner?" she asked him.

Linus had previously confirmed that the rumors he'd heard were the same as what Meera had overheard about the prisoner. He chewed for a minute before he could reply. "Last I heard, they are," he said, swallowing his remaining bite of pasty and licking grease off his fingers. "Folk are starting to say he must not be human the way he's held out against torture. They're saying he must be ... you know, *knell.*" Knell, like raeken, were a taboo subject—illegal to read about, and for the most part, unmention-able unless one was renouncing them.

Meera lowered her voice even though no one was around them on the winding path to the canal and asked, "What makes knell ... different? Do you know?" She knew only vaguely from her reading that the knell had magic in some capacity. The rider, Kallan, from her favorite story was knell, but the story hadn't actu-ally included any mention of magic or any other unusual charac-teristics.

"I heard from another guard that they have special abilities and live a long, long time. He also said they have fangs and red eyes, but I think he was just trying to scare me. I heard the pris-oner looks normal, so either he's human or knell look the same as we do," Linus answered with a shrug.

"How long is a long time?" she asked.

"Like—forever," he replied. "They're like gods on land, only evil."

Were gods never evil? Meera didn't know much about religion. Her father had always said, "faith is the enemy of learning." He believed absolute certainty of anything prevented people from thinking and discovering new things. He would also say, "being a scholar doesn't mean I know everything or even many things, it means I'm painfully aware of how little I know." Meera missed his jovial philosophy, and she wondered for the first time how soldiering might change him. She hoped his sense of humor would remain untouched by the horrors of war.

When they reached the canal, Linus left with a wave and a loping run up the hill, and Meera proceeded to feed Cerun chunks of what she thought was venison through the slits of his muzzle. Studying her raek friend, she noticed his large eyes were glassy and despondent. "Cerun, I spoke to King Bartro yesterday," she said uncertainly. She wanted to tell him there was hope but didn't want to mislead him, either. "I explained why it might be prudent for him to remove your muzzle. He didn't seem pleased by the suggestion but didn't dismiss it outright ... He said he would consider it."

She knew Cerun heard her and understood, but he didn't blink. And before the contents of her bucket were even empty, he laid his head back down on the ground, refusing to eat more. Meera had wanted to ask him questions about what Linus said of knell but decided against it. Instead, she took some extra time wiping his feathers clean and used a brush she'd borrowed from the stables to loosen the caked dirt from his claws. Humming while she worked, she hoped to infuse a small amount of joy into the raek's day.

Eventually—though she had not enlivened Cerun's spirit at all —she decided it was time for her to go, and she put some of her supplies neatly against the right-side wall and others back into the cart to wheel back to the butcher. Engrossed in her work, she hadn't noticed him approach. Then she glanced up and started— Prince Phineas stood at the tapered end of the left-side wall. Hesitantly, Meera wheeled the cart over the threshold of Cerun's beach, but the prince strode in front of her, blocking her path. She froze, and as her body stilled, her heart raced. The prince's hands were in his pockets, but he looked anything but relaxed; the set of his shoulders was tense—predatory—and his chin was raised as if he were scenting the air. His golden hair gleamed in the sun, loose on his shoulders, and his lips were curled in a charming smile that did nothing to dispel Meera's unease. Bobbing a perfunctory curtsy for him, she said, "Your Highness," avoiding eye contact and hoping he would move aside. He didn't.

"I thought I'd come down here and get a look at my father's pet," he said with a strangely boyish, innocent glint in his eyes. "And I haven't looked upon the raek in some time either," he added, laughing with seemingly true joy and tossing his head back even further. Meera didn't care what he called her, but she hoped he wasn't aware that the king had asked her to spy because then others might know. No, she thought; he was probably referring to the interest the king had shown in her when the royal family was at lunch the other day. "Well don't just stand there," he continued, raising his fair eyebrows in an approximation of interest completely at odds with the sneer evident in his tone of voice. "Impress me with your grace and wit! You were much more interesting at lunch."

Then, to Meera's horror, he took two steps closer to her. He was just one man, but it felt like he obstructed the entire width of the beach. He was a blockade in himself—a hulking beast more menacing than the truly large animal behind her. His hands didn't leave his pockets—he didn't need them to assert himself; he was plenty threatening without them. She wanted to pass him—to leave. Her eyes shifted side to side, but her legs felt loose and weak from fear. She didn't think she could dart around him even if she abandoned the cart. He took another jaunty, teasing step closer, creeping into reaching distance, and she took a very small step back, bumping her heels against the cart's wheel. She was trapped.

"Your Highness, is there something you need from me?" she

asked, her voice quavering. She had managed to keep it steady through two meetings with King Bartro himself, but just a few moments in Prince Phineas's presence had completely unnerved her.

"Need? Perhaps not, but I'm always in search of new entertainment. I find life at the palace can be taxingly boring," he replied, lowering his honeyed voice like he was sharing intimate secrets with her. He leaned forward slightly and smiled what—if she didn't know better—she would call a friendly, handsome smile. Under the circumstances, however, the prince baring his white teeth felt like an animalistic threat.

Meera gripped the cart's wooden handle so tightly splinters bit into her palm. Then, glancing around once more, she decided to make a break for it. She started to move to her right, saying, "Pardon me, Your Highness. I have other duties to—"

But like a cat playing with a mouse, the prince's left hand shot from his pocket and clamped over her mouth, fingers and thumb pressing into both cheeks. Meera gasped an ugly sound of shock as his fingers squeezed her lips into an absurd pucker. "You don't go unless I say so," he purred calmly into her face.

Losing all sense of decorum, she struck out with both arms and stumbled backward, away from the prince. Tripping on the cart's wheel, she fell on her butt just over the first claw marks in the dirt. Prince Phineas stepped forward, hand outstretched to claim her again, but Cerun moved behind her. Faster than Meera would have thought his bulk and chains would allow, the raek lunged forward and swiped at the prince. A single claw found its mark, slicing open the prince's fine, belled sleeve and gouging into his skin.

The combined rattle of the raek's chains, the low rumbling of his warning growl, and the prince's howl of pain and outrage bombarded Meera's ears. She felt as if the world were exploding around her, and she sat dumbstruck with her hands over her ears and her heart in her throat. The noise only lasted a moment, however, and she lowered her hands shakily to her sides. Cerun stood protectively behind her, and Prince Phineas had a hand clasped over his bleeding arm.

Flashing his teeth in a mockery of a smile without any of its earlier charm, the prince opened his mouth to say something then seemed to reconsider and shut it. Quickly, he smoothed his expression back into one of cool indifference and remarked, "I better get this cleaned up," before turning, inexplicably, to go.

Meera's forehead bunched in confusion, and she watched as Prince Phineas sauntered back up the hill, taking his time despite the blood dripping from his sleeve. Once he was out of sight, she sagged against Cerun's front leg and felt laughter, of all things, gurgle up from her belly. Her nerves and relief left her hysterical, and she laughed for some time, her fits coming and going in waves until she finally settled down. It wasn't funny, she knew; it was most definitely the opposite of funny. The prince had attacked her—tried to hurt her, scare her, or both. It was terrifying.

Taking several deep breaths, she sobered and moved away from Cerun to look into his eyes. "Thank you, my friend," she said. "But I don't know what we're going to do now. He'll seek vengeance for this." Phineas hadn't left her with a final word or threat, but Meera knew she hadn't seen the last of him. Shakily, she rubbed her cheeks where he had gripped her.

Cerun blinked—it was the only response he could offer.

Sighing, Meera went to the wall to get her vinegar and honey. Cerun's movements had worsened the gash under his muzzle, which was now bleeding freely. There wasn't much she could do for it, but she did what she could. After caring for the raek's wound, she was tempted to spend yet more time grooming him to avoid leaving the safety of his vicinity, but she couldn't put off leaving forever. Feeling vulnerable and afraid, she trudged uphill with the cart to the butcher.

At the butcher's hut, she paused to listen to his latest song and offer him a smile; the man made her uncomfortable, but she would choose his company over the prince's any day. The butcher bowed deeply when he finished his ballad and brought his bloody cleaver to his chest. Meera clapped her hands and shouted, "Well done!" before turning to go. The odd man was growing on her.

Leaving the butcher's hut, she kept a wary eye out on her way to the kitchen. She expected the prince to come back for her. She expected guards or soldiers to accuse her of treason and drag her away. She expected *something* but was met with nothing. Once in the kitchen, she beckoned Cook into the pantry and told them what had happened. "What should I do?" she asked. "Will they punish me? Will they punish the raek? Should I leave—run even?" Meera knew she was babbling, but the potential conse-quences—official or unofficial—of her encounter with Prince Phineas terrified her.

Cook considered her seriously but maintained a calm exterior. "You should do nothin'," they said finally.

"Nothing?" Meera repeated blankly. Nothing didn't feel like an option when her chest was clenched with anxiety and her feet were pacing the floor in a desperate attempt at action.

"Do nothin'," Cook repeated. "You did nothin' wrong. That raek out there's a dangerous animal what's been killin' men, and the prince got hisself too close. If you leave, you run, you look guilty. You're not guilty, so you do nothin'."

Cook's words sounded simple and reasonable, but Meera wasn't sure reason would protect her if the prince sought revenge. "What if he comes for me again?" she asked. "I've heard some of the stories ..."

"Them stories is awful, but them women was charmed by 'im. They went with 'im where no one was around," Cook said. "Stay out in the open where there's other people. Don't be going places alone. He's a good boy when there's people around. Rumors are rumors, but the king would skin 'im if he did that stuff where people could see. You give it time 'n' hopefully the prince forgets, gets distracted by somethin' else shiny." Cook clasped her arm reassuringly. "You understand?"

"Yes ... that makes sense. I understand," she replied, blowing out a deep breath. Now she was the woman who befriended dangerous animals, agreed to spy for the king, and had the attention of a violent prince. How was she going to perform her duties and never be alone? How had her life spiraled this far out of her control?

Afraid to be alone even in her own bedroom, Meera spent the rest of the day in the kitchen. She ate, she read, and she even spoke to some of the other staff for the first time in weeks and tolerantly answered their repetitive questions about the raek. She didn't go up to her room until she was sure Teardra would be there already and had never felt so glad to have a roommate before. Then, despite being exhausted from her constant vigilance, she struggled to fall asleep, repeatedly imagining the prince's face—his well-crafted mask of charm and what she had seen underneath when the mask had slipped for just a moment. The beast lurking behind Prince Phineas's handsome features prowled the edges of her mind, perturbing her rest and hunting her in her dreams.

8

The morning after her encounter with the prince, Meera waited in the kitchen until she was sure Linus would be outside before going out to their usual meeting bench. She was still terrified and didn't plan to take any chances by being alone.

"There you are!" Linus cried. "I was worried—you've never been late before."

She gave him a weak smile. "Let's start walking, and I'll explain." The morning was misty and grey, and as they started walking, Meera glanced around, imagining Prince Phineas materializing on every hazy garden path that intersected their own.

"Spit it out!" Linus said eventually. "You're really scaring me now. What are you looking for anyway?" He joined her in cocking his head to and fro, and the pair of them looked like twitchy roosters surveying their brood.

Meera took a deep breath and sighed it out before regaling Linus with her tale from the day before. "... So, Cook told me not to be alone. I'm scared, Linus. Do you think you could stay while I feed the raek from now on?" she asked.

Linus had stopped at some point during her story and was staring at her, wide-eyed. "Of course! Of course, I'll stay with you." He lowered his voice and leaned in toward her. "Prince Phineas ... have you heard—" he started to say, but Meera cut him off.

"Yes—I've heard," she said quickly. She didn't want to hear; she didn't want to know what heinous crimes he had committed against other women.

They started walking again and were both quiet. Linus drew himself up to his full height and strode purposefully at her shoulder, making Meera smile to herself. Of all the palace guards to have as her defender, Linus was likely the least threatening, but there was no one she'd rather have with her—except Cerun, perhaps. They were halfway down the hill when she realized that Linus hadn't brought her a flower. "No flower today?" she asked.

"No," he replied tersely, an odd note in his voice. Meera didn't press him further. She thought perhaps he felt uncomfortable after the king had noticed the flowers he'd taken from the gardens. Or perhaps he'd finally accepted her lack of reciprocated feelings for him. It would be better if he did, but the thought still made her sad. She cared for Linus and didn't want to be a source of disappointment for him. He felt so much younger than her now, but in a year or two ... Maybe, she thought.

FOR THE NEXT SEVERAL DAYS, Meera was vigilant about never being alone. Linus stood guard while she fed Cerun, then walked her to the butcher and dropped her off at the kitchen, where she spent the rest of each day. Cook let her help to keep her occupied since the palace staff had mostly lost interest in her by then, and Meera could only hope the prince would also lose interest in her.

By the fourth day after the incident, she began to think that maybe he had. She hadn't seen Phineas or even heard any whispers about their encounter, and she was beginning to wonder if the nasty incident was behind her—she hoped it was, anyway; her vigilance was becoming an issue. It had been five days since she'd met with King Bartro, and she still hadn't begun her new duties. Nobles were starting to arrive for the socializing and festivities leading up to the Summer Solstice, and she hadn't done any spying or so much as checked the urn for a message from the king. As frightening as another encounter with Prince Phineas would be, Meera also dreaded being called to the king's study and having to explain why she hadn't so much as left the kitchen in days.

After an early lunch, she resolved to find the urn with the flower on it. She felt reasonably confident she could avoid meeting the prince; the palace was large place, and she generally went unnoticed. Even so, she walked through the gardens on the most well-used paths and only took palace hallways and staircases when other people were in sight. It wasn't difficult for her to arrive at her destination while remaining surrounded by people, either—the palace was bustling with people indoors and out since the solstice would soon be upon them.

The difficult part of Meera's journey ended up being the actual act of checking inside the urn, considering how crowded it was. She found the small urn in question on a decorative table under a portrait of the current queen, Queen Magda. It was black with a white lily painted on it, and Meera wondered whether it had always been there and whether the king had chosen it because of the flowers she had worn until recently. Then, she stood there for a long time, staring at the painting and thinking how foolish she'd been to try to check the urn in the middle of a busy day. So far, she was a mediocre spy.

Pursing her lips, she studied the queen's portrait and waited for her chance to open the urn without witnesses. Queen Magda had whiter blonde hair than her son—though it still made Meera's skin crawl—and while the queen was beautiful, she wore an oddly blank expression in the portrait. Meera supposed she had never heard any strong opinions or interesting anecdotes about the queen, so perhaps the blankness was true to her character. Magda's role was to produce heirs—something she was very good at—and strengthen the ties between Terratelle and Arborea. Absently, Meera wondered whether the queen was happy or just another chained captive of the palace. Then, when the opportunity finally presented itself, she tore her attention from the portrait, fumbled the lid off the urn, and reached inside.

Pulling out a scrap of paper, she replaced the lid and immediately moved down the hall toward the staircase that would take her back to the gardens. Her heart was pounding, and she felt inordinately excited by her small feat. Forgetting to be concerned about the prince, she walked quickly through the garden to a quiet section that was seldom visited. There, she ducked behind a full, flowering bush that she habitually used as a private shelter to relieve herself behind on days when she spent time reading in the gardens. Then she opened the ragged bit of paper to find a single name written on it: Duke Harrington.

Well, she thought, she had no idea whatsoever who Duke Harrington was, so she had her work cut out for her. She dropped the paper and kicked some dirt over it before leaving her private bush to begin her task for the king. She wasn't entirely sure where to start, so she spent the afternoon in the busiest areas of the palace and gardens, learning the names and faces of as many of the noble visitors as she could. At times, she stood or sat in unobtrusive places to observe, and when necessary, she took up bottles of wine and played the part of a serving woman to get close enough to hear snatches of conversation.

The nobles were accustomed to ignoring servants and never so much as looked at her long enough to notice that her dress didn't match the outfits of the other serving staff. That evening, she sat in the kitchen for a long time chatting with the visiting staff and hearing their gossip. Most of the visiting servants weren't aware of her notoriety, so she was able to speak with them without their conversations veering into interviews about the raek. However, after a long day, Meera still knew nothing about the duke in question.

For several days, Meera spent her afternoons listening and observing and her evenings conversing in the kitchen. Slowly, she started to piece together a general picture of the nobles of Terratelle. She didn't learn anything specifically about Duke Harrington, but she was at least beginning to get an idea of who was who and the tell-tale markers of the different regions the nobles came from. For instance, those from the north wore the finest fabrics as their lands had the best grazing pastures for sheep and the best soil for cotton. Their provinces were nearest the mountains that created the border between Terratelle and Arborea, so they also benefited from trade with the Arboreans. But mostly, living in the north meant they were far from the war with Aegorn at the southern border.

There were fewer nobles present from the southern provinces as they were in constant threat of attack. Their lands had also been depleted of most of their resources over the duration of the long war, leaving the southern dukes and duchesses as the miserable proprietors of poor and disgruntled people. Meera knew from general gossip that many had fled from the border over the years, leaving cities quieter than before and entire villages deserted, and the army had taken up residence in much of what was abandoned. From what she understood, despite years of conflict, the borders between Terratelle and Aegorn hadn't actually changed much; they were locked in an even match, and neither could gain the upper hand or was willing to surrender an inch of land.

Most of the present nobles were from the regions closest to Altus since it was much easier for them to make the journey. Altus lay evenly spaced between the northern and southern borders of Terratelle but closer to the sea on the eastern coast. The eastern sea was the Cerun Sea. Meera and her father had visited when she was a child, and her ancestors had supposedly voyaged to Terratelle from across the Cerun Sea. The provinces along the eastern coast were fishing towns, whereas the western coast along the Penchin Sea dealt mostly in trade with Cesor, a land with a much hotter and dryer climate than Terratelle, which, therefore, produced very different goods. Nobles from the west coast often wore gold and brought gifts of pottery from Cesor.

Despite all she had learned, Meera had yet to figure out how Duke Harrington fit into the larger picture of Terratelle, and she was growing frustrated. One morning, before she went out to meet Linus, she asked Cook whether servants were allowed to use the palace library. Cook just barked a laugh in answer, and Meera took that to mean it was a ridiculous question that no one but her would even think to ask. However, she decided she might as well try to use the library—hoping there would be some sort of map or document outlining the Terratellen provinces and their proprietors. Her father likely had the information in their home, but the more entrenched Meera became in her new palace life, the stranger she felt going back to her empty house with its memories of her father and the person she had been when she had lived there.

After feeding Cerun, she ate her lunch and went to her room to change into one of her nicer dresses and fix her hair, resolved to go to the library to seek out the information she needed. She hoped that if she looked decently put together and behaved as if she had the right to be there, no one would question her. On her walk through the palace, her stomach twisted with anxiety in anticipation of her small quest. Opening the heavy oak double doors to the library, she beheld the wall-to-wall bookcases for the first time.

Though it was not nearly as breathtaking as the Altus Grand Library where her father worked, she still found the palace's library enchanting and beautiful. It was a quiet and dim space, with heavy velvet curtains covering the windows to preserve the delicate papers and inks from the harsh light of the sun. She only took two steps into the room, however, when an elderly, droopy-faced man in the traditional black robes of a librarian intercepted her. "Good afternoon, Miss," he said, sounding anything but welcoming. His eyes swooped down her body then back up, and he added, "Lost, are we?"

Meera felt immediately irritated with the man and had to resist the impulse to request obscure books and refer to the Altus Grand Library librarians she knew personally to prove to him that she belonged there; she was meant to be discreet, after all. With a steadying breath, she said, "Good afternoon, Sir. I am the lady's maid to the visiting Lady Valory of Greenspire. She bade me find her a list of nobles and their provinces of origin." Lowering her voice conspiratorially, she added, "She finds her tutelage to have been lacking, and is struggling to keep up with the complexities of palace life."

Lady Valory was a young noblewoman Meera had observed for some time the day before. Her fine clothes and jewelry made it likely she came from the north, and Greenspire was the only northern province that readily came to mind. Meera's heart raced from the lie—lying wasn't something she was accustomed to; she was really putting her spying abilities to the test.

"I see," the librarian replied. "I certainly have the requested information. I usually require such texts to remain in the library for study, but as the lady is not here and you surely can't copy it out for her ... I suppose you can take it for today, but you must return it tomorrow."

Meera struggled not to stare at the man's jowls when he talked. They flapped around like fish on land, and she amused herself by thinking they were as keen to be away from him as she was. "Thank you, Sir. I will certainly return them tomorrow," she said, bowing her head respectfully.

The old librarian huffed and moved away to retrieve the document. Meera assumed he didn't want her to follow as he clearly didn't approve of her presence in the library, so she remained by the doors. Then she heard the man say to himself—in what he must have thought was a quiet voice: "Just as I'm always saying ... no point even trying to educate women."

As distasteful as Meera found the librarian, she decided it was probably fortunate that he thought so little of women; it had made him inclined to believe her story, but she also thought it made him less likely to remember anything specific about her or the name of the lady she had used. In her experience, men who didn't like women didn't bother distinguishing between them. When she left the library, she tucked the scroll the old librarian had given her into her bag. Feeling giddy from her success, she practically skipped down the hallway. What had been anxiety before her venture felt like excitement in retrospect, and spying for the king, she decided, was thrilling.

Meera took the scroll straight to her room, hoping she would have time to copy it all out before Teardra came up for bed. She learned that Ned Harrington was the Duke of Harringbay, a small province on the coast of the Cerun Sea, divided from the border of Aegorn by only a stretch of rocky cliffs. The cliffs themselves, while ostensibly part of Terratelle, were uninhabited. She also learned that his wife was Duchess Kenna Harrington, and they had a daughter, who was not named on the scroll but would now be sixteen years old. Harringbay was, as the name suggested, situated on a bay, and the inhabitants of Harringbay were primarily fisher-men. Meera wondered why the king would want her keeping an eye on the duke of such a small fishing province. Then she assumed it must have something to do with the war, seeing as Harringbay was so close to Aegorn. When she was finished, she packed her new information away where Teardra wouldn't see it and went to bed.

The next day, she returned to the library and was forced to stand and wait while the librarian bent over the scroll and studied it for any damage, his jowls wobbling close to the paper. Finding the scroll intact, he begrudgingly released her, and she exited the palace through a set of back doors into the garden. She was walking quickly when, out of the corner of her eye, she noticed a man so like her father, she halted in her tracks. His black hair curled loosely at the nape of his neck over golden brown skin, and there was something about his build—his stance, even. Meera stared at the man, heart racing. It couldn't be her father, but ... could it?

The man was standing next to a fountain on the patio where a small group of nobles was having tea. It was a hot day, and while most of the guests were underneath shade canopies set out over the patio, he stood in the blazing sun talking animatedly with another man. Meera had an irrational but overwhelming desire to see his face. She knew she was being ridiculous—that it couldn't be her father—but still ... Holding her breath, she skirted the outside of the fountain as if admiring it, resisting the urge to crane her neck. Finally, she had rounded the fountain far enough and glanced up excitedly to view the man's profile. Her breath burst from her lungs, and she sagged in disappointment; it was not her father, of course.

This man had thicker eyebrows and a stronger jaw. Meera started to turn to walk away, chastising herself for being so silly, when she heard the gentleman he was with shout, "Roger, come over here! I want you to meet Duke Harrington!" She stopped short, her disappointment snapping back to excitement. Unsure of what else to do, she plopped onto the fountain's edge and brought a book out of her bag, opening it in her lap and pretended to read while she listened to the men talk.

"Ned, this is my son Roger," said the man the duke was with. From what little Meera had seen of him, he was shorter and thicker wasted than Duke Harrington.

"Well, hello Roger! It's a pleasure to meet you. Your father was just telling me how quickly you're learning the family business," replied the duke. Meera could only hear the exchange and couldn't read any of the men's body language, but she thought the duke sounded genuinely affable; she didn't detect any tone of irritation or insincere charm.

"P—pleasure to meet you, Your Grace," stuttered the young man with obvious nerves.

"Please, call me Ned," the duke replied. "I don't hold with titles —my own anyway. I wouldn't be caught calling the king, *Barty*." He laughed heartily, and the other two men gave appreciative chuckles.

"You have a daughter Roger's age don't you, Ned?" the thick man asked, making it glaringly obvious why he had been boasting about his son's work and sought to make the introduction.

"I do. Yes, my daughter is sixteen now," the duke said. "She isn't in attendance, however; Emmaline decided to stay home, and once she has decided something, nothing will sway her! Strong-willed as a wild horse my daughter." While the man's words could be construed as critical, his tone was full of warmth and obvious affection, and Meera couldn't help but immediately like him.

"Shame, shame!" said Roger's father. "I would have liked for the young ones to meet. Ah well, your wife is here, isn't she? Echem ... the duchess?"

"Oh yes, my Kenna is here with me. She was cornered by one of the Frease sisters over there last I saw her. I should probably go extricate her," replied the duke, making his excuses to end the conversation.

"Ah, I see! Well, we won't keep you, but I'll be sure to tell my wife to say hello, and perhaps our children may meet another time," said the thick man hopefully.

The conversation broke up, and the duke moved away, ostensibly to find his wife. Meera waited several minutes before rising and turning to survey the gathering. She could see Duke Harrington with a slight woman in purple, who she assumed was his wife. Duchess Harrington was very Cesorean looking with reddish brown skin and straight, glossy hair. She and the duke were in the crowd of the party, however, so Meera couldn't get close enough to hear them. Still, she took up a post on another edge of the patio in order to listen to whatever talk she could. She didn't hear anything pertaining to the Harringtons that day, but she could at least identify them, which was a start.

Over the next week, she sought them out in common areas whenever she could and kept detailed notes about them in her journal. She saw the duke and duchess walking in the gardens together holding hands and presumed the duke to have real affection for his wife, which was rare among nobles who married more often for status than love. Duchess Harrington seemed to be a quiet, demure woman but a kind one. A servant girl who had spilled wine on her told Meera in the kitchens one evening how gracious the duchess had been, even seeking to hide the girl's mistake, so she would not lose her position.

Other than that, Meera could tell the duke was a cheerful man; he was quick to laugh or tell a joke, but he didn't seem to have any especially close friends in attendance. Most of what she overheard him say fell under the realm of small talk. He seemed to enjoy the gatherings that included entertainment of some kind more than the ones that required much conversation. She saw him enjoy puppet shows, musical performances, and dances, but at social gatherings, he appeared to shy away from discussion or would make excuses to leave a conversation relatively quickly. Meera thought it was strange that a man could be both exuberant and affable and reserved and taciturn at the same time. However, despite all she had learned, she certainly hadn't discovered anything about the duke she thought the king would find valuable —not yet. She would have to keep trying.

9

———

Two weeks into her role as a spy, Meera still hadn't left any notes in the urn for King Bartro. She had only learned personal tidbits about the duke and didn't want to give the king such trivial information. However, she continued to check the urn every few days just in case he left a message for her. One day, after feeding Cerun, she ate lunch in the kitchen and thought to check the calendar Cook kept on a wall to keep track of feast days and other special events. Rising to look at it, she realized it had been six weeks exactly since Cerun and his rider had been brought to the palace; their arrival was marked with a crude drawing of the raek. Time had sped by quickly for Meera for the first time since her father was conscripted, but she imagined it must be a painfully slow slog for Cerun and didn't even want to imagine what his rider was enduring in the dungeons.

It was a gloomy day with a steady downpour of rain and the occasional rumble of thunder in the distance. Meera had already had to change her dress from getting soaked going down to the canal and back. Most of the nobles would either be spending time in the great hall or the more private drawing rooms, she knew, so she decided to take the servant's passages from the kitchen to the great hall to look for the duke. She slipped into the hall through the servant's entrance and was immediately in the middle of the action. Glancing around, she took in the array of nobles eating and talking, playing cards, and gathering to listen to a minstrel performing a love ballad.

She was about to walk across the hall to position herself discreetly behind a group of women working on embroidery projects when she caught sight of the golden-haired prince she had almost forgotten to be wary of—almost. Stiff-legged as a stork, she quickly altered her course and walked straight to the hall's main entrance and out the double doors. She had only glimpsed Phineas, but her heart was thundering with the rumblings of the storm outside. Ducking behind a large potted plant, she waited, watching the door to the hall to see if he might have noticed her—might have followed. She was so anxious, she felt like the reverberations in her chest must be echoing around the hallway for all to hear.

For what felt like an eternity but was surely only a couple of minutes, Meera waited, crouched behind the potted plant. Eventually, she determined it was safe to move and decided it was better, really, that she knew where the prince was—she wouldn't have to fear going around a corner and being surprised by him. Her plan for the afternoon was thrown, but she didn't think the duke and duchess had been in the hall regardless. Walking through the now very familiar halls of palace, she decided she might as well check the little flower urn for a message from the king. After waiting briefly for the hall to clear, she reached inside the urn. She hadn't actually expected there to be anything inside and therefore, stared dumbly at the piece of paper in her hand for a moment before remembering to keep walking lest someone see her.

Retracing her steps back toward the hall, Meera intended to pass its double doors and turn into a lesser-used hallway to read her missive, when she rounded a corner to find the prince walking toward her. He immediately locked eyes with her despite complaining loudly to a companion about the minstrel in the hall. Meera froze like a startled rabbit. Then, without any notion of shame or propriety, she turned tail and fled, running full out down one hallway and then another.

She was panicking. She didn't even know if the prince was following her—she knew only fear. Reaching the doors to the garden, she hurtled out into the rain and hid in a thick copse of trees, crouching low to the ground. Catching her breath beneath dripping leaves, her pulse steadied, and she regained her rational mind, slowly realizing how foolish she had been. There had been no need for her to flee—the prince had been surrounded by onlookers. She couldn't allow herself to panic like that; she was bound to see the prince at times and didn't want to make herself even more entertaining for him.

About to call the day a wash and return to her room for yet another dry dress, she remembered the bit of paper still clutched in her fist and unfolded the now-soggy scrap. The ink was already beginning to bleed, but she could still make out the words: *Report to me immediately upon reading.* As cold rain trickled down the back of her dress, she wondered what could be so important. With a sigh, she wiped at a rivulet running down her face.

She was soaked through and had just made a public spectacle of herself. Would the king really know if she reported immediately? Could she go to her room for today and report tomorrow? She didn't think he would know ... She wasn't expected to check the urn every day, after all. She would rather see the king dry and with a steady mind. But what if he had someone else monitoring the urn who would tell him it was empty? What if he knew she had checked it and would know if she didn't report immediately? Meera had never been one to curse, but she felt very close to it then. She couldn't ignore a summons from the king—or even defer it.

With a brisk pace—hindered slightly by the wet fabric of her dress sucking at her legs—she walked back into the palace and made her way to the king's study. Giving her name to the guards outside his door, she waited as one went in. The only sound was the drip of water from her skirt to the stone floor, and Meera imagined her hair was likely flattened to her head like a wet cat. When the guard returned, he held the door to admit her, and she squared her shoulders and raised her chin before walking into the study.

The king's study wasn't as bright on this rainy day, but it was well-lit, and rain pattered and danced off the glass-paned windows. King Bartro sat behind his desk, and Meera approached the desk and curtsied with as much dignity as she could muster, considering her soaked dress clung greedily to her thighs. Looking at the king's face, she expected to meet his eyes, but his gaze was lowered, roving over her body where the wet fabric of her dress clung to her form.

She could see the appreciation in his stare; his eyes were molten blue-green metal bringing heat to her face. Her nipples peeked—partly from her growing chill—but partly in response to the king's attention. She thought she should feel embarrassed and exposed, but strangely, she felt excited. Just as her spying challenged and thrilled her in new ways, the king's notice of her body felt like an opportunity for her to try out a different version of herself. When King Bartro met her eyes, however, his sensual gaze flickered to one of amusement. "I'd invite you to sit down," he said, "but I wouldn't want you to ruin the leather."

The king's mocking tone immediately extinguished any boldness Meera had felt. She *did* feel exposed then and had to resist the urge to cross her arms over her chest. Her earlier panic upon seeing the prince had left her emotions close to the surface, and while she knew she should exercise caution in the presence of the most powerful man in Terratelle, his derision rankled her. Wryly, she replied, "Your Majesty requested my *immediate* presence ..."

"That I did," he said, drumming his fingertips on the polished tabletop and leaning back in his chair. He sat silently for a long moment in which Meera wanted to shout: "Why am I here!?" but she merely studied the king in return. He wore a contemplative and businesslike expression, and she wondered at how quickly his demeanor could change—could flare and then gutter like the lights in his eyes that intrigued her so much. Finally, he said, "Start by reporting. What have you learned about the duke?"

With a deep breath, she replied, "I have learned some of his personal qualities and habits, Your Majesty—that he has genuine affection for his wife and daughter, that he is quick to laugh, that he enjoys spending time outdoors ..." she trailed off briefly before getting to her point: "Your Majesty, I have not learned anything pertaining to the duke's loyalties or future endeavors. Indeed, he does not seem especially inclined to speak to anyone here at the palace about anything." She felt embarrassed to admit that she hadn't learned anything useful but hoped the king would appreciate her candor.

King Bartro appeared neither pleased nor displeased. He rubbed his cropped beard at his jawline and responded, "The duke must have some reason for making the trip to Altus; he does not usually engage in palace life. If he isn't speaking to anyone here at the palace, perhaps he is speaking to someone *not* at the palace." His eyebrows rose in expectation of a reply, though he had not asked a direct question.

Maybe he was right, Meera thought; maybe the duke was biding his time at the palace for show when he really had business in the city. She didn't relish the task of attempting to follow him outside the palace grounds—possibly in the dark of night—but she didn't think she could abdicate from her role as spy just yet. "Perhaps, Your Majesty," was all she said, and she raised her eyebrows in an echo of his demeanor. For a time, they both held their tongues. It was a power game the king liked to play—being silent for so long he made people want to fill that silence, want to confess into it—but Meera had come ready to play.

Finally, King Bartro spoke: "The reason I required your presence, Miss Hailship, is actually another matter entirely." Meera's mind immediately went to Cerun, and she reprimanded herself internally for forgetting that she represented the raek as well as herself. She should be more careful of her actions in front of the king; displeasing him could have consequences for her friend.

Bartro continued: "Your ... *touch*, shall we say—with the raek—has been so impressive, I thought you might have similar luck with my other prisoner." He paused and studied her as if to judge her reaction as her eyes widened in shock. This wasn't about the duke or Cerun but the prisoner? How could she possibly help torture a man? King Bartro appeared satisfied with her reaction—nodding and reclining in his chair. Perhaps he feared she was in league with the raek and his rider somehow, she thought. Her reasons for volunteering to feed the raek were flimsy—even she thought so.

Cocking his head, he explained, "For six weeks now, my best men for the job have tried and failed to extract information from the prisoner who was captured with the raek. At this point, the interviews cannot continue without risking the loss of a potentially valuable informant. I'd like you to feed and nurse the man as you do for the beast. With any luck, he will find you equally as agreeable. I hope that which my men could not do might be accomplished with a ... *woman's touch*." The emphasis he put on his final words made Meera once more acutely aware of her body under her soaked dress, making her feel vulnerable and defenseless. She walked a fine line with the king between excitement and fear. For the first time, she noticed King Bartro's resemblance to his son, Prince Phineas, in the shape of his strong jaw and the curve of his full lips.

She was to go into the dungeons to feed and care for a potentially dangerous prisoner? Somehow the danger of a man was more frightening to Meera than the raek had been. She couldn't quite tell whether the king was trying to imply anything particular with *woman's touch*, but she thought he was just trying to make her squirm. He had previously agreed that he would always allow her to keep her dignity intact, and she assumed that promise still stood. "Will I have any protection, Your Majesty?" she asked. He wasn't requesting her assistance with the prisoner, after all—it was a command. Every request from a king was a command.

"I am told you are already escorted by a member of the palace guard," he replied. "That should be protection enough." He started shuffling through some of the papers on his desk, clearly losing interest in her.

"Yes, Your Majesty," she replied. She had to suppress a shiver from her dampness and bent and flexed her stiff fingers at her sides, hoping he would dismiss her. The longer Meera spent in the king's presence, the more burdens she seemed to acquire. She didn't know how she would manage to care for Cerun, see to the prisoner, and follow the duke often enough to discern why he was in Altus. She didn't need any more duties—she needed a hot cup of something and dry clothes.

To her relief, King Bartro looked up one last time to say, "You may go, Miss Hailship." She curtsied hurriedly, dislodging more water droplets onto the floor, and began to turn when he added, "Oh, and beware my son; he chafes at his lead." Meera looked back, nodded dumbly, and let herself out of the study.

For a moment, she paused outside the door to compose herself. Then she caught one of the guards gawping at her wet figure, and she crossed her arms over her chest and quickly walked to the garden exit, choosing to walk through the rain to avoid people since she was already soaked through. As more water pelted her, she pondered the king's parting words with frustration: *beware my son; he chafes at his lead.* Why did King Bartro always leave her with cryptic warnings?

Meera assumed he meant that he only had so much control over the prince and couldn't actually prevent him from doing her harm. Under the circumstances, she resolved to renew her efforts to not be alone. Then she remembered that she was supposed to be tailing the duke, which she couldn't do with an escort and may take her away from public spaces. If Duke Harrington was doing something the king would want to know about, he would be doing it away from prying eyes, after all ...

She couldn't focus on that now; first, she would get through the next day and her new role in the dungeon, then she would make a plan about the duke. When she reached the kitchen, Cook took one look at her and pointed to the door leading to the servant's bedrooms as in, "Get yourself out of those wet clothes," and Meera smiled, knowing Cook would have something hot and tasty waiting for her when she returned. Even as her roles for the king multiplied and threatened to overwhelm her, some aspects of her life were at least still simple and enjoyable.

10

───────

The next morning, the rain gave way to a cloudless sky. Meera thought it would turn into a scorching day—summer was fast approaching. She waited for Linus on her usual bench, and when he came around the corner with a grin on his face, she smiled in return. Most of the clouds from his brother's death seemed to have cleared away, and Meera was glad to see that her friend was doing so well. Linus's honey-brown hair swayed on the sides of his face, threatening to cover his eyes as usual, and she almost reached a hand up to tuck some behind his ear but restrained herself; she needed to keep her distance to avoid giving him the wrong impression.

Then, for a moment, she wondered whether it could be the right impression. What could a life with Linus be like? He was kind and cared for her, and she wouldn't be alone anymore. His family sounded wonderful, especially his mother. What if she joined that family? She could have a mother, and she could get away from the palace. Maybe it wasn't such a bad idea ... Would that be fair to Linus, though? She did love him—in a way.

Perhaps she should reconsider marriage, Meera thought—a convention she had discarded years ago before her life had changed, before her father had left. Suddenly, her pleasant daydream of family and laughter and the warm embrace of a new mother came to an end. Her father ... Her father had gone to fight in the war, and so would Linus. It was his dream—one he spoke of often and with great enthusiasm. Meera knew what it was like to wait and to wonder, and she wouldn't volunteer herself to go through it again. She almost laughed at the thought—having volunteered herself for a far more precarious position than that already—and wondered wryly whether she had finally learned caution.

After they exchanged their usual greetings, Meera said, "Linus, I hope you don't have plans this afternoon because you're not going to believe where we're going ..."

His confusion was plain on his face when he asked, "Where?"

"The king called me to his study yesterday," she said, leaving out the urn and the puddle she'd left on his study floor. "He asked me to care for the man that was captured with the raek. He wants me to feed him and see to his wounds, and he said I could bring you for protection."

Meera expected Linus to be excited about their new task, considering how much interest he had shown in the prisoner before, but his face blanched of its usual healthy color. "We're going into the dungeon? We have to help that ... man—that *thing*?" he stuttered.

"Well, yes. At least, I'm expected to go into the dungeon to feed the man and see to his wounds, and I was hoping you would go with me, but ..." she started to say, breaking off when her voice cracked. She wanted to give him an out—it wasn't his duty to go with her—but she was afraid. She didn't know anything about this man and didn't want to go alone.

Linus stopped and grasped Meera's arm gently to stop her and pull her to face him. He looked uncharacteristically serious—his gaze steady and fixed on her—and said, "If you're going, I'm going, Meera. I'll be there to protect you." He immediately let her go and started walking again, but it took her a second to rouse herself to follow. She felt like she'd seen the future—the man Linus was going to be when his last vestiges of boyhood were gone. She could picture the strong, confident soldier he would be—tall with clear skin and a straight nose. It almost made her reconsider her earlier daydream about marriage. Almost.

Meera was glad Linus would stay by her side. It made her feel safe from the prince, and it made her feel more confident going into the unknown of the dungeon. However, having Linus wait for her every day while she fed and groomed Cerun meant she hadn't been spending as much time with the raek. Her visit that day would also be brief, but she could at least reassure Cerun that she would be caring for his rider. "I saw the king yesterday," she told him as he ate fish off the end of her tongs. "He asked me to tend to your rider. It sounded like he might be very hurt, but the king wants him to survive. I'll bring him food and see to his wounds, and I'll be able to let you know how he's doing every day ..."

Looking into her friend's immense blue eye, she wished for the hundredth time that he could speak to her in return. Cerun gave a blink of understanding and made a low rumble in his throat—not a growl but a content sound. Then he did something unexpected: he extended his left wing out, gesturing with his head to his wing tip where his feathers were most vibrant. "Are you hurt?" she asked, thinking he was asking for help of some kind, though he had never done such a thing before.

He didn't blink, and he turned his body to brush her arm lightly with his feathers. The unusual behavior caught Linus's attention, who was immediately alarmed. Pacing at the edge of the claw marks in the sand, he called, "Come out, Meera! What's it doing?"

"I'm fine!" she called back with some impatience in her voice. She knew Linus had every reason to fear the raek but felt frustrated that he hadn't yet accepted that Cerun wouldn't hurt her. Turning away from Linus, she ran a hand along the raek's feathers. They were beautiful shades of cobalt blue, deep blue, and teal. The feathers on his wings were larger than most of his others. He sometimes shed his smaller, fluffier feathers onto the beach, and Meera had taken a light blue one once to use as a bookmark. Then it occurred to her that she was going to see his rider, and Cerun might want to send him a token. "Do you want me to take him one of your feathers?" she asked.

He blinked.

Peering down at his wing, she selected one that was half cobalt and half a much darker shade of blue, part of the stripes that marked him as male. Grasping it toward the base, she pulled hard to free the feather from his wing. It wasn't one of his flight feathers at the very edge of his wing, so it didn't leave such a glaring gap. But the feather was immense—longer than her arm. She tucked it into her cart and met Linus to walk up the hill. Her chest ached for Cerun, and her fear and reservation about the man in the dungeon was forgotten; she only wanted to help him and heal him as she had done for his raek.

After they left the cart with the butcher, who was once again busily carving a hanging carcass and singing at the top of his lungs—this time wearing some sort of makeshift crown of branches on his head—Meera and Linus went to the kitchen. They each ate a light lunch—the nerves in their stomachs leaving only minimal space for food—and afterward, with Cook's help, Meera loaded up a tray of food to take to the prisoner. She had no idea what condition she would find the man in, so she brought plain broth as well as heartier foods. Cook didn't comment about her new duty; they just shook their head and emitted a disapproving hum.

"What else should I bring?" Meera wondered aloud to Cook and Linus, who both shrugged. "I suppose once I see him, I'll know what he needs and will make another trip down ... Um, where *is* the dungeon exactly?" She felt ridiculous for not asking sooner.

"When there's prisoners, the guards take the trays and don't tell me nothin'," replied Cook with another shrug.

"I'm pretty sure there's a stairway going down near the armory," Linus said.

"Where's the armory?" Meera asked with exasperation, feeling like she was already in far over her head.

"Come on," he replied, taking the tray from her and leading her down a servant's corridor. The armory, it turned out, was on a lower level where she had never been. The level consisted mostly of very sturdy-looking locked doors. "I think valuables and the like are locked down here," Linus said, whispering unnecessarily. Meera could see that there were several palace guards stationed in the hall, but Linus, it seemed, had never been stationed down there. Since he was the youngest guard, they mostly treated him like a page—having him run around delivering messages and doing other remedial tasks.

Linus greeted the nearest guard by name, explained Meera's new duty, and asked where they would find the prisoner. The guard looked shocked and pointed them to an unmarked wooden door further on. "It's the only way in and out," he said, "and there's only one prisoner down there." He didn't look inclined to show them the way, so they continued on their own.

Since Linus had the tray, Meera pulled the door open. It wasn't locked, and she stepped forward and peered inside to find a steep staircase descending into utter blackness. Damp, cold air wafted up from below, smelling tangy like stones and slightly musty. She looked around, found a lit torch on the wall behind her, and took it. She was wearing an apron with Cerun's feather tucked into the front pocket, and she fingered the feather where it lay across her chest like a sash. Then, with a trepidatious look toward Linus, she stepped down onto the staircase.

After a few steps, she found an unlit torch and lit it with the one she carried. Clearly, no one else had been down there that day; the torches were all cold, and Meera continued lighting the way on the steep, straight descent. Linus walked behind her, the platters on his tray rattling and setting her teeth on edge. When they reached the bottom of the stairs, the corridor before them was narrow with rows of iron-barred cells on their left side, but the way forward was pitch black with no way of knowing how long the row extended or what might be further on. There were some echoey drips around them, but otherwise, the dungeon was silent—silent and cold. Meera shivered, accustomed as she was to the warmth of spring and not the freezing dampness of the underground space.

Grateful for the light in her hand and the friend at her back, she continued down the row to the next torch on the wall, and the next. The cells she passed were missing their doors, which explained why the prisoner wasn't in any of them, and she thought the iron must have been repurposed at some point—for tools, chains, a muzzle large enough for a raek ... She counted ten doorless cells and three wall torches before they reached the first cell with a door, and there he was. She drew in a sharp breath— even in the dim lighting, she could see that the man's entire body was covered in wounds. He lay face down on a mat leaking straw, completely motionless and completely naked. His stillness disturbed her; it was cold, but despite his nudity, he didn't shiver.

Peering around the cell, Meera saw that were moldy bits of food that looked like they'd been thrown in for him scattered on the floor, and she caught a glimpse of a rat fleeing from her torch-light. Other than the man, the mat, and the food, there was only a porcelain pitcher of water and a hole in the back corner of the cell floor, presumably for bodily waste. There wasn't a strong stench of human excrement, so she assumed the hole was very deep or emptied out in some way. She and Linus both stood speechless for a long moment before Meera pulled herself together and started making a mental list of what she would need to do: she ought to clean out the rotten food, clean the man's wounds, dress him in something, find him a fresh mat and some blankets, and get him to eat.

The king hadn't been specific in his instructions for her, so she assumed she had free rein in how she cared for the man as long as she didn't let him out. There wasn't anyone here to make sure he didn't overpower her and escape, but she supposed his condition was so bad that they'd given up watching him. Then she realized something obvious that probably should have already occurred to her: a key. They didn't have a key to get into the cell. "We need to find the key," she said to Linus, her voice sounding overly loud as it bounced off the myriad of hard surfaces.

Linus's clouded eyes focused at the clear instruction, and he looked around and suggested, "Maybe it's further on ..." He trailed off. They had both seen enough already, but it made sense to look further down the hall before climbing the long staircase back up to ask the guards where the key might be.

Meera had the torch, so she walked ahead, moving quickly— buoyed by a sense of urgency to help the man in the cell. They passed at least as many cells as they had before if not more before they found a room branching off to the right. The room had no door. They entered it, and she could sense the room's spaciousness even though she couldn't see. She skirted to the left along the wall until she found the first torch, but it did little to illuminate the cavernous space. Her whole body shaking, she kept moving until she lit three more.

After the fourth torch, she could see the left half of the room clearly, and bile rose in her throat. There was a stone table with leather straps and a large fireplace, and hanging on either side of the fireplace was a collection of wicked-looking tools. It was a torture room. She looked at Linus; he was eyeing the table, which was crusted with dark, dried blood. Meera felt sick and disgusted, but Linus looked horrified with almost childlike confusion in his round eyes. "Do you think anyone could really deserve this?" she asked him, not trying to make a point but truly curious about his thoughts.

His mouth compressed into a tight line. "Maybe not, but maybe it's worth the lives it could save and the destruction it could prevent," he replied quietly.

She considered his answer. Was torturing one person justified if it saved many others? So far, it seemed to her that violence only begat more violence; men fought in a war, a raek was captured by force and hurt, the raek killed two men, and she knew the cycle would continue—could almost read it in Linus's face at times when he spoke of Cerun. With a deep sigh, she replied, "It hasn't saved anyone yet," knowing that the prisoner's torture hadn't resulted in any useful information.

Recalling her urgency, Meera resumed walking and lighting torches. Just past the fireplace, she found a row of pegs holding keys, and reaching her torch closer, she saw that they were numbered. "I found the keys," she said. "Do you know what number he was in?" She remembered it was the eleventh cell but wasn't sure if the numbers started at the stair end or at the other end.

"It was marked number 39, I think," Linus replied. The key for number 39 was hanging on the peg, so she took it and retraced her steps, extinguishing the torches she had lit by twisting the knobs that restricted the flow of oil to the wick. "Shouldn't you leave those?" he asked. "We'll need to put the key back."

"No," she replied in a steely tone that surprised her. "The prisoner is my responsibility now, and anyone who wants to open his cell will have to get the key from me."

Linus looked at her with astonishment like he'd never really seen her before, and Meera squared her shoulders and met his look with steady certainty. She had been thinking of her duties as tasks given to her—jobs about which she had little say—but in that moment, she realized the king had given her responsibilities, not tasks. To have responsibility meant to have control—to have power—so she decided to use her power and use it to do as much good for the prisoners as she could. She would care for Cerun and his rider, and she would endeavor to prevent them from enduring further harm.

11

When they returned to the cell, Meera tried the key in the lock. It was tricky to get it positioned right, and her attempts sent a cacophony of iron scrapes and clangs echoing the length of the dungeon. Her jaw tensed from the grating noise, but despite the racket, the prisoner lay utterly still. Meera wondered if he could possibly be playing possum to surprise and rush them when they opened the door, but when she slowly swung the door inward, he remained as he was.

Door ajar, she didn't know what to do next; she didn't have any of the supplies she would need. Linus was standing slightly behind her with the tray of food, looking just as uncertain. Take control, she told herself. Turning to Linus, she told him to leave the tray and go upstairs to get a basin of warm water, soap, clean linens, vinegar, honey, and a needle and thread. She hoped he could carry all of that at once, and when he returned with what she needed to clean and bandage the man, she would send him for clothes, blankets, and bedding. Meanwhile, she would stay to make sure the rats wouldn't spoil the fresh food and start cleaning the cell.

Linus looked anxious about leaving her. Meera—admittedly—was terrified to be left alone in the dark, dank dungeon, but she was trying to focus on the prisoner's desperate needs and not her own paltry fears. To show Linus that the man was no threat to her, she entered the cell and touched him lightly on the shoulder on a small expanse of skin not broken or damaged in any way. When he didn't stir, she shook him lightly. He was so cold and still that she began to fear they were too late to help him. Bending low over the side of his face, she listened for signs of life. His breathing was shallow, but she could hear the rasp of it in his dry throat.

The man's dark hair was loose and falling over his face, and she brushed it aside, revealing a young, handsome face that was grimy but not mutilated like the rest of him except for a bloody lip. "He's so young ... my age probably," she said absently. Linus was still loitering in the walkway with the tray, looking anxious. "I don't think he's in any state to hurt me," she assured him.

He shifted from foot to foot before setting down the tray. His hands finally free, he pushed at his hair, which hung in his eyes. "Okay," he agreed, "I'll get what you need and be back as soon as I can." Meera nodded in response, and he turned and ran as if chased by shadow monsters.

Without Linus watching her, she could unselfconsciously study the man's body to assess his wounds, and she squinted at him in the dimness. His back was covered in what looked like burns from a hot rod. They had undoubtedly been extremely painful to receive, but the heat of the rod had at least welded the flesh shut, closing the wounds. His butt and thighs appeared to have been whipped, and there were some deep gouges that gaped and oozed—those would need stitching, she thought. His calves ... She bent and peered closer, not believing her eyes. What had looked like pockmarks in the low light turned out to be nail heads —he had five nails embedded in each calf.

Meera was horrified by the damage done to the young man's body, and despite the cold dungeon air, she began to feel clammy and sick just from looking at him. The corpses by the canal had disturbed her—haunting her dreams these six weeks—but those men had at least died quickly—one instant of violence had ended their lives and their suffering. Whereas someone had been inflicting slow, meticulous violence on this man since he'd gotten there. Her mind almost couldn't grasp the amount of time he had spent in the dungeon—all the meals she had eaten and walks she had taken in that span of time, during which he had experienced only pain and darkness.

Meera didn't want to keep looking, but she had to—she was the only person who could help the prisoner. A small part of her wondered if he might prefer to ride his unconsciousness into death rather than be nursed back to health just to continue suffering, but she couldn't *not* help him; she had promised Cerun to care for him—not to mention being ordered to by the king. Taking a deep breath, she crouched and kept looking. The soles of the young man's feet were also burned, but they still looked raw. His toenails and fingernails were all removed—she discovered only bloody flesh where they should have been—and his wrists and ankles were rubbed raw where—she assumed—he had strained against the leather straps of the torture table.

Her lunch felt like pure acid in her stomach. She wasn't sure how she was going to maneuver the man's body to wash and bandage him, but she was loath to discover what injustices had been committed to his front. Since she couldn't begin cleaning the man until Linus returned, she started gathering the rotten food on the floor and putting it in the old pitcher of water, which she moved out of the cell. Then she more or less stood by the fresh tray of food to prevent rats from taking any of it and waited. She said some vague words of reassurance to the unconscious man, but the sound of her voice bouncing off the stone walls and iron bars rattled her nerves.

She had propped Cerun's feather against the far wall and standing back and observing the still-life of the cell, the feather was the only drip of color in the dungeon. Its vibrancy felt almost harsh and jarring against the other more subtle greys, blacks, and browns, and Meera couldn't help but stare at it while she waited— her eyes drawn to the relief of color and beauty over and over again rather than suffer the sight of the mutilated prisoner.

It felt like an eternity before Linus returned, but eventually, he trudged slowly down the stairs, burdened with supplies. Dropping everything outside the cell, he looked immediately ready to sprint back up to the light of day. "What else do you need?" he asked, slightly out of breath.

"I'll need help moving him to clean and bandage his wounds," she replied, already reaching for the vinegar and some linens.

"Oh ... Wouldn't you rather I get new bedding and blankets?" he asked, gnawing his lip.

After waiting in the dungeon alone for such a long time, Meera's patience was at its limit, and her frustration heated and boiled over quickly. It was one thing for Linus not to enter the raek's beach, but there was no way this man could hurt him, and he hadn't killed Linus's brother or harmed anyone—that they knew of, at least. Meera looked up at Linus's face ready with an angry retort, but her rage drained away. The man within her friend had made an appearance earlier that day, but just now he looked like a frightened child; his eyes were wide and darting around the dungeon, and he was bunching fistfuls of his uniform shirt in his hands, making the silver-stitched bear do a rippling jig.

"Okay," Meera acquiesced in a puff of air. "Go and find bedding, blankets, and clothes. I'll do my best without you, and when you get back, you can help with the rest." She didn't know how she would manage without help, but she didn't think Linus would be a great help in his current state anyway.

When he left, she got to work. She started by removing the nails from the man's calves. It was like Cerun's arrow wounds in that the nails seemed to staunch the bleeding, and when she removed them, the little puncture wounds spurted fresh red drops into the still-life picture of the dungeon scene. Meera didn't have any tools except a needle for stitching the wounds and scissors to cut linens, so her hands were quickly covered in gore. From experience, she knew it would crust under her nails and travel with her for days.

She washed all of the man's visible wounds with vinegar, letting it run onto the soiled bedding, which she would soon replace anyway. The astringent tang of the vinegar filled her nose —a relief from the man's stench of blood, body odor, and urine. He shuddered when she doused the raw burns on his feet but didn't wake, and she decided to treat the burns like she would a cut with simple cleaning and bandaging since she didn't know what else to do. Some of the gaping whip lashes on his butt and thighs required stitching. Her clumsy efforts with the needle made the man twitch irregularly, but his eyes never opened and face remained impassive.

Otherwise, she wiped him clean with a soapy cloth and lathered and rinsed his hair. Meera was warming up from her exertion, but the man lay still, naked, and now damp. She thought he must be cold to the bone, but she couldn't cover him up until she finished with his injuries and Linus returned with blankets. Wrapping bandages around his legs and arms while he lay prone wasn't too difficult—most of his injuries seemed to be on his backside, which explained why he lay face down. Then she cleaned and bandaged his toes and fingers, each individually. It took a long time, but she wanted to keep filth out of the wounds, so they wouldn't become infected. She also used honey generously to help prevent festering and was careful to wrap the honeyed wounds well, hoping the dungeon rats wouldn't notice the sweet liquid gold in their vicinity.

When it came time to flip the man over, Meera laid a large swath of cloth over his back and butt. She couldn't wrap bandages around those areas, but she didn't want them touching the soiled mat he lay on—she had no choice but to try to flip him while keeping him on the mat; the alternative was rolling him onto the stone floor, which would likely open some of his wounds on impact. Positioning her left hand under the man's shoulder and her right hand at his hip, she pushed up from her crouched position next to him. He budged a small amount, but not enough to flip over. The man was thin from deprivation but still dense with muscle and larger than she was.

Panting, she stood to stretch her back and catch her breath before another attempt, allowing herself a few uncharitable thoughts about Linus before crouching back down. On her second attempt, she focused less on being gentle and managed to roll the man onto his back. Though she positioned him on his wounds, he remained utterly unconscious—his face relaxed—and Meera studied that young, handsome face. It was paler and more angular than the Terratellen faces she was accustomed to—with high cheekbones and dark, straight eyebrows. His mouth was slightly bloodied and bruised, and she noticed for the first time that despite his long captivity, he had no beard. He couldn't be *that* young, she thought.

Her gaze continued down his body, and she realized why most of the damage was done to his back: his front had been made into a gruesome statement piece. Even given all that she had already seen, her stomach turned. Hateful words had been crudely carved into the man's body: *demon* was cut into his chest, *go back to hell* had been sliced under it into his stomach, and smaller, like an afterthought *MURDRER* was gouged slanting over his right bicep, an "e" missing from the word. While less physically gruesome than his other wounds, Meera found the hate-infused words even more disturbing.

Shaking her head, she clenched her eyes shut for a moment before opening them to resume her task. None of the cuts were very deep, at least. She cleaned them all with vinegar and stitched a few of the larger ones shut. Then she went on to clean the rest of the man's front—wiping his face and torso. She checked his teeth for damage and found them intact—not that she could have done anything for him if they had been knocked out, but she would have at least known to only bring soft foods.

The young man was stark naked, his privates on full display. Meera had seen a naked man before—her father had never been particularly bashful about nudity—so she wasn't surprised by what she saw. She did, however, feel distinctly uncomfortable touching and cleaning the man there. On the one hand, she was glad he was unconscious to save them both the awkwardness, but on the other hand, his inability to consent to her touch discomfited her. After a moment of indecision, her desire for the man to be entirely clean when he woke up spurred her onward, and she washed his whole body as best she could.

As if on cue, Linus returned just as she finished. With him, he had a fresh mattress, blankets, and clothes. "How's it going?" he asked sheepishly.

"I've mostly finished cleaning and bandaging him," she replied. "But I could use your help getting him onto the new mattress." Putting the blankets and clothes down, Linus edged into the cell for the first time. Meera took the new mat from him and positioned it next to the old one, more toward the center of the cell. "This will be good," she said. "It will be easier for me to tend his wounds if I can move all the way around him."

She laid a large bit of undyed linen over the bed to serve as a bandage for the man's back, and when she straightened up, she caught Linus staring transfixed at the words cut into the prisoner's body. She thought he looked confused or conflicted, maybe, but she wasn't sure. While she wasn't quite in the mood for another philosophical debate, she couldn't help saying, "You can't tell me *this* was for the greater good of Terratelle." She was getting tired, and her earlier irritation with him edged through her voice more than she had intended.

His scrunched forehead reddened, and his lips pressed together for a moment before he retorted, "They're our *enemies*, Meera—him and that damned raek. Our enemies! If we didn't lock them up, they would be out there killing us!" His raised voice echoed all around her, tearing at her already frayed nerves.

"But how do you know? Maybe they're trying to kill us because we're trying to kill them! How can you hate them so much?" she cried back just as loudly. What she meant was: how could anyone hate a person enough to carve their malice into their enemy's body? But her heated question came out wrong—came out personal.

"How?" Linus shouted, voice cracking and eyes swimming with unshed tears. "They killed Sam! They killed my broth—" he choked off in a sob.

Meera's irritation vanished, and she stepped toward her friend, hands up placatingly. "Linus, I—" she started to say, putting a hand on his upper arm.

"No!" he cried, shaking her off. "Sam died protecting us all! Because we had to lock them up! We had to lock them up, or they would have killed innocent people. That—That's why Sam had to go onto the beach—to keep the raek alive, so we can use it to save even more people ... by—by torturing it, or trading it, or learning from it or whatever! Whatever the king thinks will do the most good for Terratelle. That's why Sam died—to protect Terratelle. He ... he had to," Linus said, pressing a clenched fist to his mouth. Tears ran freely down his face, and Meera wanted nothing more than to hug him.

She understood now why he couldn't question the treatment of the prisoners—question the war; he needed it all to have meaning so that his brother's death, too, could have meaning. But it didn't. At least, she didn't think so. She thought Sam's death had been a pointless waste of a young life, but she didn't say so. Swallowing the lump in her throat, she tasted the tears that ran down her own face in empathy with her friend. She reached toward him again, but he was pacing the small space and slipped her grip. "Linus, I'm sorry. I didn't mean you. I ... I just don't want to see anyone hurt. Your—your brother was so brave, and ... he died doing what he believed in," she said lamely.

Linus wasn't looking at her, though; his full attention was on the prisoner, who lay still and oblivious despite their shouting. In a low voice she had never heard from him before, he asked, "If it was up to you, would you let them go?" Tearing his gaze from the prisoner, he stabbed her with it instead, and she had to look down and away from the hostility in his eyes.

Meera opened her mouth and stuttered incoherently; she felt like the conversation had completely gotten away from her, and she didn't know how to backtrack—how to sheath the steel in her friend's stare. Trying again, she said, "I—I don't know. I ... maybe." Yes, she thought; she probably would let them go if it was up to her. She didn't want to say it—she didn't want to upset Linus further when the question didn't matter because it *wasn't* up to her—but she didn't have to; he could see it in her face.

Linus nodded at first like he was coming to understand something. Then, resuming his stunted pacing, he shook his head side to side like his whole body objected to her. "Linus—" she tried again, reaching out to him, but he cut her off.

"They're monsters, Meera! Both of them—all of them! They're monsters, and they killed Sam! Whose side are you on anyway?" he asked. He kicked out angrily at the prone prisoner, clipping the man on the hip. For a brief moment, his eyes opened wide at his own actions before he quickly turned and fled the dungeon.

Meera followed him out of the cell and called after him, but he didn't slow or look back. Too quickly, he disappeared up the stairs, and she was left heaving with dismayed sobs, unsure of what to do. She wanted to run after Linus—comfort him and talk things through. But she couldn't leave the prisoner—he needed her. She was responsible for him. Torn, she looked to the prisoner, to the stairs, then back to the naked young man lying alone in the cell. She would stay—she couldn't leave the man like that. Wiping her eyes with the clean back of her hands, she grunted in frustration that she had to choose between the stranger and her friend. She didn't want to choose ... Whose side *was* she on? Meera didn't know why there even *were* sides. Still, she pulled herself together as quickly as she could to focus on the task at hand.

With some effort, she maneuvered the young man onto the fresh mattress. He would probably be more comfortable on his stomach since there were fewer wounds on his front, but she left him on his back since she wouldn't be able to feed him face down. Dragging the old mat out of the cell, she heaved it a way down the corridor and left it in one of the doorless cells. Her eyes continued to leak the occasional stray tear, but she kept moving and did her best to put Linus out of her mind. Returning to the prisoner, she abandoned the notion of clothes, knowing she would need to check and bandage his entire body every day. Instead, she left the stack of clothes on the floor for future use and used the swath of linen that had previously been on his back to cover his front, loading blankets onto the man and tucking them in slightly at the edges. Then she used a rolled-up blanket to prop under his head and did her best to spoon broth into his slack mouth.

After a long effort, she only got him to swallow a very small amount of food, and with a weary sigh, she realized that she would need to return frequently to give him more. She didn't think the man would rouse before she came back again, but she left a new pitcher of water just in case. She also emptied the broth crock into the hole in the corner and left it by the mat in case he needed to relieve himself. Then, after a moment's consideration, she pulled back the blankets to reveal his nakedness and packed extra linens around his privates in case he wet himself or worse. Once she'd bundled him back up, she took Cerun's feather from against the wall and laid it over his chest as a sort of blessing for good health. Deciding to return later with more broth and torch oil, she left her lit torch in the cell with the man. She wouldn't let the darkness swallow him again.

When she left, she removed the food tray and honey. The vinegar she could leave behind, but the rats would find a way into the honey. On the steep ascent up the stairs, she replayed what had happened with Linus over and over again in her head, but the warm air at the top shocked her out of her reverie—she had become accustomed to the chill in the dungeon and had forgotten that it was midday as well as nearing summer. She squinted from the sudden influx of light. The three guards in the hall gaped at her as she passed, and she nodded to them but averted her red eyes. She had done her best to wipe the blood from her hands, but they were red as well. Blood also splattered her face and clothes from removing the nails from the man's calves, and Meera anticipated an exasperated shake of the head from Cook for her appearance.

As she moved through the palace, she elicited many stares. Groaning inwardly, she assumed her new duty would be common knowledge by the next day, and interest in her would spike again as a result. Reaching the kitchen was a relief, and her shoulders dipped in a release of tension. Cook wordlessly took the tray from her and gave her bloody visage a frown and a cluck. Then Meera spent several long minutes scrubbing her hands and arms in the sink basin before removing her soiled apron and having Cook check her over for errant blood. Once clean, she realized how hungry she was and ate a large bowl of stew with crusty bread. She knew she should pay attention to the gossip while she ate and listen for any mention of the duke, but her mind felt too full from the day's events. She would think about the duke tomorrow.

IN JUST A FEW SHORT HOURS, Meera was back at the top of the dungeon stairs with torch oil and a bottle of broth. Her heart hammered at the prospect of going into the dungeon alone. It was an irrational fear—she had already spent most of the day alone in the deep darkness—but the stale, cold air wafting up to her and the eerie echoing of drips below gave her a visceral foreboding. As she descended the stairs, she filled the torches—a tedious job— and when she reached cell 39, she retrieved the key from her pocket and opened the door with less trouble than the first time but still a lot of jangling.

The young man was right where she'd left him, Cerun's feather rising and falling with his steady breathing. Sitting on the mat by his head, she propped his head and shoulders on her knees to make it easier to pour broth from the bottle into his mouth, and she tried to use her other hand to massage his throat and help the liquid go down. He didn't cough or choke—she didn't think he could in his state—and with effort, she got him to take in at least a small amount of liquid. With a sigh, she decided that was enough for the day, and she would return in the morning. She didn't relish her new job, but she would do whatever she could for the man regardless of her own discomfort.

When she left the dungeon, she was desperate for fresh air and went into the garden to gulp in the new smell of blooming flowers. It was evening but still light out, and there were quite a few people milling about the gardens and even more gathered on the patio. Meera wondered where Linus might be but didn't think there was any real possibility of her finding him. She would have to wait for the morning to see him and hoped to make amends with him on their walk—not that she knew what to say to him. He was right; she didn't think the prisoners should be caged and tortured.

Without thought, Meera's feet sought the quiet companionship of Cerun on his beach. They walked her through the gardens and down the hill to where he lay, muzzled head wearing a groove in the dirt between his clawed forefeet. She approached the raek, and as they were alone for the first time in a while, she embraced him around his neck. For a minute, she rested her forehead against his sleek feathers, then she scratched him in his favorite places, and Cerun hummed low in his throat like a deep purr. Finally, Meera looked him in the eye and said, "He's alive but unconscious. If he doesn't wake soon to eat and drink, I'm not sure how long he'll last ..."

Cerun shut his eyes. Meera felt tears prick at her own, but she swallowed them back; Cerun didn't keen and thrash in his despair and helplessness, so she wouldn't cry either. "I'm sorry," she whispered. She truly was sorry and was beginning to feel increasingly burdened by her responsibilities; she wanted to help Cerun and his rider but was also beholden to her king. Whose side *was* she on? She asked herself the question over and over, but all she could think was that she wanted to be on the *good* side ... whichever that was.

12

———

Meera sat on the edge of her usual bench the next morning, eager for Linus to arrive with the cart. She felt like she'd been waiting for longer than usual, but she couldn't tell if she really had or if her anxiety about seeing Linus only made her feel that way. When he finally pulled the cart around the corner, his steps looked laden, and his head hung low. Despite how tired Meera's legs were from her regular trips down the dungeon stairs and back, she sprung from her seat. "Linus! I —" she started to say.

"Sorry I'm late," he mumbled, interjecting. He stared at the ground and refused to meet her eyes.

"That's okay," she replied. "Are you alright? I wanted to find you yesterday ..." It was true she had wanted to find him, but she hadn't actually looked and felt bad about that.

"Let's just go," he said despondently, turning to drag the cart down their usual path. Meera followed and studied her friend as she walked beside him. He looked older and not in the handsome way he had when pledging to stay by her and keep her safe—he looked sunken in as if from years of hardship, though he'd been spry and boyish just the day before.

After several minutes of walking in silence, she couldn't stand it any longer. "Linus, can we please talk? I really didn't mean to upset you yesterday or accuse you of anything—" she said, a pleading note in her voice.

"Let's just forget about it," he replied, still not looking at her.

Meera wasn't sure she could forget about it; Linus was clearly still upset. It was then, however, that he heaved a heavy sigh, and she smelled the alcohol on his breath. "Have you been drinking?" she asked indignantly, forgetting that she had been trying to apologize.

"That's no concern of yours," he retorted moodily, letting his hair hang in front of his eyes without sweeping it away.

"Yes, it is, Linus—because we're friends!" she cried. Throwing out her hand, she pressed it to his chest and halted him in his tracks. With her other hand, she brushed the hair out of his face.

Peering anxiously into his eyes, she searched for the Linus she was familiar with, but he swiped her hand from his face and said, "Don't, Meera—just don't."

There was so much defeat in his voice that she obeyed. She stepped aside for him, and when he started walking, she strode next to him in silence. As she walked, she bent her own head, and they looked like two mourners, though only one wore black. Meera's lip trembled, and she bit it to clamp down her emotion. She didn't know if Linus's behavior was about their fight or his feelings for her or both, but she didn't think she could say anything to ease his pain regardless. Either way, she would have to lie to say what he wanted to hear, and she wouldn't lie to her friend—not in this case, anyway.

THE NEXT SEVERAL days were a busy blur. Meera awoke early to feed the prisoner before she met Linus, fed Cerun, ate a quick lunch, and descended the dungeon stairs a second time. Then she made two more trips in the afternoon and evening before collapsing onto her bed at night. In between her dungeon visits, she also renewed her attempts to learn more about Duke Harrington. She observed the duke later in the evening than she had previously, hoping she might see him leave the palace and follow him to discern something about his visit to Altus, but she didn't have any luck.

Feeling the need to be constantly prepared for her many responsibilities, she started keeping a bag with her at all times containing the dungeon key, a bottle of water for her, a bottle of broth for the prisoner, food in case she couldn't make it back to the kitchen, and a book in case she needed to hide her face or bide her time during her spying. Meera's walks with Linus used to be her favorite part of the day, but they soon became the least pleasant—even considering the soiled cloths she had to change several times each day from around the prisoner's genitals.

Linus wouldn't look at her and barely spoke to her no matter what she said to him. Meera knew he was struggling and didn't want to let him slip away from her, but she was already so heavily burdened with obligations that she didn't feel like she could carry the weight of their friendship single-handedly. On one of their silent walks down the slope, she released him from waiting while she fed Cerun since he wasn't accompanying her to the dungeon anymore anyway, and he didn't argue. Meera didn't mind not having Linus as a constant escort, but she missed her jovial conversations with him—she missed her friend.

Over time, her schedule took a toll on her body. She had a constant dull headache from sleep deprivation, and Cook had to shake her awake on several occasions when she dozed off eating.

Her mind and body were both pervasively exhausted, and while she was getting stronger from her frequent trips to the canal and the dungeon, she wasn't getting stronger fast enough. The stairs, especially, felt brutal after a long day, and her leg muscles would shake with effort while she half dragged herself using the railing.

As time passed, she grew more weary, but she also grew more hopeful that Prince Phineas had forgotten about her. Each passing day without trouble from the prince eased some of the tension in Meera's mind, and she became more comfortable the dungeon as she spent more time in its dark depths. Sometimes the cool air was even a relief from the heat that daily announced summer's imminent approach.

However, even as Meera became stronger and more confident—if progressively more exhausted—the prisoner's condition didn't change. He remained unconscious and unresponsive. She spoke to him sometimes, but his face was always slack—peaceful even. She wondered how he could remain in such a state when he should be feeling so much pain. His wounds were healing but slowly; he needed to eat to speed the healing process, and he needed to wake up in order to eat. Meera could only force the man to swallow small amounts of broth, which kept him alive but didn't improve his condition. His ribs already showed under his pale flesh, and she feared he would only get thinner and weaker as time went on.

ONE DAY, Meera walked briskly to the dungeon after her lunch, taking an extra roll with meat and cheese with her in case she got hungry again. She was hungry a lot lately—her body needing more food than usual to get through her long days. As she often did, she stopped briefly to duck behind a bush in the garden to relieve herself. The walk from the kitchen to the dungeon entrance was second nature to her now, and she let her weary mind wander on her way.

Absently, she nodded to the guards in the armory hallway as she passed them. She thought she noticed one of the guards avert his eyes from hers, but she was in such a hurry, she didn't pause to consider the strange moment—she merely tugged open the dungeon door and started down the stairs. The torches were already lit. She kept them lit and refilled their oil regularly. She didn't want the prisoner to awaken to darkness, and she dreaded the possibility of ever being in the dungeon herself when the light spluttered out.

Following the torches, she reached cell 39. Past the prisoner's cell was thick blackness—Meera had not progressed further since her first journey into the dungeon. Turning her attention to the prisoner, she could see that the young man was exactly where she had left him; his face was angled slightly toward the cell door, and the blankets and water bottle had not been moved. She wasn't surprised, exactly, but she kept imagining that one day she would arrive to find him awake—sitting up, even. In that moment, however, she wondered if he would ever wake again.

Undoing the clasp of her bag, she rifled at the bottom for the key. But just as her hand closed around the metal, a voice colder than the dungeon air sounded behind her: "Another funny job for a kitchen maid ..."

The voice echoed off the walls and bars, surrounding Meera—bombarding her. Her heart stopped for a breath. Then it started up again with the thundering gallop of a wild horse. It was Prince Phineas! He hadn't forgotten her—he had come for her where no one would see or interfere. Meera could tell from his tone that his usual mask of charm and innocence had been discarded, and while she didn't hear him step out from the darkness and move behind her, she could feel him looming closer.

Suddenly, fear turned her limbs weak and lifeless like the butcher had strung her up and drained her of all her blood. Aside from her pounding heart—desperate to pump life to her dangling extremities—her whole body froze. She had to do something—she should turn or run or say something to buy herself time to think—but she didn't. She did nothing. Her terror seized her and held her fast.

The prince chuckled and brushed a finger down the bare back of her neck. She trembled, and had she not just relieved herself outside, her bladder would have emptied. "You look awfully at home in a dungeon," he whispered into her ear, his breath the only warmth in his statement. "That could be arranged, you know. There are plenty of cells left … Or, we could play with some of the tools I've been meaning to try out in the other room. That might be … amusing." Meera pictured the torture room—the dangling instruments of malice, the table covered in blood—and she whimpered involuntarily. She could feel in her gut that the prince's words were not idle threats.

Phineas hovered behind her, but only her fear held her in place. Move, she thought. She needed to move! Why couldn't she move? She shut her eyes. It was all she could manage, as if not seeing would make her disappear—would make her safe. The prince brushed another delicate finger along the skin of her neck. Then, without warning, he rammed his right fist into the side of her head. The force of the blow knocked Meera off balance, and she fell forward and to the side. Clutching her bag in one hand and the key within in the other, she couldn't think or move fast enough to catch herself; her face bashed against the bars of the cell, rattling the iron as well as her head. She crumpled to the floor. The prince grabbed at her and caught the bodice of her dress, pulling and ripping it open on the side.

Meera tried to curl in on herself—to shield her throbbing head with her arms—while Phineas attempted to get a grip on her to drag her away. She had never been struck before—had never felt the sudden, violent pain of a blow to the head—and she pressed her free hand to her face as if holding it together. Irrationally, she felt like it had cracked and would break apart if she let go. Her other hand was still inside her bag. She had dropped the key at some point, but she touched one of the glass bottles within. Pulling it free, she swung it up at the prince, trying to hit him in the head with the bottle.

Phineas caught her flailing arm easily and took the bottle from her grip. Laughing cruelly at her helplessness, he dangled the water out in front of him, daring her to grab it. Meera didn't even try—she was barely in control of her body. Suddenly, she noticed she was doing a sort of heaving dry sob, and she tried to pull in a full breath of air—to steady herself. One breath ... two breaths ... three. Then she could think a little, move a little. Sitting up fully, she lowered her hand from her face, relieved that her skull stayed in place, and she didn't seem to be bleeding.

"You know, I am a bit parched," the prince said mockingly as he unscrewed the cap of the bottle to tip his head back and take a drink. That was the water, Meera thought, staring at him, but she still had the broth ... Desperately, she grappled in her bag for the other bottle, pulled it out, and swung it as hard as she could at the only part of the prince she could reach from the floor: his groin. Despite her arm feeling like jelly, she landed a solid blow. The prince spewed water in a choking grunt, and the bottle in his hand fell and shattered against the stone floor. Bending over himself, he backed away a few steps, face screwed up in pain.

Meera gripped the cell bars and used them to drag herself to standing. Her legs wobbled under her weight but held. Get away, get away, get away, she thought. The stairs—but she didn't think she could outrun him. The cell! Fumbling once more in her bag, she gripped the key to the cell. Trembling, she jammed it into the keyhole and turned, hard. The cell bars jangled with deafening reverberation, but she got the door open faster than ever before and threw herself inside. She reached through the bars to lock herself in, but the prince, having just recovered himself, looked up to see what she was doing and lunged for her.

Meera was clutching the key—turning it and trying to pull it free from inside the cell—when Phineas grabbed her hand and attempted to rip it away. She had dropped her bottle somewhere and had one free hand. With her pointer and middle finger, she thrust between the bars and rammed the prince in the eye. He cried out. She managed to pull the key out of the door, but Phineas still held her right hand and tightened his grip on her. The key was crushed in Meera's palm, biting into her skin, and he wanted it.

For a minute, they tugged back and forth, the cell door banging with every effort, and Meera's body colliding with the bars. She kept her neck arched and head held back to protect her face from further harm and scratched frantically at the prince with her free hand, but he also pulled his head back and out of her reach. He had her hand with both of his now and was slowly prying her fingers off the key. With a last, desperate move, Meera twisted her hand and used her legs to push all of her body weight backward. She wrenched free of Phineas's grasp and fell back— hard. Her tailbone smacked onto the stone ground and sent pain waves up her spine, and the key tinkled to the floor nearby.

She scrabbled back from the door on her forearms, gasping for air and shaking all over. The prince rattled the cell door violently and screamed his outrage, surrounding her in the echoes of his guttural cry. But he couldn't reach her. She had gotten away—she was safe. After a winded moment, Meera turned onto her right side to push herself up and looked straight into the prisoner's open eyes.

Startled, she thrust herself into a seated position and scooted backward, whimpering at the pain it caused her right wrist. Then she shrunk into herself and peered all around; she was cowering in a cell between an angry, murderous prince and a foreign, possibly magical, prisoner—between a definite threat and a complete unknown. All things considered, she was glad to be on the inside of the cell door, and she released a shaky exhale. The prisoner was probably too weak to hurt her ... probably.

Prince Phineas stepped all the way up to the cell door and glared at her, his mask off and the beast within him shining through every curve of his eyes and mouth. His hair was loose and dangled between the bars, a gaudy show of shining gold against the dull, rusting iron. For a surreal moment, Meera stared transfixed by his glowing waves of hair. They were so soft and bright in the gloom and so at odds with the prince's steely eyes and tense jaw. Then she met his gaze and wondered if there was any love or kindness in the man at all or if he was all impulse and aggression.

Without a word, Phineas pressed away from the cell door, which intoned one final clang of emphasis, and he stormed away down the corridor. Meera's ears rang along with the iron bars, and she couldn't hear whether or not he climbed the stairs and left the dungeon. Gazing after him, she stayed completely still and hoped, once again, to be forgotten. Then she remembered the prisoner and swiveled to look at him. He looked back with pale grey eyes.

Meera scooted herself away from the prisoner's mat but not so close to the cell door that the prince could reach her if he came back. She thought about standing up but wasn't sure if she could —she was so shaken. The key was on the floor, and she snatched it up to put in her pocket. Her bag lay outside the cell door, abandoned in her desperate scramble for safety. Breathing deeply, she took a brief inventory of herself: her right wrist was hurt from wrenching it away from the prince, her head and face throbbed painfully but weren't bleeding, and her dress was torn on the side. She was okay, she told herself—she was fine. She cradled her injured wrist to her stomach and gave her heart a moment to slow from a gallop to a trot.

When she began to feel steadier, she turned her attention to the prisoner, who lay still on his mat. He returned her gaze without expression, and for a full minute, they stared at one another. Meera swallowed; she felt as if she'd been screaming, though she didn't think she actually had. "My name is Meera Hailship," she croaked. "I've been caring for your wounds and trying to get you to eat ... I also care for your raek."

The man didn't answer and continued to regard her. His dark eyebrows caved in ever so slightly, but Meera couldn't tell if he was confused, angry, or just in pain. "Can you understand me?" she asked. Cerun could, so she assumed his rider could as well. She didn't know if another language was spoken in Aegorn. The man jerked his chin down ever so slightly, and Meera had the sudden impression that she was speaking to Cerun—as if he had just blinked at her. Attempting a smile, she said, "You remind me of him—your raek, I mean. I call him Cerun. He accepted the name."

The man didn't answer—there was only a fleeting twitch in one of his cheeks. Was it suspicion? She couldn't tell. Meera sighed. She knew the prisoner had no reason to trust her and might think this was some sort of elaborate interrogation technique. She supposed in a way it was; the king wanted her to acquire information from the man with her *woman's touch*, which she took to mean kindness. In that moment, however, she didn't care what the king wanted. She didn't care if the prisoner spoke to her—only that he refrain from attacking her. After narrowly escaped the prince's assault, she didn't feel up for a second round.

Vaguely, she wondered what the man thought of her sitting in his dank cell and felt a surge of self-consciousness. She didn't want to appear weak with her clothing torn—even in front of a man who was weaker and stark naked. Suddenly, the man lifted his head as if trying to sit up and emitted a groan, his face scrunching in agony. He quickly laid his head back down, panting. Meera pitied him for the pain he must feel, and she looked around for some way to help, glad the prince hadn't thought to extinguish the torches. There was a bottle of water by the man's bed, and the bottle of broth she had used to strike the prince was reachable through the bars.

With a glance down the corridor, she crawled to the cell door on her knees and grabbed the broth and her bag with her uninjured hand, scooting quickly away from the door again like a very uncoordinated cat batting at yarn. The man watched her, and Meera had to resist the urge to fidget or otherwise occupy herself to avoid just staring back at him. To ease her discomfort, she spoke: "Your wounds have all closed, but they're still healing. I don't think any of them are life-threatening unless they become infected, and so far, they haven't. If you move, make sure you move carefully ..." She trailed off, not sure what else to say.

Exhaustion from the attack was starting to weigh heavily on her shoulders. She thought could probably leave the dungeon without further incident, but the notion made her fear spike and her stomach turn over. The prince could be waiting on the stairs or in the hallway beyond. Meera supposed she could get a weapon from the torture room ... But if she seriously maimed or killed the prince, she would hang for treason. Being in the king's service would not protect her. Drawing her knees into her chest, she rested her forearms and chin upon them. She was safe for the moment, so she would stay in the cell.

But how long would she need to stay in the dungeon? Linus would look for her if she didn't turn up in the morning, she assured herself, and with that comforting thought, she decided to hunker down and wait. Slowly, so as not to startle the prisoner, she leaned toward him and plucked the water bottle from the floor by his mat. Then she took a long drink, which helped settle her nerves. Meera couldn't in good conscience drink in front of the man without offering him anything, so she looked back at him and said, "You should have some broth. I can help you sit up to drink it. I have some food in my bag too …"

The man didn't reply in any way, so she took the broth and edged slowly toward him. Sitting next to his mat, she shifted the bottle from her left hand to her right in order to lift his head with her left. She had forgotten about her injured right wrist, however, and the weight of the broth in her hand sent a sharp pain through it, causing her to drop the bottle on her lap. Examining her wrist, she found it was starting to swell but didn't look too horrible. It probably wasn't broken. She hoped it wasn't broken—she couldn't imagine being even more helpless than she already was while she waited for a broken bone to heal.

Noticing the man looking at her wrist as well, she said, "I don't know how much you saw … I was coming down to feed you, and a man—Prince Phineas …" she said his name with deep disgust. She didn't think it mattered if the prisoner knew. "… he attacked me. I locked myself in here to get away. I'm … not sure if it's safe to leave," she said apologetically, feeling like an unwelcome guest.

The young man's handsome—if drawn—face remained impassive, and he continued to study her. She studied him in return. He still had no trace of stubble or beard but otherwise looked normal—human, that is—though he didn't look

Terratellen. His face was more angular, his jaw and cheekbones very pronounced—very unlike her own round face. His skin was paler than hers but not impossibly pale for Terratelle, although his hair was very dark considering his skin tone. Gazing into his eyes to gauge their color, Meera could only judge them to be grey in the dimness.

Drawing in a steadying breath, she took the bottle back in her right hand, this time anticipating the pain and gritting her teeth through it. She started to slide her left hand under the man's neck to help him drink, but the second she touched his skin, he jerked his head violently back and away from her. The sudden movement made her jump and sent another spike of pain through her wrist and her throbbing head. "Really, I don't mean you any harm! I've been taking care of you and your raek. He wanted me to bring you this," she said, remembering the large feather on the man's chest and picking it up to hold it where he could see. She hoped Cerun's token would have a calming effect on him.

The man looked long at the feather, his eyes growing reflective with tears in the low lantern light, but when he looked back at her, it was with undisguised fury. Meera was surprised and a little unnerved by the obvious animosity in his expression, so when he moved slightly under his blankets, she scooted back, putting her hands up in front of her face placatingly. Slowly, she reached out to drop the feather back onto his torso, where the vibrant streak of blue settled precariously back onto its pallid backdrop.

"He wanted me to pluck the feather to bring to you," she explained, trying to guess why he was angry. Then, unexpectedly, her fear, frustration, and exhaustion gushed out of her in a torrent: "I'm not a torturer! I've never hurt anyone! I'm just a kitchen maid—a scholar's daughter. I never asked for any of this! I mean, I volunteered to feed Cerun, but I didn't know what I was getting myself into ... I just ... I just didn't want to be alone anymore! I never meant to be a king's tool or weapon or whatever!" Her voice rose and echoed against the surrounding iron. The noise hurt her head.

More quietly, she added, "I'm just a girl. I'm a good person—I think I'm a good person ... I did this to myself, though. It's my fault. I volunteered and drew too much attention to myself and curtsied too slowly in front of the prince, and it must be my fault. I'm reckless and naive just like Cook said." She wasn't really talking to the prisoner and didn't expect him to understand her; she was just flaking apart—her words detaching and falling away from her like the tears from her eyes.

Burying her wet face in her hands, she shook silently for several minutes. Then she lay down on the cold stone floor with the less hurt side of her head resting on her arm. She didn't know if the man had followed anything she'd said at all, and she didn't care. If he didn't want her help eating—fine. She couldn't care about that right now either. She was too exhausted and felt too hopeless. She lay still, and as her heart rate calmed to its usual deliberate plod, the cold crept into her body. The stone beneath her leached her warmth through the thin layer of her summer dress, and the dungeon air chilled her sweat and tears where they lay on her exposed skin.

Curling in on herself, she shivered. Meera thought vaguely about taking one of the prisoner's blankets, but she couldn't do it. He had faced far worse violence and helplessness than she had, and knowing how she felt, she couldn't imagine his own agony. She couldn't bear to take even one blanket from him. Instead, she lay still and allowed the cold to seize her as she had allowed the prince to trap her. She felt like she deserved the misery for her foolish carelessness and for all of the impulsive decisions that had led her to that moment. If the prisoner watched her, she took no notice.

MEERA'S CONSCIOUSNESS drifted a few times, but her discomfort wouldn't allow her the true release of sleep. Time was meaningless in the dungeon, and she had no notion of how long she'd been there when footsteps sounded on the stairs. Still, she didn't move. Her mind felt fuzzy with mold. She looked at the prisoner who looked back, and their expressions were mirrored blankness. A voice called, "Meera?" and her name bounced off every hard surface, pulsing like her injured face. She didn't move. She couldn't tell whose voice it was.

Then the voice was at the cell door: "Meera?" Someone touched the door and the clang of iron on iron accelerated the pounding in her head. She thought the voice was familiar, but like time, sound was different in the dungeon. She struggled to a seated position—her muscles stiff with cold, and her whole body rejecting the movement. Looking over her shoulder to view the dark figure at the door, she recognized their homely shape and simple white apron: it was Cook. Meera knew she should feel relief, but her heart was as numb with cold as the rest of her.

"Meera, you locked in? You got the key? You hurt?" Cook asked. There was an uncharacteristic tremor in their voice, and they kept glancing around uneasily. Meera had never known Cook to be frightened before, and it pushed the cogs in her mind to resume turning. Cook looked smaller, less sure of themself outside their domain in the kitchen. It was like seeing a flower in the snow ... or golden hair against iron bars.

Meera's mouth felt as fuzzy as her head, and she had to work her tongue around a bit before she could speak. "I'm okay. I have the key," she replied, fishing for the key in her pocket with stiff, lifeless fingers and slowly pushed herself to stand. "How long have I been in here?" she asked, handing over the key and watching Cook try to move the stubborn locking mechanism with it.

"How long? Don't know. Guard comes in the kitchen drunk, saying how you 'n' the prince went in the dungeon then how you didn't come out. I'm asking him why he didn't look for you, 'n' he's saying how scairt he is, how scairt they all are of the prince. Then he's saying how he didn't want to find your body 'n' see what's been done to you. I say to him 'you're not a guard, you're a drunk coward', 'n' I come to find you myself. You gonna tell me what happened? How come you locked in a cell with the key?" Cook looked behind Meera and seemed to register the prisoner for the first time, their shrewd eyes widening for the briefest moment before resuming their usual narrow gaze. The man continued to observe without any change in his countenance.

Meera picked up her bag but left the water and broth by the mat. "Try to drink something if you can. I'll be back tomorrow," she told the prisoner. She hoped it was a true statement—and she didn't. She didn't want the prince to find and detain her before she could return, but she also wished never to enter the dungeon again. Meera locked the cell behind her with an uneasy lurch in her stomach; the few hours she'd spent inside had felt like an eternity, and the prisoner had been in there for seven weeks. Seven weeks! If she could—if she wasn't captured or hurt or hanged—she would return for him.

Cook looked her up and down, and Meera realized she hadn't answered any of their questions. Taking a deep breath, she said, "I was about to open the cell. He attacked me from behind—hit my head and ripped my dress. I hit him in the groin with a bottle and locked myself in the cell. My head is hurt and my wrist but not too badly." She couldn't imagine what her face looked like after smacking it into the bars and crying for so long. It likely looked as bad as it felt.

Cook nodded and squeezed her in a tight hug, giving her the briefest consolation of warmth. "You're colder than a root from the cellar! Let's get you warm, fed, and in bed," they said. Meera wanted to smile in reply, but her lips didn't even twitch. She was numb, frozen like she had been when the prince had approached her—helpless, useless. She bowed her head in shame and acquiescence, and Cook led her up the staircase and took care of her, going so far as to walk her to her bedroom door.

She went in quietly, thinking Teardra would be asleep, but the older woman was sitting up in her bed with a candle lit, her stringy hair braided in a single plait over one bony shoulder. At the sight of Meera's swollen face and torn dress, she gasped, declaring, "A dungeon is no place for women!" And with that, she lay flat and rolled away from the light. Meera looked behind her at Cook, saw amusement on their face, and almost laughed aloud. She didn't laugh, but she did manage a small smile. Of all the shocks she'd had that day, Teardra waiting up for her might've topped them all.

13

———

Meera garnered more attention than usual in the kitchen the next morning because of the bruises on her face, but everyone assumed that the prisoner had attacked her. She didn't correct them. It was better for her if her interactions with Prince Phineas remained private—there would always be those who would believe the worst of her rather than believing the worst of the charming, golden-haired prince.

Leaving the interested crowd as quickly as possible, she sat on her bench outside the kitchen. She hadn't gone to the dungeon first thing. The prisoner was now awake and could hopefully drink something without her assistance. Plus, she hadn't wanted to go ... She was afraid and dreaded her next descent down the dark, cold stairs. Sagging on her bench, she repressed a groan; she wasn't looking forward to seeing Linus or Cerun, either.

Meera had awoken with a gut full of boiling rage. She was angry with Linus for shutting her out and not escorting and protecting her. She was angry with the guards for not warning her or helping her when they must have known what would happen when she'd entered the dungeon. She was angry with Cerun for sending her down with the feather that had clearly inflamed the prisoner. She was angry with the prisoner for not allowing her to help him and fulfill her duty. She was angry with the king for assigning her that duty. But mostly, she was angry with herself for ever volunteering and drawing attention to herself in the first place.

Strangely, the one person she wasn't angry with was the prince. Meera supposed she didn't feel angry with Prince Phineas because she had never expected anything from him to begin with. *He* was the monster in the palace—roaming free to bite at will rather than being chained to the walls of the canal. She wasn't angry at the prince, but she hated and feared him with a visceral burning in her blood; she felt she could witness any horrible atrocity befall him and not pity him. The feeling scared her. In a way, she was finally coming to understand the hatred that most people felt toward raeken. Would she join a frenzied crowd in cheering if the prince were chained and dragged before her? She hoped not.

The only silver lining in Meera's situation was her gratitude for Cook, who had—once again—cleaned her and fed her and had also wrapped her injured wrist to keep it stable and help the swelling go down. It was customary to give gifts on the Summer Solstice—which was quickly approaching—and she resolved to think of something appropriately special to give Cook. But while Cook's wrappings prevented her wrist from hurting too much, her head still throbbed, and there wasn't much she could do about that. Teardra of all people had offered her a tea to dull her pain, but Meera had declined the offer. She was afraid of dulling her senses along with her pain, considering she had no notion of what the day might bring. She could only hope it wouldn't bring another encounter with the prince.

When Linus approached Meera on her bench, his eyes were fixed on the ground, and he didn't greet her. She stood and walked up to him but didn't say anything or seek eye contact. Instead, she brushed past, starting down their usual path. If she spoke, she thought her rage would bubble up and gush out of her. She knew her behavior wasn't fair, but she was doing her best to dam her anger within herself. She had never felt like this before—she wanted to slam doors and throw dishes, do *something* to release the growing tension within her. She was so angry and so fed up with Linus's moods, and she felt like he had abandoned her.

He scurried after her stuttering, "M-Meera, wait! Your face! What happened?" She kept walking, quickly, and clenched her fists. The action sent shooting pain into her right wrist until she eased her fingers apart. Then Linus grabbed her arm—a colossal mistake. Meera whirled on him, lashing out with her good but nondominant hand, and beating it ineffectually against his bony chest. "Whoa!" he said, putting his hands up.

Drawing in her lashing limb, she restrained it at her side once more, but her outburst left her shaking with emotion. A hairline fracture ran the length of the dam penting her emotions, and when she saw the concern in Linus's puppy-like eyes, it cracked wide open. Grabbing at his shirt, she buried her face in his chest. He wrapped his arms around her, stroked her back, and made soothing shushing noises, and they stood like that long enough for her to soak the bear emblem on his shirt with tears and snot. They were in the middle of a well-used garden path, but it was early enough to be deserted—not that Meera had the capacity to care in that moment.

When she finally extricated her face from Linus's chest, she tried to turn it away, feeling embarrassed by her outburst—by both of her outbursts—but Linus took her chin and gently guided it back toward him to inspect her face. It looked even worse today, she knew; she had looked in her mirror the night before and that morning. Before bed, it had been a bit swollen, but now she had a livid purple bruise down the right side of her face and a smaller one on her forehead where she had hit two bars. The whole right side of her face was puffy, as were her eyes, which were also bloodshot from crying.

Linus's gaze traveled down from her face to her swollen, bandaged wrist, and as he looked at her, his own eyes filled with tears that she watched him swallow back. "What happened?" he asked, his voice cracking with either emotion or anger—or possibly just youth. "Was it *him*?" he asked. Meera didn't even know which *him* he meant.

"Let's walk," she said, sniffing and taking his hand. His embrace had comforted her, and she was loath to be alone in her skin again. He gripped her hand tightly as they walked, and she told him everything that had happened.

Linus was beside himself with anger toward the prince and guilt for not having been there. Seeing him upset with himself made all of Meera's own anger toward him evaporate. "You can't be with me all the time," she reassured him. She wanted to add that Prince Phineas was a prince—that there wasn't much anyone could do to defend against him—but she found that thought too unsettling to verbalize. "Why didn't the guards warn me or help me?" she asked, despising how pitiful she sounded. But Linus knew the men—was one of them—and Meera couldn't understand their inaction.

Linus averted his eyes from her. His grip on her hand slackened slightly, but she held tighter to prevent him from pulling away. "We're told that the royal family is our priority—more important than anyone and everything else," he said levelly as if reciting from a book.

"But that doesn't make sense!" Meera argued. "He wasn't in

danger—I was. He wouldn't have even known if the guards had whispered to me not to go down." Her anger bubbled back up suddenly, and she ripped her hand from his as if her hot rage would scald him.

"The loyalty runs deep," he murmured, sounding resigned.

"At least the one guard knew it was wrong and did it anyway. Is that what loyalty is? To abandon your own conscience? Would *you* have let it happen?" she asked. She knew he wouldn't have—not to her anyway—but she was trying to make a broader point. Meera suddenly felt like she was reliving their fight in the dungeon and knew Linus wouldn't understand her.

"Of course not! I would have protected you!" he cried.

"No!" she snapped, frustrated. "I mean, if it had been some other woman—some other innocent person—and the prince or the king was going to hurt them. What would you do?"

"I'm ... sure I won't be put in that position," he said after a pause.

"How could you possibly be sure?" she cried shrilly. "Three of your fellow guards were in that position yesterday. He was going to hurt me, Linus! He was going to drag me to the torture room and hurt me and maybe even kill me, and they knew! They knew, and they didn't do anything." Tears fell down her cheeks once more, and she batted them away in irritation.

Linus flinched at her words, but he continued to defend his position: "We're all under the power of the Crown! Even you! The royal family is the law, and it's not our job to question them. They lead and we follow for the good of the entire land. You need to just accept that!"

"This again? So, the man in the dungeon should be tortured because it *might* save Terratellen lives—it *might* be for the good of the land. And what? The prince should torture me? For what? To boost his royal morale for the good of the land? How would the prince hurting me help Terratelle, Linus? Tell me!" she shouted. She was flying down the hill toward the canal, her feet stomping the ground in unison with her thudding heart, and Linus scurried after her, bumping the cart along the uneven ground.

"I'm sorry, okay? I'm sorry they didn't help you! I'm sorry I wasn't there to help you. That I ... haven't been there. But you're okay, right? You're okay, and that's what matters," he said. He was trying to be placating, but his dismissal enraged her further.

Whirling on him, she shouted, "You don't get it, do you!? The king, the prince, they do whatever they want with people—torture them, send them into a war they don't understand, sacrifice them as raek bait! For what? They say it's for the good of the land, but what good has come from any of it? Why do they get to decide for everyone? It isn't right!"

"Meera, stop!" he shouted back. "That's treason! You can't say those things!"

"Exactly," she said, lowing her voice. "I can't question the Crown because the Crown is always right—anyone against them is wrong, evil. But what about what's *actually* right and wrong, good and evil? Torture is wrong, so how can the Crown always be right?" Shaking her head despite its throbbing, she added, "You just don't get it ... You're like a child playing with stick soldiers—happy to knock down the other sticks because they're the *bad guys*, without recognizing that you're killing people, and you don't even know why."

She stood her ground, breathing heavily and peering into Linus's face, begging him to understand. She wanted him to hear what she was saying—to be as confused as she was about how to live at the palace and obey the king while still following her own conscience. But all Linus heard was *you're like a child*. With glistening eyes and a flushed face, he threw down the cart handle, turned, and started running back up the hill.

So much for wanting to stay with her and protect her, Meera thought bitterly, and she snatched the cart handle from the ground and kept walking. Maybe she shouldn't have shouted. Does anyone ever agree with a person who's shouting at them? But she couldn't understand Linus's defense of the guards, and his blind obedience to the Crown ... She knew he wanted Sam's death to have meaning, but that shouldn't make him oblivious to everything around him!

After all, was it the raek's fault for killing his brother when he was approached by an unknown soldier, or was it the king's fault for putting them both in that position to begin with? It was the king's fault! For that and for allowing his son to hurt people without consequences, she decided—for making her walk around the palace alone and vulnerable as his *weapon* ... Or was it her own fault for coming to the palace, for volunteering, and for putting herself in that position? She wasn't sure.

Meera approached Cerun with his food, and if he was surprised by her appearance, he didn't show it. "Your rider is awake," she said tersely. "He was not very pleased about the feather."

Cerun blinked.

Meera studied him. She didn't know what surprise or relief might look like in a raek, but she had been able to tell when he was upset and worried, and right now, his behavior was bafflingly neutral. "Did you know he was awake?" she asked, not sure how he could conceivably know that but suspicious, nonetheless.

He blinked.

"How?" she asked disbelievingly before recalling that he couldn't answer her. "Did someone else tell you?" It had never occurred to her that someone else could be communing with Cerun, but she supposed it was possible.

No blink.

Then she wondered how raeken and their riders communicated at all. Could it be some form of magic? "Can you talk to him from here?" she asked, feeling mildly foolish for even considering such a thing.

He blinked.

Meera was astounded. "This whole time?"

Blink.

Meera's astonishment quickly shifted to annoyance as she considered all of the implications of Cerun's mental connection with the prisoner. The man should have known she was a friend —or at least not an enemy. "Right now?" she asked.

Blink.

"You tell him that I'm going down there next, and I expect full cooperation from him when I clean his wounds!" she shouted. Then she wondered how exactly it worked and asked, "Could he see me this whole time—like through your eyes?"

Blink.

Blood pooled in her face as she tried to go over her interactions with the raek in her mind for anything she wouldn't want the prisoner to have seen or heard. She felt like her privacy had been violated—like Cerun had betrayed her. She supposed he had never lied to her exactly, but to have been watched this entire time by a man she didn't know was disturbing—embarrassing too. She had spoken to Cerun and confided in him like a friend. Could that be why the prisoner was angry with her? Did he not like her befriending his raek—like some sort of possessive quality? That would be ridiculous; if he cared for his raek, surely he should be glad someone was feeding him and seeing to his wounds.

Meera didn't say or ask anything else, and she went about her task with as much reserve as possible. After feeding Cerun, she took the cart and turned to go with a sigh. It would likely be a long day, and she was already tired, her headache growing worse.

Despite the early hour, the sun was quickly heating the air and leaching her energy, and she dreaded the walk up the hill. She wished she could return to bed, sick, but a man in much worse shape was depending on her. She wouldn't leave him without food even if she wasn't pleased with him at the moment. But as Meera looked up the sloping expanse of grass that would surely feel more arduous that day than usual, she saw a figure striding down toward her.

It was a man. She froze. Could it be Linus? She couldn't tell yet. As the man grew closer, she didn't think that it was. The prince? Her heart fidgeted in anticipation. She wouldn't leave Cerun's beach until she knew who it was—and maybe not after. Finally, the man grew near enough for Meera to see that it wasn't the prince; there was no threatening gleam of golden hair. She relaxed somewhat but continued to wait, and when he approached the beach, she recognized the fussy servant to the king—Dodgers was it? He was breathing heavily from his walk and looked extremely nervous, remaining more than twenty feet away from where Cerun could reach him. Reluctantly, Meera dragged her cart over to meet him.

If Dodgers was alarmed by the bruising on her face in any way, he didn't show it. In fact, he didn't offer her any greeting whatsoever. He simply said, "The king requests your presence."

This again, thought Meera. She was in no mood to see the king. She also felt anxious to check on the prisoner's wounds and bring him food—he could have opened the injuries from moving, and it had been a long time since he had really eaten anything. After her previous rushed arrival to the king's study soaking wet, she decided she could take a little more time responding to this summons. "I will report to him after my other duties," she responded.

Dodgers looked flabbergasted and squeaked, "You—the king!

Come, come! The king requests your presence!" Then, trying to cover how flustered he was, he fluffed his ruffled collar, cleared his throat, and amended, "Miss Hailship, we do not keep the king waiting," in a more dignified voice.

Meera suddenly noticed the man's hands and realized that the paste covering the pockmarks on his face was several shades lighter than his rich brown skin. Her tired mind wandered as she wondered whether adding cocoa powder to the paste might help. But then she thought it would stain his frilly white collar ... Rubbing her eyes, she dragged her mind back to the present, thinking she really wasn't in any state to meet with King Bartro. "The king has made me responsible for the prisoner in the dungeon," she said evenly, "And as I am responsible for him, I must see to his care before I can engage in anything else." And with that, she began to walk past the sweaty man.

"*Anything else?*" he spluttered. "We're talking about *the king!* The *king!* I was sent to get you. What am I supposed to tell him?" He scrambled after her, the heels on his shoes sinking into the soft spring ground.

Meera continued onward, her own trusty leather boots finding easy purchase on the dirt path. "Tell him I will report to him after I have seen to my other duties," she replied over her shoulder, and she quickly outpaced the man on the ascent, leaving him far enough behind that she could no longer hear his huffing. She knew she should feel nervous about seeing the king and about delaying their meeting, but her rage at the world was supplanting all of her lesser emotions.

However, as she gathered food in the kitchen for the prisoner, Meera's rage was overtaken by fear—fear of the prince. What if he was waiting for her in the dungeon again? Should she bring a weapon? She considered slipping a kitchen knife into her bag, but again, didn't see how gravely injuring or killing the prince would make her safer overall; she would be hanged for it. Instead, she merely exchanged a resigned look with Cook and departed.

Her stomach churned as she walked down the hall to the dungeon door, and she gripped her basket tightly. As she passed the three guards stationed in the hall, she averted her eyes from them; the guard's presence used to give her comfort, but that comfort was gone—replaced by anger, confusion, and fear. The three uniformed men may as well have been making obscene gestures at her for all the reassurance they provided. And while they weren't, Meera still had to resist the urge to make obscene gestures back.

But when she reached the dungeon door, all thoughts fled her mind, and she froze. With her bag slung over one shoulder and her food basket in her left hand since her right couldn't support a tray, she stood and swayed. Staring at the plain wooden door, she tried to tell herself to move—to open it—but she didn't. Still and silent, she just stared and stared and started to breathe faster and faster. She couldn't seem to get enough air.

Meera had enough control of herself not to dump her possessions and run away but not enough to actually reach for the door handle. She was stuck—frozen like she had been with the prince. Helpless. Useless. She was so focused on the door and her panic, she didn't see anyone approach. Then, suddenly, a man—one of the guards—was standing next to her, putting a gentle hand on her arm. She jumped violently but managed not to drop her basket, and her eyes tore free from the door and latched on to the man instead.

It was an older guard with grey, grizzled hair and freckles on the bronze skin under his kindly eyes. She recognized him and didn't think he had been one of the guards stationed in the hallway the day before. He patted her arm reassuringly and leaned in to say, "Miss, I've been here since dawn, and not a soul has gone down there today." Then he smiled and pulled the door open for her, giving her a light push on her upper back.

The guard's words registered with Meera slowly. She was still gulping down air—her chest moving double-time while the rest of her was still—but she allowed him to guide her onto the stairs, taking one shaky step then another. When she stood squarely on the top step, she turned and peered into the man's face. He smiled and nodded as he slowly closed the door behind her, cutting her off from sunlight and fresh air. Meera told herself the old man wouldn't go out of his way to lie to her—would he? Then, with a deep breath of cold and damp, she descended the familiarly steep staircase.

14

____

When Meera approached cell 39, her boots crunched on the glass from the water bottle that had broken the night before. She had forgotten about the glass and would have to clean it up, but in that moment, she merely studied the prisoner behind the bars. He was lying on his stomach under his blankets, watching her. Even under his layers of warmth, he appeared tensely rigid—ready.

Slowly, Meera entered the cell, doing her best to jar the bars as little as possible. Her head ached less in the cold of the dungeon, but every little noise still throbbed in her skull. Taking inventory, she saw that both the broth and water bottles she had left behind were empty, and there was urine in the crock she had left by the mat, which she quickly emptied into the hole in the corner.

The man didn't acknowledge her or move. He simply watched her. He'd been watching her for quite some time through Cerun, she thought with irritation and embarrassment. She couldn't help but wonder what this handsome, foreign raek rider might think of her—a helpless, pathetic servant. Setting down her bag and basket, she pulled out bread and stew from within as well as more broth and water. The man's gaze shifted to the food and his throat contracted in an involuntary swallow. Meera also had sugary jam cookies for him but didn't pull them out yet, saving them as a treat for good behavior.

"You can have a small piece of bread and some liquids, for now," she said. "Then I'm going to start on your bandages. I'll keep giving you food, but it's important you eat slowly, so you don't get sick." Cook had told her so.

She held out a hunk of bread, and the man extricated his pale arm from his blankets to snatch it from her, cramming it into his mouth while still on his stomach. He would definitely make himself sick if she let him, she thought. After watching him chew and swallow, she handed him water, and he pushed up onto his forearms to drink. He drank so deeply, she grabbed the bottle and wrestled it away from him, lest he overdo it. Despite his general weakness, he was still very strong, and she swallowed nervously, thinking he could probably overpower her if he wanted to. She hoped he wouldn't want to—it was all she could really do. She was powerless.

After a moment of hesitation, she decided to proceed as usual. "I'm going to check and rebandage your wounds," she announced, unceremoniously pulling the blankets off the man's back. He flinched but didn't otherwise move. Meera would have gone slower with him—been gentler—had she not just learned that he'd been observing her through Cerun's eyes. As far as she was concerned, he should know that she wouldn't hurt him.

Moving from his back to his feet, she checked his injuries, adding honey to the ones that still looked raw and rewrapping them. It would still likely be a couple of weeks before she could remove the stitches from the whip lashes in his butt and thighs, and while most of his wounds were scabbing and healing over nicely, the burns in his feet still looked raw. Meera was used to handling the man's body and did so with practiced ease, but he flinched and squirmed now and then at her touch.

"You have stitches in some of the whip lashes that will need to come out eventually, and your feet are still very raw, but otherwise you're healing well," she told him. "I need you to roll over. Can you do it yourself, or should I do it for you?" She was using a brisk but not unkind tone. It was the first question she'd asked him since entering the cell, and she hadn't expected an answer—she'd thought he would just roll himself over. He didn't move.

The man was very thin, and Meera hadn't had any difficulty rolling him over since the first time. It would be tricky to roll him without the use of her right wrist, but she thought she could probably use her forearm wedged under his hip bone. Crouching beside him, she put her left hand under his shoulder, but he immediately shoved her roughly in the chest, knocking her onto her butt. She felt mild anger at the injustice, but it was nothing compared to the anger she saw on the man's face. Sitting on the floor, heart racing, she tried to look non-threatening. And as she gazed into the man's eyes, her irritation with him was quickly replaced by sympathy.

He had been through a lot. Meera wondered how he'd even done it—endured so much torture and not uttered a single word. She didn't think she could do that. Maybe he wasn't in his body at the time, she thought; maybe he had taken refuge in Cerun's mind. Could that be possible? She didn't bother asking—he wouldn't answer. Attempting a gentler tone, she tried again: "I want you to roll over, so I can check on your cuts. They were healing well before, but I want to be sure none of them have opened from you moving around. I've seen ... your front before—I know what your wounds say, I mean, and I can cover your nakedness if it makes you more comfortable."

The man continued to glare at her, so she thought she must be missing the point in some way. "If you have something to say, I wish you would say it! Otherwise, I don't know what you're glaring about," she snapped. Then she took a deep breath and let it out, continuing in a softer voice: "I'm very sorry for what's been done to you. I don't know anything about you, but I don't believe people should be tortured and left in cells. The king has asked me to care for you—he's hoping my genteel, feminine ways will elicit information from you—but I'm expecting no such thing. I promised Cerun that I would help you recover." She didn't bother concealing her bitterness toward the king.

The man appeared slightly less angry but still very suspicious, his dark brows drawing together and staying that way. "Please roll over," Meera added. He didn't move. She gave up—the man's front wasn't as injured anyway, so he was probably fine. Rolling her eyes at him, she handed him another hunk of bread. He ate it quickly, and she put the tureen of stew in front of him. He propped himself on his forearms to eat but soon tired and began shaking.

Meera took the tureen away, and over the next hour or so, she gave him small amounts of food and liquid until only the broth and cookies remained. The man's eyelids drooped once he was full of food, and while he fought to remain conscious and alert, he fell asleep in the short time it took her to pick up the empty tureen and bottle.

Meera left the cookies by his head, wrapped in cloth, hoping the rats wouldn't get to them before he could, and she left the broth where he could easily reach it. Then she exited the cell and picked up the bits of glass on the floor, trying not to relive the prince's assault over and over again in her mind. She didn't have time to cry and fall apart or time to rest her aching head—she had to meet the king.

———

MEERA RETURNED her basket to the kitchen and ate some jam cookies herself, hoping the sugar would help her get through her long day. She was so tired, and her headache grew worse by the hour, feeding off of her anger and exhaustion and threatening to incapacitate her. After washing down her cookies, she tidied the pile of curls on the top of her head—though no one would be looking at her hair when her face was such a mess—and she left for the king's study.

When she approached King Bartro's study, Meera tersely gave her name to the guards stationed outside, unable to meet their eyes. One went in and returned a moment later to admit her. The king was at his desk, and Meera was beginning to realize that he must spend a lot of his time there—going over documents sent to him from all across Terratelle. She wondered how he didn't bend under the weight of his hefty responsibility. She, herself, felt burdened being responsible for two creatures other than herself, and the king oversaw every living creature in the land. Curtsying low, she didn't manage a smile for her king.

"Miss Hailship, I do believe I requested your presence earlier in the day," he said without looking up from his desk. She didn't respond. When King Bartro did eventually glance up, his gaze alit on her bruises, but he didn't mention them and continued to rebuke her: "Being a king, you *could* say I am accustomed to my requests being followed." His tone and flickering eyes were unreadable.

"My apologies, Your Majesty. I needed to attend to the prisoner first," Meera replied evenly.

The king sat back in his chair. "In that case, I hope you have something useful to report," he said.

She should have seen that coming. Of course, King Bartro had summoned her for information about the prisoner, having heard that the man was awake. But she didn't have information for him, and she feared what the king might do if she disappointed him again—especially since she still hadn't learned anything about the duke, either. She was shaping up to be both an incompetent spy and an ineffectual interrogator. "Your Majesty, the prisoner has not spoken a single word. He is awake, and his wounds are healing, but he is unresponsive," she said, holding her spine straight and her chin up.

"Unresponsive or just not talking?" the king asked pointedly. "The marks on your face tell a story and not one that bodes well for your future prospects retrieving information from the man. Aggression toward you was not the response I was hoping for, and if you will not have success with the prisoner, I will be forced to assign the task to someone else. Time is of the essence, Miss Hail-ship. Anything that man could tell us grows staler the longer he resides in the dungeon. The enemy knows we have him, after all." He seemed to believe the rumors that were circulating about the prisoner attacking her.

Meera hadn't realized her position caring for the man was dependent on the possibility of her extracting information from him, but she probably should have. Part of her would be relieved to have the task reassigned to another, but she feared the prisoner would be subjected to more torture and cruelty. She wasn't espe-cially fond of the man, but she wouldn't abandon him.

"Forgive me, Your Majesty, but you are mistaken," she replied. "The prisoner hasn't responded to me with aggression." This wasn't strictly true, but he hadn't been the one to brutally attack her. She left it there. King Bartro would have to ask, she decided, if he wanted more information than that. He liked to play with silence, but she could play too.

The king studied her, looking unconvinced. He leaned forward in his seat, and Meera caught a whiff of his cedarwood scent. His intense stare bored into her, but she held her ground and her tongue. After some time, he relaxed his posture and smiled, igniting the twinkle in his blue-green eyes that stood out so starkly against his bronze skin. "You do amuse me, Miss Hailship. I'll bite. I'm told you entered the dungeon unharmed and exited it with injuries to your face and wrist. If the prisoner did not respond to you with aggression, how, may I ask, did you manage to hurt yourself in the dungeon? A fall down the stairs?" he asked, quirking a brow.

"Prince Phineas attacked me, Your Majesty," Meera replied. She didn't know how the king would respond to this revelation, but she took some satisfaction in telling him something he didn't already know.

King Bartro sighed and rubbed his short beard, displaying in small behaviors that he did, in fact, feel at least some burden from his responsibilities. "Miss Hailship, I apologize. I do struggle to keep my second born well in hand. I assure you, however, that this will not happen again," he said. Meera almost rolled her eyes, not believing the king had much control over the prince. "You will be compensated for the incident, as you were doing your duty to me when harm befell you. I will also give you more time to induce the prisoner to speak."

Compensated—as in more money. The king had given her more money for each new duty he had assigned her, but Meera hadn't come to the palace for money and certainly didn't think it was an appropriate *compensation* for her attack. However, if the king wanted to offer her something in reparation ... Was there something else she wanted? What she wanted was to go back in time and never volunteer and complicate her life to begin with, but now that she had, she cared too much for Cerun and the man in the dungeon to forsake them. She remembered her previous request to the king.

"Your Majesty, I appreciate your apology, but I'm not in need of more money," she began. "It would, however, please me immensely to see the raek's muzzle removed for his comfort and health." The last time she had mentioned the subject, the king had rebuked her and warned her that she was *playing with fire*. Meera decided right then that if she was to play with fire, she might as well play with raek fire. The thought made her smile, and smiling—even for a moment—tempered some of the boiling rage in her gut.

The king considered her. He didn't look angry; rather, he appeared contemplative—tenting his fingers and pursing his lips. Then he rose from his desk, strode around it, and stood very close to her. Meera turned to see his face, and her heart fluttered from his proximity—not from lust as it had before but from fear. Having experienced the strong hands of a man grabbing her— hitting her—she could easily imagine the king overpowering her. She had never known how truly weak she was before the prince had attacked her, and that knowledge did nothing to bolster what little strength she did have.

She didn't think the king would attack her, but she did think he might reach out and touch her. He didn't. The lights that usually danced in his eyes were unusually still, and in a serious but even tone, he said, "I'd like this relationship to be beneficial for both of us, Miss Hailship. If you find success in one of the assignments I have given you, I will remove the beast's muzzle. Know, however, that I grow impatient and am beginning to doubt that women can have many uses outside the bedroom."

"I understand, Your Majesty," she said, swallowing. While his parting words were threatening, they were at least not as cryptic as usual, and the threat of being tossed aside as a spy and interrogator only gave Meera concern for the raek and his rider, not herself—she would gladly slip back into obscurity. But for now, she would have to either get the prisoner to speak to her or learn something significant about the duke to earn Cerun's freedom from his muzzle.

LATER THAT EVENING, Meera decided to try her luck with the prisoner, doubtful as she was that he would speak to her. She brought him a basket of food and watched him eat. She didn't check his wounds, but she did briefly lay a hand on his head to check for fever. He scowled at her in response, and she decided to start small with her questioning. "How are you feeling?" she asked. "I can probably get you herbs if the pain is bad."

The man had been chewing on a sandwich with one arm propping up his head and the other holding the food, but at her words, he stopped chewing and looked at the food as if remembering to be suspicious of poison. She rolled her eyes at him. "There's nothing in the food," she said. "I'm not going to poison you. I made a bargain with Cerun—your raek—to feed him, care for him, and never lie to him, so long as he refrained from hurting me. That bargain applies to you as well unless you break it, so don't push me down again or anything."

The man looked at her for a second then continued eating. Meera wasn't sure if he was exhibiting trust in her or had just endured so much already that going without food was beyond him. Then, since starting small hadn't gotten her anywhere, she plunged in: "Listen, I've already told you the king wants me to coax you into speaking. That's still true, but what I said earlier about not caring whether or not you say anything isn't true anymore."

The man was expressionless but paying attention, so she continued: "King Bartro told me—and in case you're wondering, I believe him—that if I can get you to talk, he will remove the horrible iron muzzle from your raek's head. I assume because of whatever special magic you use with him, that you're aware of the muzzle."

The man's eyes twitched—like he almost blinked in response as Cerun would. Meera thought it was interesting and wondered if sharing minds for so long had instilled the blink as a habit. She hoped it would happen again—she might be able to learn something from it. Leaning toward him from her spot on the floor, she said, "I know you love your raek as he loves you. Isn't there anything you could tell me that would give the king some small piece of information without betraying your people? Your name? Where you're from?"

She looked expectantly at the man. He didn't speak—he didn't blink or twitch—but Meera did think she saw some emotion in his eyes and wondered whether she could wear him down. Then she said something that surprised herself: "If they remove Cerun's muzzle, I might be able to help him get free." The man's gaze sharpened on her, and she glanced down and away. She couldn't look him in the eye because it wasn't a promise. It was a possibility, but one she had never imagined she'd speak aloud, let alone follow through with.

Sighing, she laid the rest of his food in front of him and picked up her basket and bag to go. The heavy book inside bumped her hip, reminding her it was there, and she thought the man should have something to do with his time. Pulling the book out, she placed it somewhat reluctantly on the damp floor and said, "I've read this one before, so why don't you give it a go? It's an adventure tale. It might help you escape this cell for a while. You can read, can't you?" She didn't know why she had assumed it, but something about the young man struck her as intelligent. Not that he couldn't be intelligent and never have had the opportunity to learn to read, she chastised herself. The man blinked in reply, and Meera smiled. It wasn't much, but it was progress.

15

———————

Over the next week, Meera redoubled her efforts to follow Duke Harrington. After she fed Cerun once and the prisoner twice, she sought out the duke and observed him until late into the night, hoping to catch him leaving the palace. Despite her diligence, however—and the increasingly late hours she was keeping—she hadn't seen the duke do anything unusual or speak to anyone particularly interesting.

She could almost always find him in the great hall or on the patio having dinner with his wife after her other duties, and once they had dinner, they often partook in the festivities happening all week leading up to the Summer Solstice: watching performances and playing games with the other nobles. Then they would retire to their chamber. Meera knew where their chamber was and had waited in the hall late every night, hoping the duke would reemerge, but so far, he hadn't. She had seen a woman with short, bushy hair enter the chamber on occasion, but presumed her to be Duchess Kenna's lady's maid. In short, Meera was running herself ragged and still hadn't learned anything from her efforts.

On the morning of the Summer Solstice, she had to drag herself out of bed—exhausted from staying up every night and having so much to do every day. She donned her lilac dress to celebrate the summer holiday since it was her brightest and finest summer gown. However, when she glanced in the mirror, she found that while her bruises were dissipating, she still looked as tired and haggard as she felt—the purple circles under her eyes matching her purple dress. She also lived with a constant dull headache from lack of sleep and heaved a sigh at the sight of her messy, knotted hair. It had been a while since she'd found time to wash it, and it was getting greasy at the roots.

She gently coaxed some of the knots from her hair with a wide-tooth comb. Then she spread water and a drop of lavender oil over her hands before smoothing her hair up toward the crown of her head, twisting the curls into a loose bun, and pinning it in place. Her right wrist was still very tender, but she could use it when she had to. Once she was dressed and ready, she wiped her oily hands on her pillowcase—liking the smell of lavender when she slept—and she had to resist the urge to lay her head back on her soft pillow and shut her eyes. It would be a long day ... the longest day of the year.

Despite her exhaustion, Meera forced herself out of her room to get started with her tasks and to allow Teardra space to get up and ready herself for the day. In the hallway, she could sense more energy than usual—everyone was excited about the holiday even if they were the ones who would be doing the serving instead of the celebrating. She had to squeeze past two laundresses in the hall exchanging small gifts, and when she reached the kitchen, she was met with more noise and bustle than usual.

That day, tables would be set up throughout the gardens with food, and entertainers would be positioned throughout. Rather than sitting to dine, the royals and nobles would meander around, eating and drinking and enjoying puppet shows and minstrels. The palace festivities came after the parade that would wind through Altus, distributing candies and trinkets for the townspeople courtesy of the king. Meera had fond memories of sitting on her father's shoulders as a girl and reaching for the candy being tossed from ornately decorated carriages by the royal family. They had never stayed long, however, since the crowds made her father uncomfortable. Meera imagined the Center Square in Altus likely dissolved into eating, drinking, and dancing afterward, but she had never seen it.

Having been so busy lately, she hadn't found the time to go into town and buy gifts, and she felt terrible. She had really wanted to show Cook her gratitude and appreciation with something nice and had likewise wanted to find something for Linus, despite the awkwardness between them. Instead, she'd been forced to rummage through what few possessions she had at the palace for their gifts. For Cook, she had chosen a small pillow on which her mother had embroidered some herb leaves. She thought it was fitting and didn't have many things of her mother's, so she hoped Cook would appreciate how meaningful it was for her to give it up.

When she managed to corner Cook amidst the excitement in the kitchen and give them the pillow, she said, "My mother made this. You have cared for me like family, and I'm so grateful." Cook thanked her, gave her a big hug, and briskly sent her on her way with an armful of sugary goodies, but Meera thought she had seen a glisten in their eyes.

Outside, she gave Linus one of her books—a warrior's account of an ancient war. He looked intimidated by it. Meera secretly hoped he would read it and reconsider his choice of career. She also shared her sweets from Cook, and Linus gave her a bracelet made of small purple glass beads on a leather strap. She beamed at him, thanked him, and said it matched her dress, thinking that it also matched the half-moons under her eyes. Meera had Linus tie the bracelet onto her left wrist, and he fumbled and averted his eyes as he did so. They were both doing their best to move past their arguments, but it wasn't easy. Their conversation was halting on their way through the gardens and down the hill.

As they descended the slope, Meera frowned at the site of Cerun chained on his beach. He was looking increasingly dispirited and ragged lately. His rider waking up seemed to have buoyed his spirits for a couple of days, but he had quickly regressed— eating little and looking hopeless. More of his feathers had been falling out, and he was getting very thin. Meera had tried bringing him special food from the kitchen all week to enliven him, but while he had sometimes eaten her offerings—she had been surprised to learn how much he liked fruits and sweets—they hadn't improved his emotional state or appearance.

That day, she gave him some of her sweets from Cook and scratched around his neck under the chains of his muzzle. Becoming increasingly desperate and determined to rid the raek of his iron monstrosity, she hoped the duke would do something noteworthy that night. After all, if he was in Altus to speak with someone or go somewhere and didn't want anyone to know, the Summer Solstice would be the easiest time for him to do it. The palace would be abuzz with people, and everyone would be drinking and celebrating. No one would notice the duke doing anything unusual—no one but her, that is.

And with that reassuring thought, Meera found the boost of energy she needed to make it through another long day. She fed Cerun, retrieved the prisoner's food, and entered the dungeon. The cold air was a relief from the thick summer heat above ground, but when she approached cell 39, she found the prisoner in much the same state as his raek: thin, haggard, and unresponsive. He had been eating everything she brought him and allowing her to check his wounds once a day, but he still hadn't spoken a word to her—he hadn't responded verbally or nonverbally to any of her questions and had stopped looking her in the eye as well.

On the bright side, the man's wounds were healing a lot faster since he'd woken up and started eating. Meera had removed his stitches the day before. He was likely still in pain, but he was able to rise and move. His feet and butt were still worse than the rest of him, however, so while he managed to hobble around standing, he didn't do so often, and he never sat on his backside. Still, he was at least able to keep himself clean and dressed, and he looked less sickly thin than previously.

Meera didn't question him that day or make any attempts to persuade him to communicate with her. All of her hope for Cerun now resided in her spying on the duke, and all of her hope with the duke resided in that night's Summer Solstice celebration. Realizing it might be more difficult to locate him than usual, she decided to get started right after leaving the dungeon. The prisoner would have to make do with the food she had brought him for the rest of the day. It wouldn't be any great hardship—she had brought an abundance of feast foods including the rest of her sweets from Cook, which he had already dug into.

"I won't be back today," she told him. "You should have plenty of food, water, and lamp oil to get through until tomorrow." Her words seemed to catch the man's attention in a way she hadn't been able to all week. He looked directly at her, appearing suspicious as always and possibly confused. Meera had already told him it was the Summer Solstice and thought that should be explanation enough as to her impending absence. "Do you need anything else?" she asked, not wanting to leave him feeling confused or uncertain. He faced enough hardship in the dark, dank nightmare of a place.

The man reached for the book on the floor—*her* book—which as far as she knew had never left the stone floor next to his mat. Picking it up, he extended it to her. This was a level of interaction they hadn't had before. Usually, she told the man what to do, and he reluctantly did it, avoiding any unnecessary movements. Meera took the book and looked at it. Was he tired of having it in his cell? Gazing into his grey eyes—studying them—she saw ... something, but she wasn't sure what. She had asked him if he needed anything, and this had been his response. Could it be longing in his eyes? She had assumed he hadn't touched the book since she hadn't seen it move, but ... could he have read it and wanted another?

Meera reached into her bag. While she hadn't had the time to read lately, she was still in the habit of carrying a book around with her. The one she had now was a collection of short stories. She strongly suspected were written by a woman, though the author's name was male. Rather than put the book on the floor like the last time, she held it out to the prisoner in question, and to her amazement, he took it and gave her what could almost, maybe—in some parallel world full of sad people—be called a smile. She decided to take it as a good omen, and she left to find the duke.

AFTER TWO HOURS of scouring the gardens, the great hall, and the halls near their chamber, Meera had not sighted Duke or Duchess Harrington. Her shoulders sagged. After the solstice, the nobles would all start packing up and returning to their homes, and she was sure the duke and duchess would return to Harringbay where the sea breeze would make the heat of summer more tolerable, and their strong-willed daughter awaited them.

She could feel her chance to help Cerun slipping through her fingers.

Returning to the kitchen to eat something, it was then she saw Duchess Harrington's lady's maid in a corner with one of the palace guards. Meera had seen the woman exiting the Harrington's chamber before and recognized her short, bushy hair. The woman huddled close to the palace guard, betraying their intimacy, and Meera watched the two closely. She noticed they were covertly holding hands under the table, and the lady's maid had tears streaming down her face.

Taking her food, she sat as close to the pair as she could without alarming them and halting their conversation. She could just barely hear the maid speaking over the din of the kitchen—her words were somewhat choked and unintelligible from her emotion: "… not fair! I should have had more notice. Tomorrow is just too soon to leave you, Ben." She broke off in a bout of sniffing, and the man—Ben—said something commiserative and reassuring before a chorus of laughter from a nearby table drowned out their words.

Meera's suspicions were confirmed; the Harrington's would be leaving imminently. The thought of no longer skulking around watching the duke and duchess come morning was like an iron weight being removed from her head, but her instantaneous relief was followed by a heavy gust of shame. She wanted to help Cerun! She wanted to be strong enough—determined enough—to help Cerun and do the *right* thing … Wolfing down the remainder of her food, she set out with renewed energy.

The gardens were a heaving maze of separate feasts and entertainments, intertwined by colorfully dressed people coursing through them. There was so much noise and movement that, after stumbling through the crowds for several hours catching odd glimpses of performances and snippets of conversations, Meera began to feel disoriented and dizzy. After passing the same minstrel singing cheerfully for the fifth time, she collapsed on an empty bench and let the solid wood under her body settle the feeling she had of being tossed about in rough water. Taking several deep breaths to steady herself, she thought that she shared her father's dislike of crowds after all. An hour in a crowd was tolerable, but any more was overwhelming.

It was then, when she had finally paused in her efforts, that she first saw the delicate Duchess Harrington. The lady was standing in a cluster of women listening to the minstrel sing, sipping wine with one hand and fanning herself methodically with the other. The women around her were laughing at the humorous bits of the song and tapping their feet to the rhythm, but Kenna Harrington looked subdued—her slight body a still, leafless tree amongst a swaying copse of greenery.

Meera sighed in relief to have finally discovered at least one of the Harringtons, but she was weary and felt extremely reluctant to leave her bench. Wiping sweat from her forehead with the back of her hand, she thought dolefully that she would definitely need to wash her hair after that day. She remained where she was until the duchess and her group moved on, then she planted her feet and heaved herself off the bench. Slinging her bag over her shoulder, she followed the women fairly closely; it was crowded enough for her not to be noticed, and she wasn't willing to lose them.

Duchess Harrington reunited with the duke shortly thereafter. He was smiling and laughing freely, as usual, and taking what looked like generous swigs of wine. The sun was almost completely down, but servants had lit torches all along the garden paths, and lanterns hung from many of the tree branches. The many small flames danced and curtsied, each putting on its own performance for the onlookers. Meera longed to be lulled into passivity by the lights' elegant pirouetting and to forgo the constant action that had been required of her that week, but she needed to keep moving—keep acting. She needed to figure out what the duke was up to for Cerun's sake.

Ned Harrington and his wife left the festivities once it was dark, though most people were still celebrating. Rather than follow the pair through the palace and risk detection, Meera decided to take a different route to their chamber, and she walked briskly down hallways and up staircases, hoping to hide in their corridor before they arrived. By the time she reached the Harringtons' door, she was panting and sweating even more profusely, and she sidled further down the hall and ducked behind a cabinet in an unlit nook. She had moved the small cabinet there previously and had broken two of the nearest lamps. Drinking from the bottle of water she carried, she waited only a minute before the Harringtons appeared.

Both the duke and duchess entered the chamber, and Meera figured she would be spending another long, miserable night on the floor. She knew it would be a struggle not to fall asleep, but even so, she shut her eyes and rested her head against the side of the cabinet, listening for doors or movements. The minutes ticked by, and she was imagining taking a long, warm bath and scrubbing the unending week out of her hair when she started to drift into sleep. Startled by the click of a door and the shuffle of footsteps, her eyes flew wide, and she wiped drool from the side of her open mouth. Peeking around the cabinet, she expecting to see another of the hall's residents returning from the revelry in the garden, but instead, she saw the duke's familiar frame disappearing down one of the staircases. Her stomach lurched.

Pushing unsteadily to her feet, she took off behind him, torn between staying quiet and catching up to where she could keep him in view. She could normally guess where the duke was going from his routine, but this was new territory—if she missed a turn, she would lose him. Two landings later, she caught up to him and followed him down one of the larger halls to the palace's main entrance into the courtyard. Duke Harrington was moving at a quick pace but one that was easy and natural for him; he didn't look nervous or suspicious, she thought. Meera had to rush to keep up with him and remained in plain view if he were to turn around, but he didn't turn around or so much as swivel his head from side to side.

With a confident pace and steady gaze, the duke exited the palace, crossed the courtyard, and left through the front gate. Meera followed. The guards at the gate didn't question them; they didn't care who left the palace grounds nearly as much as who entered. If anything, the guards looked sulky at being unable to celebrate the solstice themselves. Meera passed them without stopping and continued to follow the duke down the palace road that led into the city. It was a familiar route, and there were others walking to and from celebrations, so despite the darkness, she felt reasonably safe and comfortable. Then they reached the crowded city square, and Meera scurried to tail the duke even more closely, afraid of losing him in the throng.

Altus's center was raucous and lively with merrymakers. However, it was not so late that the partying had turned rowdy and sour, yet—there were still many women and children around, and everyone looked jovial. Neighbors shared food with one another, and musicians played somewhere Meera couldn't see. Skirting around people, she continued to follow the duke closely. Meanwhile, the air cooled as night took over from day, running fingers along her sweaty neck as if curious as to why she was out of bed. Meera's brisk pace kept a chill at bay, and the many lights and revelers around her helped her feel secure—for a time.

When the duke turned down an unlit gap between buildings, a more insidious side of night obscured her vision and rattled her heart in her chest. It took her eyes a moment to adjust to the denser darkness, so she hung back from the duke, waiting to be able to see where they were going. Once her eyes adapted, she found she was in an alley between two rows of buildings. It wasn't wide enough to be a road, but there looked to be some business up ahead—at least, several lanterns swung over signs.

Meera wasn't a savvy city-goer, but she could deduce that any form of business being conducted—quite literally—off the beaten path must be suspect in some way. She suspected the businesses might be brothels, and her heart sank—no longer sure the duke was doing anything the king would be interested in. She could still see Duke Harrington walking ahead, but he was moving slower now, his head swiveling. He was clearly seeking out a particular establishment—one he likely hadn't visited before, she realized. But which one and for what purpose?

She followed the duke down the alley and began to regret the cheery choice of lilac dress she had chosen for the Solstice. The light fabric practically glowed in the dimness, calling out to anyone looking that she didn't belong there—that she was a young, innocent woman in purple, alone in the dark. She fiddled with the wrapping on her right wrist, her injury making her feel even more vulnerable. Then she put her left hand into her bag and gripped the glass bottle within; it had saved her once.

The duke paused in front of a building, turned, and lifted his face as if to double-check the sign. He had found what he was looking for, but what was it? Meera could vaguely make out Duke Harrington's expression in the lantern light and didn't think he resembled a man out looking for a good time. His usual easy smile was gone, replaced by lowered brows and a slight frown, and he clutched his hands in fists at his sides. Was he angry? Anxious? Squaring his shoulders, he entered the building.

16

———

Meera stopped in her tracks to think. She was in a dark alley—alone—the duke had likely just entered a disreputable establishment of some sort, and she was very conspicuous in her lilac dress. She felt vulnerable, but she couldn't turn back now. She needed to know what kind of business Duke Harrington was visiting—maybe even follow him inside. He had entered a door on the right side of the alley, so she sidled up to the sign along the right wall, hoping she wouldn't be visible if the building had a front window.

Just a few feet away from the door, she peered up at the sign to make it out. Laughter sounded down the alley, and she jumped and rammed her elbow back into the wooden building. Looking around frantically, she didn't see anyone, but she was so anxious, she felt like her heart was attempting to escape from her body through her throat. Rubbing her offended elbow, she gazed back up at the small dangling sign. Strangely, the sign didn't have any words—only a small, crude painting of ... a fish? She thought it was a fish, at least—she could make out what looked like a tail and a dorsal fin. But what did that mean? There wouldn't be a fish market this far from the river, and a market wouldn't be open this late.

She bit her lip in indecision. What now? Should she wait? If she stayed where she was, the duke would see her when he left. Not to mention, she hadn't learned anything, and this might be his only destination. Meera imagined writing a note to the king saying: "The duke went into an establishment with a fish sign. I don't know what kind of establishment it was or what he did within," and she knew she needed to learn more—to do more if she was to free Cerun of his muzzle. She would have to go in. What was the worst that could happen? The duke seemed like a genuinely kind man with a daughter close to her age. Even if he learned she had followed him, he wouldn't hurt her, would he? She could walk in, say she was lost, and ask for directions. Everyone was out celebrating the Summer Solstice, so it was plausible ...

With a deep breath and a growing uneasiness deep in her bowels, Meera faced the door, turned the knob, and pushed it open. The space within was dimly lit yet bright compared to the alley, and she was smacked in the face by a strong smell of beer. The establishment looked like a tavern but was very small and had only a few patrons at tables—all men and all sitting alone. One man glanced up at her as she entered but quickly looked away. Strange, she thought; she had never seen a tavern so small, and aside from that, it was oddly quiet—the patrons looked miserable; no one spoke to one another, let alone celebrated the Solstice. Each man was fully absorbed in his own cup.

Meera had never seen such still, sad drunks before and furrowed her brows at the scene. The duke, she saw, stood opposite the door at a makeshift bar consisting of a slab of raw wood propped on two large barrels. He was speaking quietly with the man behind the counter—a man with dark brown skin, contrasted by his exceedingly white facial hair. He had a long, unruly beard that dangled down his chest—Meera's father would have called it a *widower's beard* because after her mother had died, he had stopped grooming himself properly for a long time. Her father always insisted that a man without a well-trimmed beard was a man without a woman to impress—a sad man.

From what Meera could see, the duke was doing a lot of talking, and the barman was listening but with reserve—his face expressionless and his arms folded across his chest. She couldn't make out any words, so she moved to the table nearest them and sat down, facing the room with the duke to her right. The strange little tavern was silent except Duke Harrington's low voice, so he wasn't difficult to hear. "... why, then, cut it off the map? My father said you had the same suspicions, so join me! You're a bit long in the tooth, but I won't find a better captain, Mel. Come have one last voyage!" The duke was whispering but with passion, his arms gesticulating his words in foil to the barman's stillness.

The barman—Captain Mel, apparently—braced his hands on the counter and looked down between them for a moment before he answered in a low voice: "I put all that behind me 'n' you know it, lad. It's a mystery to be sure, 'n' one I wouldn't mind knowin' the answer to before I go, but I've got my place here to see to now." He glanced over at Meera, caught her staring at him, and waved. "Be right wit'cha, Miss!"

Meera was startled but managed to nod and avert her gaze. She hadn't even realized she'd been gaping right at them. She gazed down at the floor but could still make the men out at the edge of her vision. The duke hadn't turned to look at her, thankfully; he might recognize her from the palace if he did, considering how often she had loitered near him recently. All of his focus remained on the bearded barman—his body tense like he might leap over the counter, his arms and legs fidgeting at random as he tried and failed to hold in his frustration. "Come on, Mel! I've come all this way to see you, and this place?" he gestured around the quaint tavern, his voice rising in volume and pitch. "*This* is what's keeping you here?"

"Now you hold on there, lad. You think insulting me 'n' my livelihood is any way to convince me?" Mel asked. He sounded stern but like a man used to commanding other men, not like he was truly angry. "Folk need a place they can drink their sorrows and be left to it. A place they won't be questioned or seen by their gossipin' neighbors and the like. I give 'em what they need, 'n' there ain't no shame in that—no shame!" And with that, he made his way over to Meera.

She was nervous, but after what the barman had just said, she hoped he would take her order without too much curiosity about her. "I won't ask what a pretty young thing like you is doing in the likes of this place," he began, "but you best be watchin' yourself on these streets, Missy." Meera nodded dumbly. "Now what can I get'cha?" he asked, and she ordered a beer even though she had never had a beer in her life.

When the barman brought her beer, she thanked him and handed him money. Then she wrapped her small left hand around the enormous mug and struggled to lift it to her mouth. She had to assist her left hand with her right, making her injured wrist twinge in pain, and when she got the mug to her mouth, she took a much larger swig than she'd intended and struggled to swallow it without choking. Barely refraining from grimacing at the taste, Meera swiped the back of one hand across her mouth to wipe away stray foam and disguise her distaste for the beer. Then she smiled at the barman, who gave her a bemused snort and went back behind the counter where the duke was waiting, his head hanging low.

"You're right," the duke said, "and I apologize. I didn't come here to insult you. A man has a right to do whatever he thinks is best ... at least he should. Just consider it. Consider it, and you know where to find me if you change your mind."

The two clasped hands, and the duke left ... just like that. Meera remained at her table and continued to sip her beer, trying to look lost and morose like the other drinkers in the tavern. She didn't want to leave right after the duke, and—she admitted to herself—she was a little afraid to leave at all. She didn't know what time it was exactly, but it was late. After the Summer Solstice celebrations, there would be plenty of drunk men hanging around town, and she dreaded walking back to the palace alone.

For a time, she just sat and considered what she had overheard: Duke Harrington wanted the barman, a former ship's captain of some sort, to take him on a voyage to solve a mystery. She recalled the first thing the duke had said about a place cut off of a map, and she wondered whether he meant literally cut off a specific map or generally left off of all maps ... She tried to think of the maps she'd seen before, but she'd never been especially interested in geography. She was mostly familiar with Terratelle, but if the duke were embarking on a sea voyage, the mystery place must be across the ocean somewhere.

Meera tried to deduce why Duke Harrington would risk a sea voyage to find an unknown place and could only imagine that he sought to profit off of whatever he found somehow. He was certainly trying to hide his plans from the king ... Could this be war-related? Somehow, she didn't think so. If anything, the duke's agitation and desperation had felt personal. Could he be looking for someone? He had mentioned his father having an interest in the aforementioned map as well, so maybe it was a family matter. But why would the king care about the duke's family matter?

Meera's head swam from exhaustion—and possibly from what

little beer she had choked down—so she left off of her contemplations, and after what felt like an acceptable period of time, she rose from her table and went out the door. The darkness groped and menaced her once more, and she clenched her fists at her side and walked briskly away from the little tavern. Her fear—and also her excitement to return to the palace and report what she'd learned—quickly grew and spurred her into a run. She ran back up the alley and through the city square. She wasn't accustomed to running, but her fear made her fast—her boots pounded the uneven cobblestones of the street, and when several revelers shouted after her, she pushed herself even harder and sprinted even faster.

When she reached the long expanse of stone-paved road leading to the palace, she ducked to the side and behind a tree before stumbling to a stop. The woods were dark and foreboding, but Meera would take the threat of animals over the threat of men any day—or night. Her chest squeezed and lungs burned from her exertions. Bracing her hands on her knees, she gasped for breath, hoping it would calm her churning stomach and racing heart. But she was fighting a losing battle and soon retched the beer in her stomach all over the ground at her feet.

While vomiting was never pleasant, she thought it was probably for the best that she'd regurgitated her beer; she wanted a clear head for what came next. Because there was a next—even though she felt like she'd been awake for days and had exerted herself more than ever before, her night was not over: she needed to get back to her room safely, write a note to the king, and deliver it to the floral urn. Meera hoped she had learned enough to free Cerun of his muzzle. She couldn't make sense of the duke's meeting, but perhaps the king could.

After a drink of water to clean out her mouth, she crept out from behind the tree. Staying off the road, she walked parallel to it on the edge of the woods, and whenever she heard the sounds of voices or saw anyone, she moved quickly behind a tree or bush to hide. It took her a long while to reach the palace gate in that manner, but she arrived safely. When she identified herself to the guards as "Meera Hailship, the raek caretaker," they stared at her in interest but thankfully didn't harass her with questions about the raek or her late-night activities.

By the time she made it to the kitchen, it was completely deserted, giving her an eerie feeling—she didn't think she'd ever seen the kitchen empty before. But Cook always left bread out and stew over the fire for anyone who might get hungry, and Meera ravenously helped herself to a full meal. The large clock in the kitchen displayed that it was three in the morning: almost time to wake up, she thought miserably. But this would be her last late night; the duke was leaving that day, and her spying would be over. She only hoped it had all amounted to something—something for her king and something for her raek friend.

She entered her room as quietly as possible to retrieve the fountain pen the king had given her and a piece of paper. Teardra was asleep, snoring rhythmically—either unaware or unconcerned about Meera's nightlong absence. Bringing her supplies back to the empty kitchen, Meera sat and wrote a note to the king. It felt strange and exciting to be addressing King Bartro so informally, and the sense of adventure and importance she had felt early in her spying returned to her. Her note read:

> *On the night of Summer Solstice, He went to a small tavern in Altus with a fish sign. He spoke to the barman, a former ship's captain named Mel, and implored the barman to sail with Him somewhere. The captain had known His father, and He suggested that they both wanted answers to a mystery involving something or somewhere being cut off 'the map.' It was unclear whether He*

*meant a specific map or all maps in general. The captain declined
the request.*

Meera read the note over several times before deciding it was
good enough. Then she dragged herself from her seat, her leg
muscles protesting the movement, and walked the note to the urn.
Task accomplished, she sighed in relief; she could finally get some
sleep.

17

───────

Meera was only able to sleep for a couple of hours before the staff bell woke her. She groaned, feeling like she could have slept through the entire day and not arisen until the next morning. Stretching, she turned toward the center of the small room where Teardra gave her a look that clearly denounced her as slothful before the older woman left, clicking the door shut behind her.

Meera dragged herself from the bed. Then it took her longer than usual to get dressed—her entire body was sore from running the night before, and her head ached from lack of sleep. She had to sit on the edge of her bed to pull on her boots, finding herself unable to balance on one leg as she normally would. Her hair was so filthy at this point that she wrapped a bandana around her head to conceal the grease, and her face was still a little bruised. She consoled herself by thinking that she wouldn't be the only ragged victim of the Summer Solstice—though most people had surely enjoyed themselves more than she had.

Linus was waiting for her by the time she arrived outside, and he looked more cheerful than he had of late; he had spent the Solstice with his family, and visits with his family always enlivened his spirits. Meera smiled at him, hoping their friendship could return to its former easy companionship in light of his good mood. However, when Linus looked her over, his cheer dissipated. "Rough night?" he asked, a note of accusation in his voice.

"I didn't get much sleep," she replied evasively. "Did you have fun with your family?"

"Yes," he said tersely, and they began their walk.

Meera sighed. Now that her spying was over, she hoped she wouldn't need to hide anything from Linus anymore. She didn't like keeping things from him, but she was also growing impatient with his moods and was too exhausted to attempt to cheer him back up. They walked in silence—their new normal. Her thoughts drifted sleepily as she walked, and she was imagining Cerun's heavy muzzle falling to the ground and how happy and proud she would feel at the sight when Linus exclaimed: "Who is he!?"

Startled, Meera looked around wildly, not understanding the question, and her heart rate jumped from a doze to a run. "Who is it you're seeing?" Linus clarified. "I realize I'm young, but I'm not stupid." Meera turned her attention to her friend, still confused. He had stopped in his tracks and stared at the ground with an increasingly red face. Then, very quietly, he finished, "I want to know who he is."

Meera wrinkled her brow, her tired mind working hard to catch up with Linus. He thought she was seeing a man? "What are you talking about?" she asked wearily, her shoulders sagging.

"You're tired every morning, and some of the guards have seen you sneaking around—I heard you went into the city late last night. As your friend, I think I have the right to know if you're seeing a man and who he is," he replied, clenching his fists at his side as anger replaced his embarrassment.

He's a duke, Meera almost said. She laughed at her inward joke, but seeing Linus's stricken face, she quickly tried to mollify him: "Linus, I'm not sneaking around at night *seeing* a man—whatever that means—and frankly, I don't appreciate the accusation. You *are* my friend, but I don't think that means I have to answer to you." She hoped they could leave it at that and move past it, but Linus continued to sulk.

When they reached the slope down to the canal, they walked the narrow path through the tall grass. They were later than usual, and the sun was already starting to heat the day, turning the moisture in the grass into a thick mist. The curls escaping from Meera's bun reached tendrils of hair out to touch the humid air. Soon, the raek came into view, as well as a cluster of men standing before him. Surprised, Meera and Linus stopped. "Who is it?" Linus asked, momentarily forgetting to sulk.

Meera sighed. "Only one way to find out," she replied, pressing onward. As they walked toward the beach, she could see that Cerun was agitated—his head lifted despite the heavy muzzle cutting into his flesh, and his long tufted tail swishing back and forth. However, the men before him didn't seem to be doing anything other than looking and talking. Meera felt too tired to deal with anything out of the ordinary, but she and Linus continued to approach the group of men.

The misty air dampened their sounds as well as their skin and clothes, so they remained unnoticed despite the clamor of the cart's wheels. It wasn't until they were just a few paces away that the men finally turned to face them. Meera recognized the king and the captain of the guard, and there were also two other men she didn't know, both well-dressed in unfamiliar styles. One of the strange men had striking blonde hair and blue eyes, and the other had silky black hair, reddish brown skin, and wore a lot of gold.

Meera could tell the paler man was from Arborea and the darker one from Cesor.

People from both lands had settled Terratelle long ago, which was why Terratellens tended to have middle-tone hair and skin, ranging from light brown hair to black and light beige skin to dark brown. Most of the blonde hair, blue eyes, and lightest of skin had been overtaken in time by browns—or so her father had told her. Prince Phineas was the palest Terratellen Meera had seen, presumably because Terratelle was more closely aligned with Arborea, and Arboreans often married into the royal family. Cesor lay across the Penchin sea, making it more difficult to visit and trade with, though they were still a close, long-term ally.

Meera curtsied to the group at large, saying "Your Majesty, Captain" in greeting. Then, noticing Linus standing with his mouth agape, she nudged him with her elbow. He bowed awkwardly, his muttered greeting inaudible. Meera supposed he had never stood before the king before despite having lived and worked in the palace for over a year. Then she wondered whether this was how most people behaved upon first meeting King Bartro. If so, it was no wonder the graceful curtsy and intelligible words she had managed on their first encounter had caught his attention, she thought wryly. If she could go back in time, she might choose to faceplant into the king's plate of food instead.

"Miss Hailship," King Bartro greeted her, ignoring Linus. "These are emissaries from Arborea and Cesor, come to see the prized beast I have acquired in our war," he explained, gesturing to the two men. Meera found it interesting that the king would market raeken as demon creatures to Terratellens and *prized beasts* to foreign lands, but she assumed he wanted to impress them or sought their aid in the war. Mostly, however, she just wished she could have gotten more sleep or at least washed her hair before being presented to emissaries.

"I have just been telling these men of your success with the beast, which we had previously believed could only be mastered through ... unnatural means," the king continued. She supposed by *unnatural means* he meant magic. "I have decided that the emissaries' arrival is the perfect opportunity for an overdue test of your mastery over the beast," King Bartro concluded.

Test? Mastery? Meera didn't know what was happening. Then the king moved toward her, produced a large iron key from his pocket, and extended it to her with a fiery gleam in his eyes. Having the king in such close proximity made Linus stiffen, and he performed a jerky little bow unnecessarily. Distracted by Linus's movement, Meera took the key offered to her without processing what it was. But when realization slowly dawned, a full smile illuminated her face, and her exhaustion was forgotten: it was the key to Cerun's muzzle!

The king had received her intelligence on the duke, and this was her payment—though he was passing it off as grandstanding for the emissaries. "Am I to remove the iron muzzle, Your Majesty?" she asked, unable to hide the childlike enthusiasm in her voice.

"At your leisure," the king replied, the lights of his eyes flickering over her face in a way that suggested he was still wary of her motives.

Arborea's emissary stepped forward, looking curious but apprehensive. He addressed Meera, asking, "Are you not afraid, Miss? My people once hunted raeken in the mountains north of our lands, and the destruction they wrought in consequence was so terrible that no Arborean would dare to approach one of their species. We now leave them to themselves. We have never considered trying to capture them alive and tame them."

Meera shifted awkwardly on her feet, not wanting to encourage anyone to capture and chain wild raeken. "I cannot pretend to know anything about this raek, Sir. I don't know whether it was born in the wild or has always lived among ... people," she replied, almost saying humans but realizing that wouldn't be accurate. "But I'm not afraid of it," she concluded. She wanted to add that Arboreans should leave raeken alone, but it was not her place to have opinions in the present situation. She wouldn't want the king to rebuke her and change his mind about Cerun's muzzle.

The Arborean emissary nodded, then he stared at Meera expectantly. Glancing around, she realized that everyone present except Linus was waiting for her to act. Forgetting the cart in her excitement, she walked without hesitation across the claw marks in the sand to where Cerun was swaying anxiously, and she held the key where he could see it and beamed at him. If she weren't being watched, she would have run to her raek friend and given him a celebratory hug, but she restrained herself.

The raek kept his head held high and his gaze focused on the men behind her as she approached. When Meera was close enough to speak without being overheard, she said, "Cerun, the king has given me the key to remove your muzzle! He is repaying me for information I gave him about a visitor to the palace. The other men are here to be impressed by you—I don't think they will bother you at all. Are you ready?"

Cerun finally looked at her—he gave her a long, steady look as if trying to decide how much he trusted her. Then he blinked and laid his large scaly head at her feet. There were locking mechanisms on either side of his face where the chains that wrapped around his head were held in place, and Meera crouched, fit the key easily into one side, turned it, and released the mechanism. Hurrying to the other side, she released that mechanism as well. Then she took a moment to remove the heavy chains from around Cerun's head and neck, tossing them to the ground.

The raek remained perfectly still, waiting. "Okay," she said when she was done, and Cerun arched and retracted his long neck, sliding his snout slowly from the muzzle. Meera could now see clearly how raw the skin of his face was and cringed, but she would at least be able to tend to it properly going forward. She took a step away to retrieve her cart but hesitated when she saw Cerun move and watched to see what he would do.

The raek lifted his enormous head, stretched his jaws wide, and emitted a loud, squawking roar, his sharp teeth bared. Meera jumped at the noise but didn't retreat. Then Cerun bent, grasped the muzzle in his mighty jaws, and tossed it into the canal with a heaving sweep of his neck. She was amazed that he could hold the dense piece of iron with the strength of his jaws and not break his teeth. The cursed contraption sent a great splash into the air and had already disappeared under the water's surface by the time the droplets settled. Despite Cerun's ragged feathers and thin frame, his grace and strength were now visible in his posture, and Meera smiled at the sight.

Turning away to get his food, she saw that the group of men had retreated away from the beach somewhat, awe and fear written on their faces. Meera supposed King Bartro was certain that raek fire could not melt chains, considering there was not an entire army of archers present with him; he surely had full access to the information about raeken that his people were banned from reading. Then her attention was caught by the blonde Arborean emissary, who clapped his hands delightedly like she and Cerun had put on a choreographed show. The emissary from Cesor nodded his head in approval as well, but the king's gaze— even at a distance—looked still and calculating.

Meera chose to ignore the men and carry out her usual duties. First, she retrieved the cart from where Linus had dropped it— Linus had retreated further away with the others, and Meera almost laughed at the sight of him standing among the group of older, more important men looking gangly and awe-struck. Then she gave Cerun his food—not needing to feed it to him piece by piece anymore—and promised to bring him something larger to sink his teeth into next time. She also retrieved the vinegar and honey crocks she had left near the wall and bid him lower his head so that she could attend to his face. Now that the muzzle was gone, she hoped his skin would heal quickly. Forgetting her audience, she scratched her raek friend's neck briefly and bid him farewell for the day.

Cerun immediately started to pick at his teeth and lick his feathers clean, desperate to groom himself but keeping a keen eye on the king and his entourage all the while. Then, as if to prove he could, he lifted his head into the air, unhinged his jaws, and emitted a raging ball of blue fire. It was not a long stream like Meera had imagined raek fire would be—it was spherical and mostly contained within his jaws, but that didn't stop it from being both dazzling and terrifying at the same time. The orb consisted of many small fires swirling within it as if they were lighting the air itself with no beginning and no end, and she could feel the intense heat radiating from it.

Cerun clamped his jaw shut with a smug click, and Meera exited the beach. She found Linus staring at the raek with a mixture of fear and hatred, but her friend quickly blinked away his expression and took the cart from her hand. The king dismissed them both, and Meera found herself ascending the grassy slope with an enormous grin on her face. Seeing Cerun freed of his muzzle had raised her spirits immensely, and she didn't think anything could possibly spoil her good mood that day.

MEERA CARRIED a full basket of food down to the dungeon with her since she had only visited the prisoner once the day before, and she brought him another book in case he was ready for it. Even though she knew the man would already be aware that she had removed his raek's muzzle—a fact that continued to amaze her—she still felt excited to tell him the news. She also anticipated a long afternoon nap after her dungeon visit. Now that the duke had left the palace and her spying was over, she could finally get the rest she so desperately needed. She knew she should prioritize a bath, but she just didn't have it in her.

When she reached cell 39, however, her excitement fled her mind. The prisoner was standing, wearing the pants, shirt, and sweater Linus had found for him. He had his arms crossed over his chest and was facing the cell door as if waiting for her. Meera hesitated and stared at him. She was holding the basket of food in her left hand and the key in her right, but rather than reach toward the lock with it, she froze and clutched it in her palm. The man's behavior unnerved her. Looking him up and down, she noticed that he had tied his hair back and also that she had failed to give him any socks, and she thought his feet—though bandaged—must be cold on the stone floor.

While the man's figure was diminished from his long imprisonment, he was still impressive—his posture intimidating. Meera regarded his steely grey eyes, which betrayed nothing of his emotions or intentions. With his hair tied back, the angularity of his bone structure was even more pronounced, and she found that in addition to feeling unnerved by him, she was also having a difficult time taking her eyes off him. But why the change in demeanor? Would he rush the door? Did he think that without his muzzle, Cerun could escape and get them both away?

Despite the prisoner's ever-healing and strengthening body, Meera had never requested the presence of a guard, and in that moment, she thought maybe she should have. But she wasn't afraid of the man hurting her, so much as she was afraid of him getting himself hurt. "I hope you don't think you're going anywhere," she said, before swallowing, tearing her eyes from him, and beginning to fight the lock with the key—rattling it back and forth until she felt it catch.

She opened the cell door and stepped inside, not bothering to lock it behind her. She never did. If the man wanted to overpower her and take the key, he could, and if he wanted to be foolish and run out of the dungeon, she would rather not get hurt in the process. She even stepped slightly to the side to leave the way free and clear rather than risk being shoved. With the man standing, the cell felt considerably smaller than usual. He wasn't much taller than her—maybe four inches—but his presence filled the space.

Putting down her basket, she straightened up to find him still staring at her. His dark brows were pulled down slightly, and he wore a frown. She thought he looked annoyed. But she always thought he looked annoyed with her, and this felt different—like he was considering something, but what? He hadn't run ... "What?" she finally asked, lacking anything more poignant to say. She didn't expect a verbal answer, but he could gesture if he wanted something.

To Meera's complete disbelief, the man swallowed and cleared his throat like he might speak. Her eyes widened, wrinkling her forehead, and she felt like her heart and lungs stilled in anticipation. Then, with slow exactness like he had practiced in his head, the man said, "I have a message from *Cerun*—" He said the name like it tasted foul on his tongue but continued without pausing: "He says you should not endanger the lives of others on our behalf. Do not sell your soul for us."

18

———————

He spoke! He spoke, Meera kept thinking over and over —the thought preventing her sleep-deprived mind from processing the actual words he had used. Standing across from the young, handsome, strangely beardless—possibly knell—prisoner, who had not spoken a word in the eight weeks he had been at the palace, she gaped at him. He stared back for a while, lips pressed firmly together in a declaration of his reclaimed silence. Then he crouched over her basket and began pulling out food.

Meera watched him start to eat and tried to remember what he had said to her. She wished her mind weren't so foggy and resolved to go from the dungeon straight to her room to take a nap when she was finished there. She was accustomed to being physically weak, but mental weakness felt unbearable. What had the man said? She racked her brain. It had been a message from Cerun ... not to endanger anyone on his behalf? He didn't want her to *sell her soul*, she recalled.

As she watched him eat and tried to puzzle through what he

had said, she had a feeling he had used as few words as possible to express Cerun's message. For weeks, she had been wishing that her raek friend could talk back to her, and she regretted his choice of messenger. But why had he sent her this message? Thinking back to that morning, she realized she had alluded to spying for the king when speaking to Cerun—had vaguely told him that her information for the king had bought his freedom from the muzzle. She had been trying to reassure him that the king wasn't attempting to deceive him in some way ...

Meera didn't think she had endangered the duke with her information—he hadn't mentioned the war and didn't seem to be aiding the enemy in any way. If the king prevented Duke Harrington from taking a sea voyage, he would stay in his comfortable house with his loving wife and willful daughter, safe and happy. She hadn't endangered him—he was on his way home. Taking a deep breath, she sighed it out. She had spied for the king, but that was over now. Her soul was still her own. All was well.

The man was halfway through a crock of sausage and hash by the time she finished her reverie. "You know, if you had spoken to me before, I wouldn't have had to do any spying to get Cerun's muzzle off," she said bitterly. He merely glanced at her above his food, and she self-consciously straightened the bandana covering her filthy hair. She would normally see to the man's wounds, but she assumed his whiplashes were mostly healed since he was sitting on his butt to eat. Sighing again, she decided she didn't want to spend any more time with him that day. She was about to tell him so, when the crock he was holding fell to the stone floor and shattered, scattering glass shards and sausages.

At first, Meera thought the man had smashed the crock on purpose because of what she had said and was about to rebuke him. Then she saw thick rings of white showing in his wide eyes as his back arched and arms drew into his chest, hands twitching uselessly up by his face. He began to fall over, and she lunged for him, grabbing his head to make sure it didn't hit the ground. He fell onto his side on the mattress, and his whole body tensed and scrunched. He breathed in panicked, staccato bursts through his nose, and the visible strain in his neck and jaw suggested he couldn't open his mouth to gulp in more air.

What was happening? She didn't know what to do. She let go of the man's head and hovered her hands over him, desperate to help but useless—so completely useless. Bending close, she looked into his eyes, babbling futile words of reassurance— telling him he would be okay and encouraging him to slow his breathing. She could see beads of sweat forming on his forehead from the straining of his muscles, and she herself broke into a cold sympathy sweat. Then she started breathing loudly and slowly through her nose to set a pace for him, though in truth it was also for her—to keep herself from hyperventilating or screaming.

Finally, as suddenly as they had clenched, his muscles released: his arms dropped, his head fell fully to the mat, and he gasped shakily through parted lips. His whole body trembled. Meera sagged to the floor next to him in relief, and for several moments, the only sound was their panting. She could see weariness and confusion in the man's unguarded expression, but when he looked at her, it quickly turned to anger. Still lying on his side, he reached out and grabbed her upper arms—hard—shaking her and rasping over and over, "What did you give me? What did you give me? Tell me!"

Meera struggled and tried to free herself of his crushing grip, but she couldn't—she was helpless as she always seemed to be. Tears immediately filled her eyes. What did she give him? She hadn't given him anything but food! "Nothing!" she yelled over his voice and the rattling of her brain in her head as he shook her. "I didn't give you anything! Stop!"

He did stop and release her arms, but he still looked murderous. She scrambled away from him on the floor and used the cell bars to haul herself to standing. In her hasty retreat, ceramic shards from the shattered crock stuck in her palm and sliced her legs. Yanking out the fragment in her hand, she bit her lip, but her tears ran unchecked down her cheeks. Her palm seared with pain, and yet, it seemed so trivial compared to what the man had endured in his torture ...

She swiped the tears from her face—she couldn't bear to cry in front of him. Then she pressed her injured hand into the fabric of her dress, which was covered in bits of potato hash and sausage grease anyway—and stared uncomprehendingly at the mess on the floor. How could someone have poisoned him? They couldn't have; Meera had gotten the crock out of a cabinet and taken the hash and sausage herself from the large tureens meant to feed the palace staff. "You couldn't have been poisoned," she said, "because I got the food meant for everyone and brought it straight here. I never left it alone, and no one else touched it. I ate some myself earlier ..."

In a spike of fear, she wondered if she would be next to fall on the floor and convulse. It made her stomach turn and bile rise in her throat. Then she remembered her old neighbor's husband, Mr. Leaven, who used to have convulsions. At the time, her father had told her that Mr. Leaven had lockjaw from a large wood splinter he had gotten while trying to fix his kitchen table. Meera had been very young, and the idea of a person's jaw locking had plagued her. For months, she had thought about it before going to sleep, had ground her teeth in the night, and had awoken with a sore jaw, convinced that she, too, would die of lockjaw ... Because he had died, she remembered; eventually, one of Mr. Leaven's convulsions had prevented him from breathing for long enough that he had died. She recalled the funeral.

"It must be lockjaw," she said to the man still trembling on the mat before her. "It's probably from the nails that were in your calves. I cleaned them as best I could ... but puncture wounds are hard to clean ..." she trailed off, feeling like she should have done more and wondering how she was possibly going to help him through this.

At her words, realization dawned on his face. "Where I am from it is called the splinter fits," he said quietly, still catching his breath. She had forgotten he was from Aegorn for a moment. He did have a bit of an accent. It wasn't as pronounced as people from Cesor, but his words sounded lilted, almost sing-song to her. Splinter fits was an apt name, but no matter what he called it, Meera knew the man's chance of surviving it if he remained in the dungeon alone wasn't very good. Still, people did survive and recover from it, she reassured herself.

She started to clean the mess on the floor and handed the man the basket in case he wanted more food. He put it to the side—his appetite apparently gone—and she couldn't blame him. Meera was so used to his silence, that it didn't occur to her to try to keep him talking now that he had broken it. Instead, she left him to contemplate his fate on his own and returned to the kitchen dirty, bleeding, and more exhausted than she would have thought possible.

***

MEERA SLUMPED into a chair at one of the kitchen tables with some vinegar and bandages and began tending to her cuts. She started with the one on her palm—which was still bleeding freely —and hoped she wouldn't need to stitch it; she had had enough of tending wounds. Pulling up her skirt to check her legs, she ignored the stares from the people around her. She knew it wasn't appropriate for her to bare her legs in front of men, but she couldn't find enough energy within herself to care.

Cook walked over and gave her a look that clearly said, "Again? You're hopeless," before helping her clean the cuts on her legs and instructing her to eat something before going upstairs. "And don't you come back down 'till you's well rested and clean," they said, "I hear the muzzle's off your beast, so that guard boy can throw his food to him in the morning. I'll send word you isn't well."

Meera felt beyond relieved to have a large chunk of time to herself to sleep and bathe, but then she felt a pang for the prisoner. While he had plenty of food for the day, she worried about him having another convulsion. But it wasn't as if she could live in the dungeon with him and monitor him every second of the day … She put the prisoner and his lockjaw out of her mind and focused on chewing and swallowing her food so she could get to bed. Her eyes and head both drooped, but she doggedly filled her stomach, hoping to sleep for a long time without hunger forcing her to rise.

At the table next to her was the palace guard she had seen consoling Duchess Harrington's lady's maid the day before—Ben, was it? Poor Ben looked miserable and was sipping a cup of tea, though Meera suspected there was more than tea in the mug, knowing the habits of many of the palace guards. She felt sorry for the man, who looked genuinely depressed to be parted from his lover—even if she was glad the Harringtons had gone home. She was just about to take her dishes to the sink and finally get some sleep when another guard burst into the kitchen. The guard's head swivelled until he found Ben, and he rushed over to the sad man. "There you are!" he said excitedly, "Have you heard?

The Harringtons were robbed on their way out of Altus—just past the city! The duke was killed!"

"What?" Ben asked in alarm, standing and grabbing the other guard by the shirt, shaking him lightly. "Adrianna? Was Adrianna hurt?"

"I don't think so," the other guard replied, patting Ben on the shoulder awkwardly while trying to extricate himself from his friend's grip. "Word only came that the duke was killed."

"Is she here? Did they come back? They should come back! It's safe here!" Ben shouted, sounding hopeful and determined.

"Sorry brother, sounds like the duchess took the duke's body and wanted to go straight home," his friend said, crushing Ben's hope of seeing his lover again.

Meera stopped listening. She had heard enough, and her tired mind was slowly registering the truth of the situation: the duke was dead. The kind, smiling man with the booming laugh who had doted on his wife and missed his daughter was dead. She pressed a hand to her mouth. She couldn't believe the healthy, vital man from the night before was now a cold, lifeless body. She had liked the duke—she had never met him, of course, but she had certainly watched him enough to judge his character and had thought he was a good person.

Abruptly, she bent forward in her chair and pressed her hand into her abdomen instead. The food she had just eaten curdled in her stomach as she realized: the duke was dead the day after she had reported about him to the king—the very same day the king had repaid her for her information. She had spied on him, informed on him, and now he was dead, not twenty-four hours later ... Was this because of her? Had she done this? The king had called her a *weapon* ... She had thought it a turn of phrase at the time, but he had used her as such. Worse—she had let him. She had willingly spied for him, and he had killed the duke because of her report. King Bartro had killed the duke because of her ... She had killed the duke. It was all because of her—it was all her fault.

Suddenly, Meera lurched to her feet, abandoning her dishes on the table to flee to her room. She couldn't do this right now—she just couldn't. In her room, she hastily undressed and flung herself into her bed, burying herself under her blankets despite the heat. For once, she was glad Teardra had shuttered the window to the outside world and the bright light of summer. Curling herself into a tight ball, she squeezed her knees into her chest and threw one arm over her head like a shield. Tears trickled lifelessly from her eyes. She lay perfectly still and wished for sleep—wished for oblivion to take her. Oblivion took her.

19

Meera didn't awaken until the servant's bell chimed the next morning, and even then, she just rolled over and went back to sleep. She wasn't willing to face the day yet, and Cook had promised to get a message to Linus about feeding Cerun ... A few hours later, she got up, drew herself a bath in the bathing chamber down the hall, and gave herself an overdue scrubbing. She focused only on rubbing soap into her scalp and brushing the dirt from under her nails; she could process everything else later. Her cuts from the day before stung from the lye in the soap, but she embraced the stinging pain as a distraction from the dark thoughts threatening to burst forth in her mind.

After her bath, she slowly detangled her hair and pressed most of the moisture out with a towel, leaving it down to dry. Then she dressed in a clean blue dress and peered into her small mirror. Her bruises were almost entirely gone, and her hair was finally clean, but her brown eyes betrayed the feelings she was pushing down. She quickly looked away—it could all wait until after she'd eaten something, she told herself. Before she left her room, she pinned back the front pieces of her hair to keep it out of her face while it dried, and on a whim, pulled out a pair of her mother's earrings: two dangling circles with pale blue stones surrounded by small white pearls. She put them on—not for vanity's sake—but for the small comfort they provided her. Then she tied on the purple bracelet Linus had given her.

After meandering down to the kitchen, Meera nodded a greeting at Cook and took a large plate of food to one of the tables to eat alone. She almost always ate alone, and it was her choice—but one she made to avoid the judgment and bullying of the other staff. And on that day, she would have given anything to have a group of friends around her—women especially—chatting and gossiping to distract her from herself. Having lost her mother young and grown up without aunts and sisters, Meera had always craved the warmth and empathy of women—at least those characteristics most commonly attributed to women.

Her father was warm and loving but also single-minded about his work and often flighty ... Unable to bear thoughts of her father, Meera looked around for old Mrs. Henderby—Mrs. Henderby was always kind to her. However, now that she thought of it, she hadn't seen the older laundress in some time. She felt a rush of shame for not noticing sooner that Mrs. Henderby hadn't been in the kitchen lately. Where had she been? Was she not well? Why hadn't she noticed her absence and sought her out? Were Meera's father there, he would have tried to comfort her by reminding her: *people are as multi-faceted as the eyes of a dragonfly but much less perceptive.* But her father wasn't there, and she couldn't seem to offer herself that same level of comfort and understanding.

Squeezing her eyes shut briefly, she opened them and looked across the room at Cook. They were in the middle of frosting and decorating a cake for one of the royal children's birthdays, and Meera watched their calm efficiency as they spun the cake rounds on a turntable and expertly smoothed over the creamy frosting. She gave her mind over to watching Cook, letting herself be fully absorbed in the actions of their hands. While the rest of Cook was lumpy and homely—not exactly the epitome of elegance or beauty—their hands moved with subtle confidence and grace.

Watching Cook stack and frost the cake layers soothed Meera even as the constructed layers within her mind crumbled apart, and when Cook finished their task, she blinked and finally rose to go into the gardens and process everything, her life—what she had let her life become. Cerun had been right; she had sold her soul to the king. She had endangered the life of the duke—a good man—to get the raek's muzzle off. She had wanted to help Cerun, but she had also wanted feel better about leaving him on that beach ... Even though she knew it was wrong. It was all wrong—the imprisonments, the torture, the spying, the murder.

Meera had thought she'd been acting for herself, but she hadn't—not really. She'd been doing exactly what she had accused the guards of doing when they hadn't saved her from the prince: blindly following the king rather than adhering to her own moral compass. She had been a tool, a weapon, a soldier—exactly what she didn't want Linus to become. She had been a self-righteous fool! Her newly-full stomach soured with shame and guilt. Why had she felt so certain that she was a good person? Why had she taken that belief for granted and stopped questioning her actions? She felt like she, herself, had killed Duke Harrington, and the raw disgust burgeoning in her chest was nearly enough to send her right back to her bed and the fetal position. But somehow, it didn't—she wouldn't let it.

Meera told herself she had to keep moving forward, keep trying to be the person she had thought she was. She didn't want to feel what she was feeling, but her feelings wouldn't change anything anyway. Crying and falling apart wouldn't bring the duke back to life or make up for her many mistakes. For a moment, she wondered what her father would think of her life now; he had always wanted her to be her own person, to read everything and learn everything, and draw her own conclusions about the world around her ... And she had let herself be a tool, *a weapon.* She had never disappointed her father before, so she couldn't think what quippy saying he might use for the occasion. Fingering one of her earrings, she wondered what her dead mother would have thought of her daughter, but that was something she would never know.

Meera kept walking through the gardens, berating herself repeatedly for the decisions she had been making. She had read stories of heroes and had always imagined that she would be the kind of person who was strong enough to do what was right even when it was difficult—that she would be a hero if a situation called for it. She had imagined that she would be brave like the raek rider, Kallan, when he flew out to sea to single-handedly rescue Queen Thea from pirates. Now she wasn't so sure ... Maybe she was the kind of person who would have cried for the queen and stayed at home, leaving her to her fate—or worse, maybe she would have been one of the pirates, letting their pirate captain make their decisions for them.

She didn't want to be a bystander or a follower, and she wasn't willing to have been wrong about herself. Her betrayal of the duke was a misstep—a mistake—and she *would* make up for it. Except —how could she make up for a man being dead? Death was permanent, unalterable—not a wrong she could make right with apologies. Forcing herself to picture the duke, to remember him laughing with his wife and holding her hand, she resolved never to forget him or what she had done to him. She couldn't make up for her mistake, but she would hold herself accountable—she would be better going forward.

But how could she be better? Should she leave the palace? Go back to her solitary life waiting for her father to return? Who would that benefit? Suddenly, Meera had a thought, one that both terrified and thrilled her—one that had been lingering at the periphery of her mind for weeks but had gone unacknowledged: she would free the raek. She would free the raek and his rider if she could because it was the right thing to do—she was certain of it—and she wasn't going to let her fear stand in her way. She wanted to be a hero, not a weapon. She wasn't a raek rider like Kallan or a warrior, but she could still be a hero—she could still free the unjustly imprisoned, even if she was freeing them from a king instead of pirates.

As she meandered the gardens, the heat and humidity dried her hair in tight, fluffy ringlets. She was sweating and didn't want her bath to have been a complete waste of time, so she found a shady bench on which to plant herself for a while and continued to think. She was sitting on the very bench by the stables where the fussy servant, Dodgers, had found her weeks ago to present her to the king. Meera recalled how proud she had felt to stand in front of the king and the royal family and conduct herself with decorum and intelligence. Then she had felt proud when the king had noticed her—had acknowledged her potential and chosen her to spy for him. She was no longer proud of herself, but she would be when she betrayed her king to free her friend.

Chewing the inside of her cheek, she considered what to do next. She needed a plan. Cerun's muzzle was off, but he had confirmed that raek fire wasn't hot enough to melt metal. Otherwise, he would already be free. Linus had said that fire could only melt iron with the use of a bellows ... Meera had used a small bellows to stoke the kitchen fire at times and raise the temperature of the flames, and from what she understood, feeding air into the fire made it hotter. She wondered whether stoking Cerun's fire with a bellows would be hot enough to melt his iron chains. It might be worth a try. Would it be easier to steal the key to his chains? She had no notion whatsoever where such a key would be kept and didn't want to be caught sneaking around the palace, trying to get into the king's study. She decided it would be easier to carry a bellows down to the beach at night and much less risky.

What about the prisoner? She had the key to his cell, but she didn't think she could smuggle him past the guards in the hall. She could give him a weapon to fight his way out, but she didn't want anyone else to get hurt because of her; she wanted to free the raek and prisoner, but she wasn't at war with Terratelle or the Crown. She wasn't even angry with the king—she was only angry with herself. The king had used and manipulated her for his own gain, but he had never lied to her; she had just been foolish enough to flop unwittingly into his gaping bear mouth.

Meera didn't want to be a fool again ... How could she get the prisoner out of the palace without getting herself caught and hanged for treason? She considered taking Linus into the dungeon, taking his guard's uniform for the prisoner, and locking her friend in the cell, but she wouldn't do that to Linus. She also assumed that he wouldn't help her free the prisoners—the thought of Linus committing treason was absurd. Would he turn her in if he suspected what she was planning? She didn't think so —at least, she hoped their friendship was stronger than his stubborn loyalty.

Suddenly, she had an idea, and she leapt from her bench to enact it. Walking swiftly back to her room, she opened her chest, pulled out paper and her pen from the king, and wrote a brief note. Then she walked through the palace halls to deposit her note in the flower urn. She didn't know if her idea would work, but having a plan—and more broadly, having a purpose—was a welcome distraction from her grief and guilt. On her way from the urn back to the kitchen, she took a sharp turn around a corner and nearly walked into someone. Stepping back hastily, she began to apologize when she registered the haughtily raised chin and shining gold hair of Prince Phineas. Meera's eyes widened and chest constricted, but she didn't have time to decide between fight or flight before the prince coughed, averted his eyes from her, and said, "Pardon me, Miss," stepping around her and turning the corner.

Meera whipped around hastily, wondering if he meant to attack from behind again, but he was gone. Clutching her hands to her wild heart, she looked all around to find that the hall was deserted, and she leaned back against a wall to catch her breath. What had just happened? It had been just the two of them—she had been completely alone and defenseless—and the prince had neither touched nor taunted her. Taking a deep breath, Meera held it for a beat and sighed it out with a woosh. It was a relief to know that the king had meant what he'd said about Prince Phineas not bothering her again, but it was also eerie; what had he done to his son? What had he threatened?

Whatever it was, she couldn't bring herself to feel sorry for the prince. She did, however, have a growing fear of the king's ruthlessness. King Bartro ordered those under him to spy, torture, and murder, seemingly without remorse. Meera didn't fully understand the king's actions or his motivations, but she hoped she understood him well enough to manipulate him. Then, returning her mind to her present task, she flicked her hair behind her shoulders and off her sweaty neck to fill a basket with food for the prisoner. Perhaps today she might learn his name.

ENTERING the dungeon brought the instant relief of cool air, but as Meera stepped carefully down the stairs, she remembered the young man's fit the day before and grew increasingly apprehensive about the state in which she might find him. She wanted to rehearse what she would say to him in her head, but visions of him dead on the stone floor plagued her too much to concentrate. By the time she made it to cell 39, she simply exhaled her pent breath and said, "Good, you're alive."

The man was lying face down on his mat with his elbows propped under him, reading her book. He looked vaguely startled by her words, then his face cracked like he might laugh. He didn't. "Good, you are clean and well-rested," he replied.

Meera was glad the man hadn't retreated back into total silence, but she started at his notice of her appearance. While he had always observed her closely, his silence had given her the illusion that only she had been watching and discerning. She supposed he knew her about as well as she knew him, which, granted, wasn't well at all. She entered the cell, handed him his food, and asked, "Have you had any more convulsions?"

"Not yet," he said, his eyes darkening.

There were a million and one things Meera wanted to ask this strange man from a strange place now that he was talking, but instead, she dove straight into her plan: "I'm going to free you—both of you. Well, I'm going to try, at least, but I need you to cooperate."

The man pushed himself to a sitting position, intensity in his vaguely slanted eyes. He didn't ask if he could trust her, but she could see the ever-present suspicion in his compressed lip; he just asked, "How?"

"I've written to the king. I told him that your ... condition is potentially deadly and has made you desperate to see your raek—that you've started speaking and are asking about his welfare and whether you can see him one last time," she explained, hoping the man wouldn't view her use of the truth as a betrayal. He looked intent upon her words but not angry, so she continued: "If asked, I need you to promise to give the king information if you can see your raek one last time. I'm hoping I can help Cerun melt his chains in the night. Then, when you're brought out to say your goodbyes, Cerun can fly you both away—you shouldn't actually have to speak with the king at all. It's not a perfect plan..." she started to say, doubting herself, but he interjected.

"How would you melt the chains?" he asked.

"If I use a bellows, do you think Cerun could sustain his fire long enough?" she asked, wondering if she should have sussed out that important detail before writing to the king. She hadn't left herself any time to make another plan; she would have to act tonight just in case the king responded immediately.

The young man's eyes went slightly out of focus, and she presumed he was communicating with Cerun. "He can sustain his fire as long as you need," he said. "It may work." His tone was neutral, but there was a new light in his eyes: hope, she realized, and it made the man look younger yet.

"What are your names?" she asked him.

"I am Shael," he said, "and my raek is Borteus, though he tells me that if you free us, he will keep the name Cerun in your honor." He sounded slightly annoyed at that, but he smiled at her. It was a small, closed-lip smile, but it lifted an iron load from Meera's shoulders; they were good, she thought—this rider and his raek. She didn't know the details of their lives, but she had a strong feeling that they were good—she always had—and she intended to save them.

As she left Shael's cell, it occurred to her to consider her own fate. Would the king know or suspect that she had helped Cerun, or would he think the raek had melted the chains on his own?

Since she wanted to leave the palace anyway, she thought it was perhaps time for her to go. But would leaving soon after look more suspicious? Surely the king could easily find her home in Altus.

Suddenly, Meera realized that without meaning to, her plan would probably uproot her entire life. If the king was suspicious, she would have to leave and go somewhere he wouldn't find her. But where would she go? And if the king couldn't find her, then how would her father? A part of her didn't think her father would ever return from the war, but the rest of her adamantly refused to believe that he wouldn't one day walk into their house again, arms open to embrace her. If she ran away, how would they be reunited? Then she had an even worse thought: what if the king punished her father for her actions?

She wouldn't run, she decided. She would play dumb and go back to working in the kitchens with Cook, and hopefully, as time passed, she would be forgotten and be able to safely return home. Rather than working at the palace, she was sure there must be charities where she could lend her time and accomplish some good in the world ... Why hadn't she thought of that before? Why had she taken a servant's job when she hadn't needed it? Why had she volunteered to feed a dangerous animal? Was it to prove that she could? Had she been reading tales of heroes and warriors her whole life and had wanted to prove that she, too, could toil under difficult conditions and take on dangerous tasks? Meera laughed at the irony; she had been anything but a hero.

20

Meera climbed to the top of the dungeon stairs, thoughts swirling in her head, and as she swung open the door, she nearly walked into someone for the second time that day. King Bartro's fussy servant, Dodgers, was standing at the door to the dungeon, ostensibly waiting for her. He was clutching his hands before him and sweating profusely, and the paste he wore over his pock scars ran in rivulets into his unnecessarily frilly collar. Meera wondered randomly how many of those ridiculous collars he owned or whether he rushed back to his room each night to launder his only one. Then she blinked and focused on the fidgety man's face.

"Good, good!" he kept saying, "There you are! The king requests your presence." Sighing, he dabbed his brow with a handkerchief, clearly relieved he had not needed to enter the dungeon. Then he squinted at her, resembling a mole that had just emerged from the ground with his narrowed eyes and overlong nose. Meera suspected he meant to look intimidating because he leaned forward and added in a stern voice: "This time you will go to him straight away—straight away! Come, come!" Without waiting for a reply, he scurried down the hall.

She followed, thinking that her plan was moving swiftly. She hoped she could convince the king to let Shael see Cerun—but not today; she would need that night to break the chains ... if she *could* break the chains. If not, Shael wouldn't hold to the manufactured bargain, she would be removed from dungeon duty, and he would probably be tortured once more. Meera thought of the hope in his eyes and knew she couldn't let that happen. Dodgers deposited her in front of the doors to the king's study, and she dropped her basket and bag on the floor against the wall so that she could enter unencumbered. Then she stood before the two guards stationed at the door and stated her name unnecessarily. One entered and promptly returned to hold the door ajar for her.

Meera found King Bartro sitting behind his ornate wooden desk, going through papers as he usually seemed to be at that time of day. His smooth, brown hair was tied at the nape of his neck in a neat tail, and his beard was cut short, accentuating his strong jaw. She took note of his features before he glanced up because once his eyes alit on her, she could never seem to look away—she always felt caught by them as they burned into her soul and exposed her. When the king's gaze finally rose to hers, she dropped into a slow and deliberate curtsy, forcing herself to maintain his look and hoping her deceitful intentions didn't shine through her eyes. "Afternoon, Your Majesty," she said with a smile that didn't part her lips.

"Good afternoon, Miss Hailship," he replied, reaching across his desk and picking up what she recognized to be her letter. "It was a most interesting missive I received from you," he said, appearing to reread the note before looking back at her.

"Oh, Your Majesty?" she asked uncertainly. She couldn't read the king's mood yet, and he had the habit of flickering from one to the next with little notice.

"Lovely," he said, vaguely.

At first, Meera thought he was referring to her note—that he was pleased by her progress with the prisoner or initiative in suggesting a bargain with him. Then she noticed his heated gaze spreading over her. Her loose hair was curling thick and wild upon her shoulders, caressing the sides of her breasts before tapering off just above her waist. It was pulled back in the front just enough to keep it off her sweaty face, while having the added effect of revealing her mother's pearl and blue earrings, which were dangling from her ears and kissing the sensitive sides of her neck. The king's bold scrutiny seared along her throat, and she swallowed convulsively. She felt his eyes follow her swallow down to her collarbones and spark along the very tops of her breasts, just visible over her summer neckline. She felt as if her chest rose to meet his gaze, and she was certain that the king could see her heart fluttering behind its cell of bones.

Meera would have thought her knowledge of King Bartro's ruthlessness would have dampened her physical reaction to him, but her mind couldn't seem to control the excitement in her body. She regarded him in turn: he reclined in his chair as if at ease, but there was tension in his muscles, and his pulse throbbed in his own neck in the shadow of his jawline. She could sense his attraction to her, and her body responded to it. When he stood slowly from his chair, the movement sent a waft of his cedarwood scent to her, and the smell of him sent a jolt through her core. She wanted him to come around the desk—well, her body wanted him to come around the desk. Her mind didn't.

This was the man who held Shael and Cerun prisoner, she reminded herself—the man who killed the duke for his interest in a map. Meera sought her hatred of the king to smother her physical reaction to him, but to her surprise, she found she didn't hate him. She didn't like how he and his predecessors had used ignorance and propaganda to manipulate their people. She didn't like how he used assassins in lieu of fair trials. She didn't like that he had mocked her on occasion. But she didn't hate him; he was shrewd and observant—he had seen her and respected her in a way that no one else had before. She had fed off of his notice and strived to meet his expectations of her, and she hated that she had. But she didn't hate him.

She was there for a reason, she reminded herself: to redeem herself—to be a hero, not a weapon. The king walked around the desk and reached out, taking one of her curls gently in hand and wrapping it around his finger. "I like your hair like this," he said.

While the king's closeness set her heart racing faster, Meera had never been susceptible to flattery. "Your Majesty, may I ask your thoughts on my note?" she asked, voice shaking slightly.

King Bartro released her ringlet, grinning at her, and Meera was once more reminded of the bear on the king's personal sigil with its mouth agape, ready to catch the leaping fish. Drawing in a deep breath, she hoped she could avoid his powerful jaws. He reached a hand forward again, this time running a finger down the length of her throat, and her flesh tingled at his touch, making her shiver involuntarily despite the heat. She stayed very still like a mouse unsure of whether the fox had seen it yet—only she knew she'd been seen. Seen but not yet caught, she thought, taking a deliberate step back.

The king chuckled; he enjoyed this game of theirs. But when he spoke again, his voice was all business, the slightly husky, teasing tone gone: "So you've used your feminine wiles to get the prisoner to speak at last, Miss Hailship. You really have been useful to me of late. Well done. Tell me, though: what makes you think the prisoner would uphold a bargain? What if we show him his beast, and he still doesn't talk?"

Meera needed to convince the king that the bargain would work, and she knew what might do it—what scrap of information might validate her plan—but it would also expose her ... She didn't need lies to manipulate him when she could use the truth. Anxiety fidgeted in her stomach as she tried very hard to keep her body still. She shifted her weight on her feet but managed to keep her hands and eyes steady.

"Your Majesty, there's something I haven't told anyone for fear of being accused of something ... *unnatural*," she began, remembering the king's own use of the word when referring to magic. His relaxed posture immediately tensed—sharpened. Hoping the king was more susceptible to flattery than she, Meera continued: "But as we have been working together successfully ..." she cringed inwardly at referring to the duke's murder as success, "... and I feel you understand me on a personal level, I trust that you will forgive my former hesitancy to share this with you." She paused and took a deep breath, straining not to pant with the increase in her heart rate, all the while searching King Bartro's face for anger and preparing herself to grovel at any time. Should she drop to her knees? Cry and beg for his forgiveness? The king remained a fine-tuned blade ready for battle, but his steel was not yet directed at her.

Clearing her throat and shifting her weight again, Meera admitted, "The very first time I approached the raek, I made a bargain with him. I spoke to him and promised to feed him, tend his wounds, and never lie to him if, in exchange, he promised not to harm me. While he could not speak his answer, he made himself understood, and we have both upheld our bargain ever since. I trust that a bargain made with the prisoner would be upheld with the same level of honor."

She tried not to hurry through her confession, but her heavily pounding heart made her rush to each pause in her statement to gasp for breath. As she waited through the king's silence, she fretted about her statement and wondered whether she had shared too much. But her truth was her weapon. She knew she could not lie to the king—he would see through her—so she hoped to shield her betrayals behind this small spark of truth; she endeavored to catch the king's eye with the tiniest flame in order to blind him to what lay in the darkness beyond it.

King Bartro studied Meera with so much intensity that she imagined it heating the air in the room. A salty bead of sweat trickled down her throat where the king's finger had only just skimmed. Finally, leaning toward her—his blue-green blaze searing her flesh—the king rasped his fingers in his beard at his jawline and asked, "How exactly did the beast make itself understood? And on what authority do you believe it is male?"

He stood as still as a predator in the grass, watching her and determining whether or not she was prey. He was so close, and Meera couldn't prevent herself from occasionally glancing at his hands, fearing a quick strike. She longed to retreat back and back until she crossed the line in the sand marking the end of the king's reach, but the king's reach extended all through Terratelle; she was stuck within striking distance—unchained but imprisoned, nonetheless.

She stood her ground with a straight back and uplifted chin. "The raek blinked in response to my proffered bargain, Your Majesty, and the prisoner referred to the beast as male," she replied.

The king didn't immediately respond, and his silence gushed around her, filling the room, and threatening to surround and drown her. Meera wanted to keep babbling explanations—to fight the void with the sound of her voice—but she knew that she shouldn't. Don't speak, she willed herself; don't speak. She couldn't yield to his silence; she couldn't confess and plead into it. The king's lips pursed before he finally replied: "I see," he said, "and what else has the raek communicated to you?" His arms hung loosely at his sides, but Meera saw his hand twitch and almost flinched in response.

She took a beat to think before answering; she didn't think *nothing* would satisfy him. "Your Majesty, as he can only blink in response to my questions, the raek has not communicated very much to me. He confirmed that the prisoner was his rider, which I assumed you were well aware of. He also confirmed that raek fire could not melt iron; otherwise, I would not have requested the removal of his muzzle ... Often, he ignores my questions," she added, though that was only true on days when Cerun's spirits were at their lowest. She was telling the truth, she told herself— not the whole truth, but enough. At least, she hoped it would be enough truth to distract the king but not enough to condemn her.

There was another unbearable stretch of silence, filled only with the king's burning contemplation. Meera remained as still as she could, resisting the urge to swallow despite her dry throat. Then, with the smallest sigh of breath, the king's posture relaxed, and he walked back around his desk and sat heavily in his leather chair, tenting his fingers in front of him. "Well, Miss Hailship, I did always suspect that you were keeping something from me ... But you're a clever girl and clearly recognized that this informa-tion was best kept from the people of Terratelle for their own good," he said, raising one eyebrow pointedly.

"You were likely also right that I would have seen your knowl-edge of raeken as a threat to our land." Meera did swallow at that, knowing what the king did to perceived threats. Then she pushed the duke from her mind. "Luckily, you have proven your loyalty and use to me these past weeks and, as always, your discretion," King Bartro concluded.

Meera released the breath she was holding, and her shoulders sagged an inch or two. She was safe—he still trusted her. She hadn't fully realized how close she would come to risking her own neck for the sake of her plan; she hadn't thought it all the way through. She should have known that the king would want every detail, she supposed, studying him at his desk where he sat surrounded by neat stacks of papers covered in the minutia that made up the whole of Terratelle. He was a details man. "Now, to the matter at hand," he continued, once again fingering the note she had left in the urn. "How exactly would you propose we handle *this*?"

Meera tried to swallow again and the dry edges of her mouth and throat rasped together painfully. "Your Majesty, I believe the prisoner trusts me—at least to some extent. I would suggest that on my second visit today, I'll offer him the bargain: he will be reunited with his raek in exchange for information that would help Terratelle's war effort. I believe we should be very specific, though; I suggest we tell him that he would be brought out to see the raek tomorrow morning, that they would be given ten minutes of privacy, and that he would then be sat at a table outside of the dungeon to be asked questions in a civilized manner, to which you would expect full and honest answers."

As she spoke, the king leaned forward in his chair and tented his fingers once more in thought. "What precisely do you mean by privacy, and why do you suggest it?" he asked in a neutral tone. Meera was relieved that he didn't sound suspicious or accusatory.

"I believe, Your Majesty, that in light of the prisoner's lockjaw, he recognizes that he could possibly die soon and wishes to say farewell to his raek. By privacy, I mean only that he be allowed to approach the raek—in manacles, of course—and that all accompanying him stay back a short distance to allow him the facade of privacy. I believe that would go a long way in gaining the prisoner's trust," she explained. She didn't add that she didn't want anyone to get injured when Cerun lunged for his rider to fly him away.

"Hmmm. Well, Miss Hailship, I consent to this plan other than the matter of *privacy*—facade or not. Should the prisoner approach the beast beyond where it is safe for my men, we might not be able to coax him away. I do not wish there to be a spectacle. Guards will walk him to the edge of the beach, and he can say his farewells from there," King Bartro replied.

It had worked, she thought; she had convinced him. She was so shocked, she momentarily forgot to answer. "Yes, Your Majesty," she breathed, holding back a grin of triumph.

"Very well, then. Leave a note if the prisoner refuses the bargain. Otherwise, I will assume that we proceed with this plan," the king said, already finding his next order of business on his desk. Meera curtsied another "Yes, Your Majesty" and was about to go, when he added, "Oh, and Miss Hailship? Should your act of kindness toward the prisoner be unsuccessful, we can always make him watch while we torture his beast. His fondness for the creature will be valuable either way. Also, seeing as your duty with the prisoner is almost complete, report to me the day after tomorrow for your next assignment."

21

———————

As Meera moved through the palace halls toward the kitchen, the words *next assignment* haunted her, echoing against her skull over and over again. She was working toward freeing two prisoners, but who would free her? How would she get out of her role as the king's weapon? She couldn't—she knew too much. She either belonged to the king or was a liability to him. He had forgiven her lie because she was useful to him, but if she stopped being useful ... She shuddered, and a bead of sweat ran down her back.

Even if the king didn't suspect her of freeing the raek, she could never go back to working in the kitchen—she could never go back to her simple, quiet life. She should have been elated that her plan was working, but she felt only a bone-deep dread. Once again, she had made a decision without fully thinking through its implications on her life ... But this wasn't about her life, she reminded herself—freeing Cerun and Shael was about doing the right thing. Still, she couldn't help but wonder what would have happened to the rider, Kallan, had he freed Queen

Thea but not escaped with her … She wasn't ready to die for her beliefs.

By the time Meera made it to the kitchen, she knew she would have to run—to get as far from the palace as she could and try to make a life for herself somewhere new. She hadn't left herself any time to plan or to return to her house one last time, and she started to panic. Her heart and lungs tried to jump ship by means of her throat, and she swallowed them back down as best she could. One move at a time, she told herself, taking a deep breath.

First, she needed to see Shael again and tell him the plan. Then she would wait until the quietest time of night to go to Cerun, and she would hide a bag for herself in the woods behind the butcher's hut. She hoped fleeing through the woods and not the city would buy her time since no one would know she'd left the palace grounds. She repacked her basket to take to Shael, and she forced herself to eat a plate of bread and cheese. But she felt so much like she was consuming her last meal that she could hardly swallow down the lumps of food.

Entering the dungeon, Meera wondered whether she would end up thrown into one of the cells. If Shael got away, would they put her in cell 39? If not, would they be housed close enough to at least provide each other with company? Would the king let Prince Phineas drag her to the torture room? Meera's morose thoughts evaporated the second she reached Shael's cell and saw him lying on his mat, gasping for breath. "Are you alright?" she asked, hurrying to unlock the door and rushing to his side. He was sweating despite the coolness of the dungeon and could barely focus his eyes on her. "Did it happen again?" she asked, already knowing the answer.

Shael nodded shakily, and she held out her hand to help him sit up. He took it, and she heaved him into a seated position, putting the food down next to his legs. "It's happening," she said to reassure him. "I spoke to the king. I'm supposed to be down here making a bargain with you—that you'll answer the king's questions if we take you to see Cerun in the morning. I'm going to go to Cerun tonight to break his chains."

"And what if you and Borteus cannot break his chains?" Shael asked, using his own name for his raek. Cerun had only pledged to retain the name Meera had given him *if* she freed them, after all.

She sighed. "Then the king will expect answers from you, and if you do not give them to him, he will torture Cer—Borteus until you do or until one or both of you dies," she answered, looking him square in the face. There was no point in trying to hide the horrors that would await him if she failed, and she tried not to imagine the horrors that might face her if she succeeded. Shael merely nodded, expressionless, and she couldn't tell if he was masking his emotions or just too exhausted from his fit to express them. After staring into his eyes a beat longer than felt comfortable, she looked away and rose to leave.

When Meera reached her room, she opened her trunk and peered inside, wondering what to pack for her new life. Then she almost laughed at the absurdity of what she was doing. Where would she go? What would she do there? She didn't know how to navigate across the land or take care of herself in the woods. Even so, as terrifying as being helpless and alone in the wild was, the prospect of swinging from the noose in the palace's front court-yard was frightening enough for her to take her chances in the woods.

Quickly, in case Teardra came in, she packed a bag with two dresses and her warmest clothes. Just in case, she decided to keep her money, fountain pen, and mother's earrings in a pouch under her dress, so they couldn't be easily stolen. Touching the bracelet Linus had given her on her left wrist, she left it where it was. Leaving her books behind would break her heart, but Meera didn't think she could carry them far and was more concerned with survival than anything else at the moment. There were also so many things of her mother's and father's that she wished she could take, but she didn't have the time to walk to her house and back.

Staring at her measly bag of belongings, her thoughts spiraled, and she fretted once more about her future: How far should she go? What name would she use? She had some money but would need to find lodgings and work quickly. Who would take her in? How would she ever know if her father returned home? Shaking her head, she decided she would keep herself safe for now, and maybe in a year's time, she could risk returning home to check for her father. She would see him again, she resolved.

Since her hair had fully dried, she tied it up, and the thought of standing near raek fire with her loose curls blowing in the wind motivated her to spend extra time tucking and pinning all of her unruly ringlets. Afterward, she lay down in bed and waited. Not wanting Teardra to see her go to bed fully clothed, she had to lie with a blanket pulled over her despite the suffocating heat in the room. It felt like an eternity passed before Teardra finally came in and went to sleep. Then Meera continued to lie there, unable to sleep and unwilling to think about what her future might look like.

Eventually however, she dozed off, and sometime later she jerked awake with no notion of how long she had slept. It was still dark, and the halls were silent, but for how long? Panicking, she leapt out of bed and grabbed her bag, hurrying to the kitchen. It was 2 in the morning; she still had time. She filled her bag as much as she could with food and water. Then, unhooking the kitchen bellows from its place next to the fire, she dashed into the night to stash her bag behind the butcher's hut.

The butcher, thankfully, was nowhere to be seen or heard—presumably asleep inside—and Meera tucked her bag in a tree branch, hoping it would be safe until the next day. She planned to return her cart after feeding Cerun and go straight into the woods. From the butcher's hut, she hurried through the gardens and down the hill with the bellows, tripping on the long grass and her own feet in her haste. When she approached the beach, Cerun's head whipped around, and he emitted a low warning rumble in his chest. Then he either saw or scented that it was her and relaxed. Meera crossed over the claw marks in the sand without hesitation and gave his neck a shaky hug that was more for herself than it was for him. "It's time," she said. "Are you ready?"

He blinked, his large blue eye reflecting the near-full moon.

Looking around to decide where and how to get started, Meera reached down and grabbed the large, heavy chain attached to the raek's right forefoot. Finding the enormous chain too heavy for her to lift, she bent over and dragged it toward the water somewhat. Then she had Cerun position himself facing the water, hoping that the bulk of his body would block most of the light emitted by his fire. She didn't think they would be visible from the palace, but they would be from the edges of the garden if any guards were station overlooking the canal.

Cerun spread his great feathered wings as a shield, and Meera stood behind his head, crouching low with the bellows pointed at the chain. It was a small bellows, but she hoped it would be enough. "Okay" she said uncertainly, and Cerun opened his scaly jaws wide, producing a torrent of swirling cerulean blue fire, roughly spherical in shape.

Meera was blinded by the unnaturally bright fire in the darkness, and she blinked and blinked, desperate to clear her eyes. Squinting into the blue light, she noticed, as before, how the fireball was not one mass of fire stemming from the raek's jaws; rather, it appeared to be many small swirling fires igniting spontaneously in the air. Unlike a normal fire that consumed wood or coal, the raek fire didn't seem to need fuel, and the flames swirled in spirals rather than rising into pointed tips. She could only hope the bellows would help heat the strange flames, and she positioned it as close as she could to the inferno without singeing the device, pumping it furiously to blow air where the raek fire engulfed the chain. She could see the swirls of fire grow larger as a result of her efforts and willed them to grow hot enough to melt iron as well.

The heat emanating from Cerun's fire was intense and nearly debilitating. Meera was sweating and breathing hard, but she couldn't seem to get enough air. She was sucking in the stifling air that the fire had already chewed up and disgorged, and she quickly grew light-headed. It wasn't long before her arms ached from the effort as well, and the cut on her palm stung painfully, slick with either blood or sweat—she couldn't tell in the light of the flames; everything glowed an eerie blue. After a while, she shut her eyes against the harsh light and aimed her bellows blindly. Cerun could evidently maintain his fire for a long time, but while Meera tried to match him, she grew increasingly faint and slowed drastically. "Stop!" she finally gasped.

Cerun stopped immediately at her call, plunging the beach into total darkness and leaving Meera with the spirit of the blue flames burned into her gaze. She tried to check the chain but couldn't see anything—not even the enormous blue raek next to her. "Did it work?" she asked Cerun dumbly, forgetting that he couldn't speak and that she couldn't see his eyes. The ground shook as the raek backed away. Then she heard the whip of the chain as he yanked it hard, as well as the resounding ringing when the taught chain held together. Cerun tried several more times to pull the weakened chain links apart, but the iron held. Meera still couldn't see anything and grew frustrated with her blindness and her failure. Tears stung her bleary eyes; she had given it all her strength, and it hadn't worked.

She walked toward the canal to get a drink of water and to splash her hot, throbbing face, but she didn't realize Cerun still held the chain taught. Hitting the chain at hip height, she bounced off of it, barely managing to keep her feet under her. She felt the searing heat of the chain through her dress and patted at her hips and abdomen surreptitiously, but she didn't think she was burned. Cerun nuzzled her arm in apology and to let her know she could get by.

Meera patted his head and went to the canal, practically dunking her head in the cool water and splashing it all over herself. Cupping her hands, she drank greedily, and the cool, crisp water soothed her. With a calmer mind, she realized that when she had hit the chain and felt its heat, she had been far from where Cerun had focused his fire. Heat traveled through metal— she knew that sure enough from working in the kitchen and getting several burns on her hands early on. She hoped Cerun's ankle hadn't been burned by their effort, then she wondered whether the heat was dispersing as it traveled through the long chain, rather than staying directed at a single area.

As she stood and thought, her vision started to clear, and she could see a blurry outline of the chain, glowing yellow where they had focused their efforts before fading into orange then red further out, confirming her suspicions about the heat disseminating through the chain. They didn't need to melt the whole thing, she thought; they only needed to weaken a single link enough to break it. How could they concentrate the heat to one area? What might prevent it from spreading? Meera swiveled her head as if she was looking around and taking inventory of their space even though she couldn't see anything other than the chain's faint glow. Still, she was familiar enough with the beach that she didn't have to see it; all they had to work with was sand and water—and water wouldn't help.

Telling Cerun her plan in the process, she directed him to align both of the chains on his right side together. Knowing how much effort this would take, she would rather break two chains with one try. Then she had him scratch sand over them, leaving a small sliver in the middle exposed. She hoped the sand would get in between the linked pieces of iron and slow the spread of heat down the chain. Meera was careful to stay clear of the glowing iron while she waited for Cerun to work sand around each chain link with the tips of his claws, and when Cerun rumbled that he was finished, she took a deep breath and positioned herself by his head once more, bellows at the ready. This time, she shut her eyes tight preemptively, knowing that the harsh light of the flames would still penetrate her eyelids. Mustering her reserves of strength and determination, she called "Now!" and they both got to work.

Meera pumped and pumped, her arms trembling from effort and heat. She labored for what felt like an eternity but was probably only a few minutes, and just when she swayed on her feet and thought she might faint, Cerun threw his weight away from the wall, snapping the chains taught while they were still as hot as possible. Meera fell back in surprise and curled in on herself to avoid being hit by anything. She still couldn't see, but she could sense Cerun's position and heard the clang as he pulled the chain tight, and the links held. For a brief, horrible moment, she despaired, thinking it hadn't worked. Then she heard Cerun fall sideways and felt the ends of the heavy chains thud to the ground. The hot, softened chain links had given way!

Cerun righted himself quickly and buffeted his wings in a triumphant but silent cheer, and Meera laughed and pumped her tired arms in the air with him. They had done it! Two chains broken and two to go. They took a break, each drinking their fill of water before moving on to the second side. Knowing they were almost done was the only thing that kept Meera from throwing the bellows to the ground and herself down next to it; she was exhausted. The muscles of her arms burned and shook, the cut on her hand stung aggressively, and the persistent heat of the flames had left her feeling sick. Her head ached and throbbed, and her stomach was nauseous. But she took a deep breath and positioned herself on Cerun's other side, bellows at the ready.

After another mighty effort from them both, Cerun threw his weight against his chains and broke the softened links on his left side, freeing himself fully except for the bits of heavy iron chain dangling from his manacles. Meera assumed he would still be able to fly with the extra weight, and she could practically feel his longing to do so vibrating through his body. She trembled as well but with exhaustion; she was completely and utterly spent. Wading blindly into the canal, she submerged herself under the cool water. She didn't care about her hair and dress getting soaked through—all she cared about was cooling off. She felt like her brain had been baked.

After spending several minutes in the canal, she began to feel better and started to shiver, so she waded back out. Wringing out the heavy skirt of her dress, she pulled the pins from her sodden hair to wring that out as well. Then she sat on the beach facing the water, pulled off her boots to press the water from her socks, and waited for her vision to clear. As she sat, her excitement quickly waned, and the weight of anticipation and fear settled over her once more; she had no idea what the next day might bring.

Meera felt Cerun come up next to her. "We did it," she said, groping for him in the dark to scratch his neck. The feel of her wet hands on his dusty feathers was unpleasant, so she only patted him briefly. "I'm going to miss you, my friend," she added, feeling a lump rising in her throat. She would be completely alone now—parentless, friendless, homeless, even—but at least Cerun would be safe and happy.

When her sight finally returned, she peeled herself from the ground, now covered in a fine layer of sand. "Let's make it look normal," she said to Cerun. The raek grudgingly moved back into his usual position, and Meera searched for the severed chain ends on the ground. Finding them hot but not too hot to touch, she dragged the chains together and carefully hooked the broken, deformed links back onto their iron brethren. "Try not to move too much, so they don't come undone," she warned Cerun.

He blinked and rumbled. Then he leaned his snout into her abdomen, which she took as a thank you.

"I hope you make it home and live a long and happy life," she told him, stroking his forehead. Selfishly, she wished that he could offer her some words of comfort as well—she could use them.

Suddenly, Meera felt a pressure in her head. It felt like hanging upside down from her bed as a kid only more intense. Then, inside her mind, she sensed the touch of something unfamiliar, and she heard—without really hearing—a clear, resonant voice say, "Human Meera, I thank you for your kindness and bravery. You have the heart of a raek. Fly free and live well." The disembodied voice was strangely even in tone and rang with an almost harsh clarity. She shuddered as the presence—as Cerun— left her mind.

He *could* speak, she thought. At first, she was giddy with the realization and grinned into his moon-filled eyes, but when she stepped away and turned to trudge up the hill, her giddiness soured with the bitter realization that Cerun could have spoken to her that whole time and had chosen not to. Their friendship had been this pure thing in her mind—felt and reciprocated equally by each of them—but the fact that he could have been communicating with her and hadn't proved that it wasn't. The realization stung her throat, though she supposed their friendship could never have been equal, considering Cerun was a captive and she his caretaker.

Morosely, Meera wondered whether she would ever find a true friend in the world. Her mind strayed to Linus, but she always felt that Linus loved the idea of her more than who she really was. She suspected his crush on her was shallow—childish. She never felt like he really saw her—or at least understood who she was and how she viewed the world. Maybe he did; maybe she was underestimating him ... But there had been a growing chasm between them for so long, and she couldn't seem to close it. They disagreed about so many things—too many, probably.

With a sigh, she wondered what she would say to Linus the next morning, but she quickly pushed the thought away as it churned up all of her grief and fear about leaving. When she got back to her hallway, she shucked her wet dress and slip and put them down the laundry chute so Teardra wouldn't see them. Then she crept quietly into their shared room and lay down on her bed, so exhausted that she went right to sleep. Her wet hair splayed across her lavender-scented pillow and dried while she slept, leaving no trace of her nighttime excursion.

22

____

The morning bell startled Meera awake too soon after she fell asleep, but she wasn't groggy; she knew exactly what day it was and what lay in store for her. Teardra was the first out of bed, so Meera stayed still and waited for her roommate to dress and go. Just when Teardra was reaching for the door, however; it occurred to her that she might never see the woman again. "Have a nice day," she called, *and a nice life*, she thought. Teardra turned in surprise, stared at her for a moment, and then ... smiled, before brusquely turning to go. The small gesture shocked Meera, who thought maybe she should have tried harder to connect to her dour roommate.

Getting out of bed, she opened her chest to find that in her haste to pack the day before, she had packed all of her practical-colored dresses, and what remained staring up at her was her lilac dress. It wasn't ideal, but it felt almost fitting since she had already worn it on two especially pivotal days: the day the king had recruited her as his *weapon* and the day she had tailed the duke into Altus. She supposed both days had brought more complications to her life—not to mention resulted in the duke's death—but the dress wasn't bad luck; it was just a dress, right?

First, she tied a small pouch containing her money, the king's pen, and her mother's earrings around her waist for safekeeping. Then she donned her purple dress. She was still wearing Linus's bracelet from the Solstice and was glad that she would always have a token to remember her friend. Once she pinned up her hair, Meera crossed for the door, but she hesitated, retrieved her ornate little mirror, and left it on Teardra's side table as a gift for her.

In the kitchen, Cook busily laid out breakfast for the staff. Meera ate as much as she comfortably could, knowing she might have a long, arduous day of travel ahead of her. And while she ate, she watched Cook, admiring their competent grace and kind authority. She would miss Cook and tried to think of some way of saying goodbye without really saying goodbye, but she couldn't think of anything. Cook, of all people, would see right through her and know that something was wrong. Meera couldn't take any risks that day, so instead of saying goodbye or anything especially profound, she took a proffered pastry from a pan Cook held out to her and said, "Cook, you really do make the best food."

Cook snorted and yelled "Off with ye, you panderer! You're not gettin' anymore!" No, she wasn't, she thought sadly before going outside.

Waiting for Linus, she bit back her tears; she hated goodbyes, and this day was stacking up to be just as difficult as the day her father had left for the army. He had packed himself a bag the night before—which Meera had repacked, removing several books and adding in more socks and packages of nuts and dried fruit. She had cried the whole week in anticipation of him leaving, but he had remained stoic for her. It hadn't been until he was standing at the door ready to go that tears had spilled down his cheeks. Then he had held her for a long time before letting go and saying, "I'll do my best to come back, but if I don't, know that you have been my greatest joy and accomplishment."

Meera had sobbed and shaken her head saying *no* over and over again. She hadn't even managed to say *goodbye* or *be safe* or *I love you*. Her mind had just screamed *no!* and nothing else had seemed to make sense. Afterward, she had felt ashamed of herself —for not saying something more meaningful, for not doing her part to comfort her father when he was the one going unprepared into war. Now, as she sat on her bench, she thought that if she was to be his greatest accomplishment, then she had to be a hero— had to do good in the world.

Linus arrived looking sheepish after their fight the other day, and for a time, they walked side-by-side without speaking. But Meera couldn't stand it; this was it—their last walk to the canal together. She didn't know what to say, but she had to say something. "Linus, you were right that I have been out late doing things … but I wasn't seeing a man," she started, taking a deep breath. "I was doing something for the king … spying for him."

Linus was so shocked that his mouth actually dropped open. Meera would have laughed on any other day. He tried to speak, but she interrupted him: "Please, let me finish. I didn't tell you to keep you safe, and I still won't tell you any details for the same reason. But you should know that I don't want to do it anymore, and the only way I see out is to leave. After we feed Cerun, I'm going to leave the palace and make a life for myself somewhere else."

Linus stopped in his tracks, and she turned to look him full in the face. She saw several emotions play out in his features while he processed what she had said, but then he frowned and seemed to land on confusion. "But why, Meera? Why won't the king let you stop spying if you don't want to do it anymore? Can't you just work in the kitchens again?" he asked. He looked like a child with big button eyes asking why every day couldn't be a holiday.

"Linus, if I'm not being valuable to him anymore, then he'll ... see me as a liability. I know too much—Just trust me; the king won't let me stop, so I have to leave," she replied, knowing he still probably wouldn't understand the danger she would be in for even suggesting to the king that she go back to working in the kitchen. She did; she knew King Bartro.

"You could stay with my parents," he suggested hopefully. "I'm really sorry about what I said the other day—really—and I've told my parents all about you, and I'm sure they'd love to have you—"

Meera cut him off. She couldn't bear to hear the lovely picture of an impossible life he would describe to her. "Linus! I have to run away where the king won't find me. I won't put you or your family in danger. If anyone asks you about me, just play dumb, okay? Keep yourself safe," she pleaded. She wondered if she should have just left without saying anything, but it was too late; she had already said something. Starting to walk again, she added, "We need to feed the raek. The king is bringing the prisoner out to see him today—they made a deal—and I'd rather we feed him and leave before that happens." She didn't add that she had orchestrated the whole thing—she tried to sound neutral, so Linus wouldn't suspect her involvement and blow her plan.

He put his head down and kept moving. If he was surprised to hear about the king's bargain with the prisoner, he didn't show it. Meera couldn't tell if he was thinking, sulking, or both, and she kept pace with him, not knowing what to say—how to transition to a more heartfelt goodbye from where they had left off. Then they reached the canal, and she wheeled the cart all the way to Cerun, knowing he couldn't move without risking undoing his chains. Peering around, she thought they all still looked intact. So far, everything was going well, but that didn't stop Meera's heart from beating against her ribs, trying to flee the scene before it could unfold.

Walking the cart back to Linus, she turned to watch the gruesome spectacle of Cerun ripping into the deer carcass she had given him with his sharp teeth and powerful jaws. It took him only a minute or two to devour his meal, then he picked his teeth with a claw. She knew he would normally drink after eating, but —again—he couldn't risk moving. Her task accomplished, she turned to Linus. He wasn't looking at her, but she could see the grief and conflict etched across his face. His forehead creased, and she imagined those creases would one day be permanent. Then she sighed because she wouldn't be there to find out if they ever would.

Stepping forward, Meera threw her arms around Linus's neck and clutched him to her. For two beats of her heart against his, she wasn't sure he would hold her back, but he did—his arms wrapped around her back and pressed her even more tightly into him. Neither of them seemed to find the right words, so they just held each other and swayed slightly. Meera was about to speak, but Linus stiffened and pulled away. When she searched his face, she found he wasn't looking at her but was gazing over her shoulder toward the hill. Without even looking, dread filled her stomach; Shael was coming out, and she shouldn't be there. She should have left already—she should be in the forest behind the butcher's hut, grabbing her bag and running for her life. She hadn't considered this possibility ...

Turning to stare up the hill, she watched as the king, the captain, two guards, and Shael approached the beach. Shael's wrists were in manacles, but his ankles were not, she was relieved to see. Hopefully, he would be able to ride Cerun with his wrists bound and get help removing the manacles in Aegorn. For the first time, Meera wondered how long it would take them to fly to Aegorn—she had never thought to ask. Then she shifted from foot to foot and contemplated walking up the hill and trying to casually pass the king and his prisoner—to flee. But how could she do that without raising suspicion? She had no other job to get to ... the prisoner was right there.

Uncertainly, she just stood and stared while the party approached; the king and the captain walked in front with Shael behind them, flanked by guards on either side. There must have been another key to his cell, she realized suddenly. Her key to cell 39 was still in her small bag in her room. The king had never asked for it, and she hadn't had the foresight to offer it to him. The amount of details and possibilities Meera had overlooked was beginning to pile up, and she started to sweat—though the sky was cloudy, and the day hadn't heated up yet. What else had she missed? What should she do? She would have to stay, she thought; she would have to stay and hope to be forgotten in the ensuing confusion—to slip away after they escaped.

She wanted Linus to leave—to be safe from whatever might happen next—but he remained where he was, all of his attention on the king. When the procession neared, Meera curtsied, Linus bowed, and King Bartro nodded to them in return, briefly searing Meera with his fiery gaze before turning to motion the guards forward with Shael. Shael was squinting considerably despite the low light of the morning, and he kept his head bowed, eyes on the ground. His feet were still bare and bandaged around the middles, and Meera cursed herself for continually forgetting to bring him socks and for failing to find him shoes for that moment. She reassured herself that he wouldn't need shoes for flying.

Despite the two months he had spent in a cell, Shael cut a fine figure compared to the guards on either side of him. He was thin, but he still retained lean muscle all over his body. His scars and mutilations weren't visible under his clothes, and his dark hair was tied back and shone glossy in the outside light. Meera had never remembered to ask him why his face remained smooth and beardless after all that time or whether he was human or knell. There were so many things she wished she had asked him ... But at least she had done this much—at least he would soon be free.

As the guards propelled Shael toward the claw marks in the dirt, he hunched and dragged his feet, appearing much weaker than she knew him to be. Each guard had a lazy hand on one of his upper arms, presuming him to be feeble and defenseless, and Meera stared at Shael's limp arms, waiting for them to come to life —waiting for him to find his moment. Cerun hadn't moved from his position in the center of the beach, and he watched the men approach him with a sharp predator's eye, head raised. Even though he remained perfectly still, Meera kept glancing at his chains, wondering if they had come undone. They hadn't. Everything was going according to her plan—except there she was, watching.

King Bartro and the captain of the guard positioned themselves slightly behind and to the left of Shael to observe the proceedings. Then the king turned, beckoning Meera close to him with a graceful wave of his hand. She obeyed. She tried to act normal as she walked to him, but the harder she tried, the more stiff and unnatural her legs felt under her. The king didn't seem to notice. Standing near enough to him to smell his cedarwood scent, Meera clenched her fists in anxiety, wishing she was already far away from there. A part of her wanted to see Cerun fly free, but mostly, she fought the urge to run—to flee to safety and never look back. Her legs shook, and her heart flapped against the metal chains in her chest. Then, in unison, everyone faced the raek as if ready for a performance ... And a performance they would get, she thought.

"Well, Miss Hailship," King Bartro whispered, his mouth against her ear. "It's the moment of truth."

23

T*he moment of truth?* Meera assumed King Bartro meant it was the moment they would find out whether the prisoner would uphold his bargain. Then again, she could never quite tell what the king meant when he was being vague. Fiddling with the fabric of her lilac dress, she hoped he didn't suspect her. He couldn't; if he did, wouldn't he have called everything off? Or brought more guards—soldiers even? The king didn't wait for her to respond to his statement, calling to his prisoner: "Go ahead, say your piece!"

Meera's attention snapped to Shael, who stood slightly stooped with his head down. If she didn't know better, she would think he looked defeated and resigned to his fate. The guards seemed to think so, only holding him loosely by his arms. For a long moment, Shael stood motionless. Meera tried desperately to stand half as motionless, her arms and legs longing to squirm in time with her churning insides. Then, in one fluid movement, Shael swept out his left leg, caught the left-side guard behind his knees, tore his left arm from the man's grip, and drove both of his fists together into the right-side guard's head.

Both guards lost their balance—teetering comically as they tried to right themselves—and without pause or hesitation, Shael ran for Cerun. The raek extended his wings, emitted a shrieking roar, and shook his legs to undo his loosely hooked chains. The captain and king both shouted orders as they realized what was happening, but the guards scrambled away from the raek in fear instead of rushing toward their prisoner. Meera felt the king shift in agitation next to her, but her eyes were riveted on Shael, who— with more grace than she would have thought possible— launched himself onto Cerun's back, using the raek's knee as a stepping off point.

Movements limited by his bound wrists, Shael landed on his stomach but quickly maneuvered into a straddle with his legs on either side of Cerun's neck. They were free, she thought triumphantly. They just needed to leap into the air and disappear into the distance. There were no soldiers or archers to force them back to the ground once they took off—the two guards present had their swords drawn but were too afraid to cross onto the beach and stood looking uncertain. The captain attempted to rally and instruct his men but to little effect, and Meera glowed, confident that Cerun would successfully depart at any second. Goodbye, she thought.

Now it was her turn to flee. On shaky legs, she backed two steps away from the king, readying herself to run, but she hesitated; she wanted to see Cerun fly away—she wanted to see her friend soar free at last. Cerun launched from the ground and beat his wings into a hover just as the king turned and clasped a hand around Meera's throat, shouting, "You!" in her face. She was caught! A deadly inferno raged in the king's eyes a moment before they were both whipped with sand from Cerun's flapping. Meera squinted against the barrage, groping uselessly at the king's iron grip. She couldn't breathe, and panic roused her limbs into action —scratching like an animal and kicking out at random, she struggled to free herself.

The king only squeezed harder, cutting off her breath completely. Her chest exploded with need, and her movements became more desperate but just as futile. A resounding thump announced Cerun's return to the ground, and his chains rattled as he lunged for the king. Meera could barely register what was happening in her panic, but at the edge of her vision, she saw Cerun's mouth gape, and his unnaturally bright flames swirl closer. The king saw too.

With a sweep of his outstretched arm, he vaulted Meera by the neck into the fire's path, released her, and ducked. Meera barely stumbled before Cerun's blue flames were upon her. She opened her mouth to scream but didn't have any breath with which to make a sound as the fire engulfed her right shoulder, upper arm, chest, and neck. It burned only for a second against her flesh before Cerun retracted the flames and withdrew. But that second was a slap of raw pain. It was there, and then gone—except around the edges, where it continued to devour her, sinking unrelenting teeth into every nerve it could reach.

Meera fell to the ground on her left side, rolling onto her back. She gasped for breath—the need in her lungs taking precedence over her burns. Arms and legs strewn around her, she sucked and sucked in air until she finally satiated her hollow chest. Then there was only pain. Agony bit and tore her flesh where the flames had licked her. Moaning piteously, she tried to lift her head to inspect herself, but she couldn't move. She couldn't look at her burn to see how bad it was, but it felt bad— debilitatingly, dangerously bad—except for her shoulder, which was a puzzling void of nothingness. She lay completely still, immobilized by fear and pain—a captive in her weak and searing body.

Staring up from her prone position, she could just see the edge of Cerun's hulking shape; he had moved around her, still intent on smiting the king with his blue blaze. Whimpering from the pain it caused her neck, Meera managed to jerk her head to the side and watched helplessly as the scene progressed. Cerun's bulk blocked out the sun as he moved above her toward his target. King Bartro was on his feet, facing his attacker but backing swiftly away, when Cerun lunged again. He almost had his prey in his jaws, but Linus—from outside of Meera's vision—flung his body before the king, left arm raised but shieldless.

The blue flames swelled in Cerun's throat, and Meera screamed but couldn't hear herself over the raek's war-cry. Cerun's sphere of fire swallowed Linus's arm and side, blue flames reflecting horribly off the wide whites of his eyes. Cerun retracted his neck and raised a large, clawed foot, bearing an iron manacle with a dangling length of heavy chain. He was about to swipe the life from Linus as he had done to his older brother only months before, his teeth bared in a demented battle grin. But he hesitated —stopped.

For a moment, Cerun stood perfectly still with his foot raised to kill. Linus remained standing protectively in front of the king, miraculously holding himself upright despite the deep red of his charred skin from his left cheek down his left arm and side. The black scraps of his guard uniform hung off of his torso, and his skinny adolescent frame barely blocked the king's more developed body from view. Swaying ever so slightly like a blade of grass on a mild day, he refused to move, and Cerun lowered his foot, choosing to spare him. The raek started to dodge around Linus for the king, but the captain had rallied his two guards; they rushed at the raek from the side, swords drawn. With a screech of frustration, Cerun backed away, retreating toward Meera.

Meera was observing the scene before her while laboriously attempting to stand. Mustering her strength, she had pushed herself to a seated position. Gasping from pain and exertion, she got her feet under her and tried to stand, to get to Linus—to help. She fell to her knees once, then again, but she eventually thrust herself upright. Then she stood precariously and uncertainly, her stomach roiling in objection. But what could she do? She had already failed to protect Linus, and it was too late for her to run. She stood, blinking—her mind as dusty as the air around her and her dirt-lined mouth. She felt simultaneously acutely aware that she needed to do something, as well as like she was floating outside herself and couldn't reattach to her body. Her burns seared in never-ending agony—drawing her attention again and again to her injury—but she couldn't bring herself to look.

Cerun backed away from the guards and crouched in front of her, bunching his legs under him and preparing to leap into the sky. In her daze, Meera noticed Shael looking down at her. He was frowning, his dark brows drawn together, and she found herself thinking that he looked like an avenging angel atop Cerun's back. In a flash of decision, Shael's brows unfurrowed, and he leaned down toward her, extending his manacled hands. Meera stared at them, registering that he offered her a way to run—to leave—but she couldn't leave, could she? The image of Linus's burns flashed in her mind. She started to turn her head to search for her friend, but Shael yelled, "Now!" forcing her attention back to him. Weakly, she reached up for him, and he engulfed her left hand in both of his.

Before she could even attempt an awkward scramble up Cerun's back, the raek pushed off from the ground and flapped his great, feathered wings, moving them skyward. She dangled from

Shael's grip, and his strength kept her from falling as she hung and swayed precariously, dizzy with pain. Cerun's wing brushed against her with every beat, threatening to toss her to the ground —which she couldn't see but was rapidly receding beneath them. When they steadied and soared through the clouds, Shael heaved her over Cerun's neck in front of him.

Belly-down and limp, she lay still, unable to do anything but shake—her face pressed into the smooth feathers of Cerun's shoulder. Her right arm, shoulder, and neck were a terrifying combination of scorching pain on the edges and befuddling lack of sensation in the middle. Meera had no idea how badly she was burned, but she was too exhausted to move, let alone do anything about her injury. Bowed over Cerun's neck, blood pooled in her head, and she let the darkness take her.

WHEN MEERA CAME TO, it was the pain she noticed before the voice. She wanted to flee from the overwhelming agony—to cower behind unconsciousness rather than feel it—but Shael kept saying her name, kept pulling her back to the world: "Meera?" It sounded strange in his accent; he had never spoken her name before. She cracked open her eyes and tried to move her head, but it felt oddly heavy. Then she remembered that she had been thrown over Cerun's neck and was still partially upside down. Turning her face, she found Shael standing on the ground next to Cerun looking up at her. "I am going to pull you down," he said, and without waiting for an answer, he used his manacled hands to grab her under her arms and drag her off the raek's neck.

Falling awkwardly into Shael's chest before her feet hit the ground, Meera's burns chafed against his shirt, and she let out a strangled scream of pain. The sound would have embarrassed her had she been of sound mind, but her awareness was limited to her agony and confusion. Her legs buckled under her weight, and Shael lowered her to a seated position against Cerun's foreleg. Even seated, her dizziness threatened to spill her over, and Shael had to catch her and prop her up once, then again. As the blood in her head drained, she slowly regained her senses and looked around, seeing only greenery without distinguishing characteristics. "Where are we?" she rasped, looking to Shael for answers. Blearily, she registered that his eyes appeared more green than grey in their current surroundings.

"We have stopped at a stream to drink and rest," he replied, but he wasn't looking back at her face; his green eyes were directed at her shoulder. Meera couldn't quite read his expression, but she didn't think he looked concerned—which might have been reassuring, except that he probably didn't care enough about her to feel concerned.

Drawing in a shaky breath, she ducked her chin to finally look down at her injured shoulder, causing the burns on her neck to scream from the movement. She stared and stared, barely comprehending what she was looking at: from halfway down her upper arm to what she could see of her chest was a patchwork of dark leathery red, wet-looking brighter red, and areas of yellowish white. There was one especially white spot at the edge of her shoulder, which she focused on for several moments before registering: it was bone. A piece of her shoulder bone was exposed through the melted mess of her flesh. Meera leaned to the side and heaved, puking the contents of her stomach onto the ground next to her. Then she shook and started to sweat.

Whimpering, she swallowed down the foul taste in her mouth and forced herself to dip her chin and look again. Once more she stared at her wrecked body and tried to reconcile what she saw with how she felt. She couldn't believe how damaged she was; it was too much for her to process. Her skin and the flesh underneath were so decimated that she couldn't feel most of it. Her pain stemmed from the outer edges of the burn, which were less intensely injured but still a bright, blistering red. On her second look, she saw that her singed lilac dress hung open, revealing most of her right breast, but she didn't especially care; that was the least of her concerns.

Shael stooped next to her, cupping a large leaf filled with water in his hands. He brought it to her lips and tried to help her drink, but she mostly spilled it down herself. Undeterred, he carried the leaf to the stream and back several more times until she had consumed a small quantity of water. Meera felt hot and cold at the same time and almost regurgitated the water she had just swallowed down.

Her pain was almost all-consuming—almost. Fear crept up on her, then the bone-deep terror of knowing she would almost certainly die. Even if they reached Aegorn—reached help—she probably wouldn't survive her wound. She imagined she could already feel her body faltering ... She had considered the possibility of her death before—at the hands of the king, at the hands of the prince, at the end of a rope, swinging for treason. She had considered—like all people do—that they would one day die, but considering something and being confronted by it were not the same. Not now, she thought pitifully; she couldn't die *now*. Clutching at Cerun's clawed foot beside her for support, a single tear leaked from one of her bloodshot eyes, but she held the rest in. She had to keep it together because she was afraid—she was afraid to die, and she was afraid that if she made herself any more trouble, Shael might decide to just leave her behind.

Meera had absolutely no idea what the strange, possibly knell, man thought of her. She had cared for him as best she could—for Cerun's sake—and because she would probably help just about anyone who was injured and needed assistance. He, in turn, had tolerated her and spoken to her once he had realized she was trustworthy and might actually help him—well, after he had accused her of poisoning him. Shael was still a stranger, and as much as Meera had liked believing she and Cerun to be friends, Cerun was also a stranger; he had kept his voice from her and may have just been tolerating her as well. Cerun had been the one to burn her, after all. Meera believed that had been an accident, but she still didn't know whether he truly cared for her or not. With a shuddery exhale, she removed her hand from the raek's foot. She was going to have to take care of herself if she wanted to live.

Biting her lip through the pain, she rocked forward onto her hands and knees and slowly forced her wobbling legs under her. Standing, her head spun and vision grew spotted, but she stayed upright. Oddly, despite the cacophony of pain overwhelming her senses, Meera was still acutely aware of sweat dripping down her back—she was already growing sick and feverish from her injury, she realized in a flash of fear. What if she got worse? Who would take care of her? Doing her best to swallow her fear, she felt how dry her throat was. She needed more water, but the thought of getting it herself was daunting.

Glancing toward the stream, she found Shael watching her. He had been trying unsuccessfully to pick open his manacles with a stick or smash them open with rocks. Meera returned his gaze as steadily as she could, attempting to appear strong and capable even though she was anything but. Then she turned her attention to the stream—to the nourishment that would hopefully prevent her ravaged body from failing. On legs like a newborn fawn's, she staggered toward the stream one step at a time until her boots squelched into the muddy water's edge. Looking down, her head rushed and vision blurred, and she collapsed onto her knees.

Cold water soaked her thin, summer dress and creeped into her boots.

She tried to cup her hands and lean forward to drink but repeatedly fell to one side or the other, unable to balance on her knees. Finally, she planted both of her hands in the squishy silt of the bank and bent all the way forward to drink like a forest creature. Tears slid down her cheeks into the water, and she hoped Shael wouldn't notice them. After drinking her fill, she crawled away from the stream until she reached firm ground, caking herself with mud and ripping her dress open further until only the tatters of her slip underneath covered her right breast. When she finally struggled to her feet again, she looked at Shael, opened her mouth—then quickly shut it, fighting down the nausea that threatened to undo all of her hard work. Once she regained equilibrium in her stomach, she looked at him again and said, "I'm ready when you are."

His dark brows were furrowed in his usual inscrutable look. "Then we will go," he replied, and Meera sighed a breath of relief; he would take her with him. She didn't know where they were going or whether she would survive regardless, but at least she wouldn't be left behind—at least she wouldn't die alone.

Between Shael's manacles and her injuries, getting onto Cerun's back was a tedious affair. Eventually, Shael pushed her up by her backside and held her steady while he clambered up behind her. Then he looped his arms over her body. When his shirt brushed against her burns, she whimpered involuntarily. Shael held on to Cerun's neck feathers in front of her, his arms steadying her on either side of her waist, and Meera did her best to sit straight and still. Clasping her hands together in her lap, she squeezed them tightly to distract herself from her pain and fear. She was already wet and chilled, and she shivered, dreading the flight to come.

Cerun took a long drink from the stream before launching himself up and over the trees. His dangling chains snagged and ripped at branches as they lurched upward, and the force of the departure shoved Meera back into Shael—her weak muscles helpless against the pressure of their trajectory. Her stomach leapt into her throat, and she clamped her mouth shut in an effort not to vomit. When Cerun evened out in the sky, she thought to pull away from Shael, but she didn't have the strength; she merely allowed her head to loll back against his chest. She was vaguely aware of the sense of flying being like running down a hill on a windy day, but she was too disoriented to pay much attention to her surroundings and kept her eyes screwed shut against the harsh sunlight of midday. The wind buffeted her face and chilled skin, and she huddled closer to the man behind her. Shael's warmth and steady support were her only comforts.

24

———————

Meera fell in and out of consciousness as they flew, unaware of how much time passed. Once it was dark, they stopped briefly to relieve themselves, and Shael had to rouse her and carry her off of Cerun's back. Every part of her body ached, and her burns screamed with each movement. Unable to see, she simply crouched where Shael dropped her, deciding her dress was privacy enough. However, she barely managed a trickle of urine, having sweated out all of her water. Meera knew she was in rough shape and wasn't sure how much longer she could bear another cold, turbulent flight, but there was no alternative.

Shael pushed her back into position on Cerun's back and resumed his place behind her, and she sagged against him, shaking. When Cerun leapt into the air, she moaned and clawed at her own forearms, in so much pain she couldn't think. She retched, but her stomach was empty. Breathing felt like an immense effort. Meera hoped to fall asleep or slip back into unconsciousness—even death might be a relief. For a time, she huddled and shivered, staring wide-eyed into the blackness around her, but eventually, her eyes drifted shut.

When she next awoke, it was from being squeezed and jerked backwards. Her eyes flew opened to daylight and blue skies stretched out all around her, but she didn't have a chance to be unnerved by how high up they were—Shael's arms pulled his manacle chain taught against her middle, digging it into her ribs. Meera blinked to find that his hands were splayed grotesquely, and she felt him arching and convulsing behind her. Groggily, she realized he was having a fit and knew that his whole body was tensing, including his neck and face, making it difficult for him to breathe. Straining her ears over the wind, she heard him gasping for air. Then he jerked again and unbalanced them both. Meera felt herself slide to the side and scrambled desperately to grab some of Cerun's neck feathers, clinging to them with all of her diminished strength. Shael was like an iron anchor tied around her waist and pulling her overboard.

Just when she started to lose her grip and looked down to see that the ground was merely a pale green swath through many layers of cloud, Cerun nose-dived, causing her to lift from his back. She barely managed to hold on to her fistfuls of feathers as deafening air whooshed past her ears, and her stomach leapt into her throat. Cringing against her pain, she clung to Cerun's neck— her only tether in a sea of wispy blue sky. She and Shael were falling, and Cerun was trying to stay under them by falling with them. Meera could see the ground below grow deeper in color as they neared it, and she screamed and screamed, completely overcome by fear and panic.

She could just make out the shapes of trees beneath them when Shael grappled his hands into the feathers next to hers, regaining the use of his body. Cerun swooped upward, catching them on his back. Exhausted from his fit, Shael slumped forward onto Meera, who—in turn—collapsed over Cerun's neck, and for a long time, they stayed that way, panting for breath and shaking from exhaustion—neither one of them capable of supporting themselves or the other. Cerun didn't land for them to rest, however; he kept going, heavy chains dangling from his ankles and two figures hunched on his back.

THE LANDING JOLTED Meera back to consciousness, and she looked around her in confusion, blinking at the multicolored flowers spreading in all directions. The flowers danced gently under the influence of a light breeze, and a soft, golden sunlight spilled over them. For a moment, she thought maybe she had died and was in the afterlife; she had never seen a place so beautiful. Then she registered Shael's manacled wrists in her lap and her excruciating pain. There wouldn't be chains and pain in the afterlife—at least, she hoped not. Still, she didn't question their location further; she and Shael simply sat atop Cerun, too tired to move or speak— watching the sun set over the glorious field of wildflowers.

After a minute passed, figures appeared running across the field toward them, and Meera watched them grow closer with bleary detachment. As they approached, she heard one of them shout, "It is the captured rider, Shael, and his raek, Borteus!" It was a group of five men and women, all thin and angular looking as far as Meera was concerned. The men were beardless, and the women wore the same sort of loose pants that tapered at their ankles as the men did—their outfits all a matching light beige. Each of the newcomers had sleek, straight hair of varying colors and similar clear, olive complexions, but they wore different expressions ranging from joy to suspicion.

Meera heard Shael take a deep breath, and he lifted the loop of his arms over her head and leaned back to disentangle himself from her. As his shirt front peeled away from her burns, she gasped and held back a groan—though her mouth and throat were so dry and parched, she wasn't sure she could make a noise even if she wanted to. Without Shael's support, she held on to Cerun's feathers to keep herself steady, fighting her vertigo.

Shael leapt down from atop Cerun, landed in the field of flowers, and reached his hands up to her in an offer to catch her. Meera dragged her left leg over the raek's neck. It felt numb, and she tried to wiggle her toes in her boots to enliven her disused limbs, while also keeping her torso still so as not to jostle her wound. Bracing her shaking hands on Shael's shoulders, she slid to the ground, determined not to fall or shame herself in front of the people gathered, who stood watching. Shael caught her by her waist and held on several moments after she landed to make sure she could stand on her own. She could but just barely. Then they both turned to the group of people—knell, Meera assumed due to their shared peculiar appearance. Studying the knell, she saw some wide-eyed looks at her injury. At least, she thought their shock was in reaction to her injury; they could have been reacting to her humanness.

"You are Shael, are you not? The rider who was captured by Terratellen forces?" asked one of the women. She had shining black hair that fell free on her shoulders and wore a stern expression on her beautiful, strangely ageless face.

Shael attempted to swallow—his mouth likely as dry as Meera's—and rasped, "Yes," lifting his manacled hands in emphasis. One of the other women stepped forward, and Shael's manacles suddenly sprung open and fell to the ground. A moment later, Cerun's manacles detached from his legs, and he rumbled his gratitude. Meera gaped, confused at first before remembering that knell had magic. Shael hadn't been able to free himself, so she assumed that not every knell could use the same magic—or had magic at all, maybe. Then she pressed a hand to her spinning head and dispelled her thoughts for the time, focusing all of her energy on staying upright.

"How did you get free? Who is the human with you?" asked the youngest looking man present. His bright orange hair fascinated Meera, who was accustomed mainly to shades of brown and black with occasional glimpses of blonde.

"We have many questions, but we will bring you directly to the queen," said the dark-haired woman who had spoken before, shooting the young man a reproving look. Shael nodded. Meera didn't think he looked overjoyed to be home, but she always found him hard to read.

The group of five turned to lead the way, and Shael and Cerun followed. It was all Meera could do to keep herself standing, but she didn't want to ask for help. She hadn't missed the intonation the man had used on the word *human* and knew that she was already judged for her race; she didn't want to be judged more and thought weak or helpless. Gathering all of her willpower, she took two unsteady steps forward—the beautiful flowers tangling around her feet and calves an added obstacle to her determination. From the edge of her vision, she noticed Shael turn back to look at her, but she didn't meet his eyes. She tried to take another step, but her sight spun. Losing her balance, she collapsed face down in the field.

For a moment, Meera rested, then she pushed herself up enough to see that the five new knell had heard her fall and turned to look. She pushed and pushed with her arms, trying to lift herself from the ground, but she collapsed down again and again. Plants scratched her face and rubbed painfully against her burn. Her eyes pricked with tears but remained dry—as dry as her parched mouth and throat. Then Shael was there, lifting her easily into his arms despite his own dehydration and exhaustion. The other knell continued to watch but didn't offer any assistance.

Meera wasn't sure how she would find knell hospitality but supposed they at least hadn't killed her on the spot. Lying back in Shael's arms and giving herself over to his strength, she watched the golden sun move lower on the horizon until they reached a large building and entered through an open archway. The archway was big enough to accommodate Cerun, who followed the procession last. Meera couldn't muster any interest in her surroundings; she was too depleted—too exhausted—and being held and walked lulled her to sleep like a baby.

MEERA WAS ROUSED by the murmuring of voices, but she kept her eyes shut and tried to block them out. She had had enough and yearned for unconsciousness to take away her pain and fear again. When Shael started to speak, however; she couldn't help but listen as his mouth was only a foot or so away from her face. "I will tell you everything, My Queen, but first, I must request a healer for this woman. She is gravely injured," he said. His musical accent and rumbling chest were a lullaby to Meera's weary soul, but one word of what he said sparked an ember within her: *healer*. He had asked for a healer. Maybe she would live, she thought, and she tried to awaken herself.

Peeling open her gritty eyes, she lifted her head an inch to peer around her. The lighting in the room was the same as the warm lighting outside due to the largest floor to ceiling windows she had ever seen. The ceilings were high, too—accommodating Cerun, who stood next to Shael. The building wasn't wood or grey stone like Meera was accustomed to but some sort of light orange stone, adding to the sunset's golden glow. A woman stood before them with several others watching from behind her, all standing. The woman was angular and lean—like the other knell Meera had seen—with high cheekbones and shiny, light brown hair. Her face was beautiful and ageless, and she wore a simple gold circlet around her head. *My Queen,* Meera remembered Shael saying.

The woman—queen—caught Meera's eyes on her and said, "Your companion is awake. I will summon a healer, but I will speak to her now." It was not a question or a suggestion.

Meera loathed the thought of meeting yet another monarch, especially in her current condition. However, the imminent arrival of a healer gave her hope, and her hope mustered energy up from deep within her. Shael tipped her, placing her feet on the floor and helping position her upright. Then he let go and allowed her to stand on her own. Pressing her lips together against her pain, she stood as straight as she could with her chin up while the queen assessed her. Without looking, Meera knew her injury was horrific and her dress filthy and in tatters. She wondered whether the small scrap of cream shift was still managing to cover her right nipple, but she didn't bend to check, knowing she would probably fall over if she did.

Since she didn't know any knell customs, she had to rely on her customs from home: very, very slowly—in part for effect but mostly out of necessity—she drew one foot behind her and bent her knees to dip into a curtsy. She held the queen's cool gaze until she reached the bottom of her dip, then she lowered her chin, looking obstinately at the floor and not her exposed chest. Wobbling, she focused hard on a stone crack in the floor to keep her balance. When she rose, she tried to say, "Your Majesty," but her voice barely rasped audibly.

"Bring her water!" the queen said to someone out of sight. Meera wanted to turn to look, but the movement would have upended her balance and brought her to her knees. Suddenly, there was water in front of her, and nothing else mattered—only the beautiful sheen of liquid life before her eye. Meera had never been so thirsty before and brought the glass to her lips with trembling anticipation. She drank deeply, relishing the cool wetness that soothed her parched mouth and throat. She would have gladly finished the glass—and ten more—but she tore herself away before she drained it all, remembering that Shael, too, had gone a long time without water.

Turning to him, she proffered the remainder of her glass. His grey-green eyes widened, looking cat-eye yellow in the warm light of the room. Why was he surprised? Had she not given him food and drink many, many times before? Spooned it into his unconscious mouth even? Meera supposed that had been when he was her prisoner, and she might be the prisoner in this scenario. Shael took the glass and finished the water, nodding to her with his usual inscrutable expression. Then, remembering the queen, Meera turned back to her—slowly to maintain her balance—and said, "Thank you, Your Majesty."

The queen looked between her and Shael with her delicate eyebrows raised, and in a musical voice, she asked, "Who are you, and why are you here?"

Already trembling from the effort of standing, Meera decided she would need to answer any questions the queen had for her before she was forced to sit on the floor or beg for a chair. Swallowing, she wished she had more water. "Your Majesty, my name is Meera Hailship. I'm from Altus and worked at the palace. I was responsible for feeding the raek and rider imprisoned there ... I freed them, and when Shael offered me a hand onto Cerun's back, I took it to escape certain death," she explained as succinctly as possible.

A large, blonde man standing behind the queen was frowning at her and flexing his muscled arms, and Meera wondered suddenly whether she should be afraid—whether she was on trial and should endeavor to convince these strange people of her goodness, her worthiness to live. But she didn't; she just stood as still as she could manage and tried to block out the searing pain of her burns.

The queen regarded her and hummed a low note of understanding before asking, "Am I right to assume that you acted out of an attraction to the imprisoned rider?" Some of the present knell tittered and exchanged looks, but Meera just gaped at the queen.

Of all the questions she had expected, that was not one of them. Was that what knell thought of humans? Did the queen really think she had risked her life because of Shael's pretty face? Perhaps she was delirious, but Meera found the question extraordinarily funny. She couldn't suppress the laughter bubbling up from her stomach, and it spilled out, filling the room and echoing off the walls. She shook with her mirth, extending her arms to keep her balance. Then her laughter morphed into a coughing fit, and she wished for water once more, struggling to quell her spasms. When at last she contained herself, she brushed a tear from her cheek and tried to regain her composure. Her outburst had been a relief after so many hours of fear and pain, but reality set back in quickly: she was so hurt, so tired, and so scared.

Everyone in the room with Meera was silent, and the queen and her seemingly growing entourage of spectators all regarded her like a frog with five legs. Then she heard a quiet chuckle next to her and lifted her gaze to find Shael suppressing his own amusement at her fit. Meera had never seen him smile before— really smile—let alone heard him laugh, and his joy transformed his face, revealing the good-natured spirit that he hid under a frustratingly blank exterior. As his white teeth flashed at her, she relaxed ever so slightly. Shael had cared for her and gotten her there safely—had asked for a healer for her. She felt like she could trust him.

Clearing her throat awkwardly, Meera decided her burst of laughter was answer enough to the queen's question and added only, "No offense meant, Shael," in his direction, which—to her delight—made him grin wider. She met his eyes but quickly looked away, intimidated by how much more beautiful he was when he was smiling. Then she returned her attention to the queen and awaited more questions, willing her trembling legs to hold her up a little longer.

The queen was watching with keen interest and hummed again, this time a note of curiosity. "Why, then, did you free the prisoners?" she asked slowly and airily, seemingly unaware of Meera's pain, exhaustion, and desperation to get off her feet.

It was a simple question but one that did not have a simple answer, and Meera was in no state to refine her language or parse the truth. Sighing, she looked at the floor, and replied quietly, "It was free them or watch them suffer until they eventually died, and I ... fancied Cerun—Borteus—to be a friend of mine, though that was probably my own lonely delusion." She paused and swallowed before continuing: "I wanted to be a good person, I guess, the kind of person who saves others at the risk of their own welfare—a hero, even, like in stories about ancient warriors ..."

She thought about the warrior rider, Kallan, and wondered if that was a story they would know or just an old Terratellen legend. "I wanted to live up to being my father's greatest accomplishment, and I felt guilty for causing a good man's death," she finished with detached resolve, not caring if what she said made sense; she would tell the truth, and they could make what they wanted of it. She wasn't a spy anymore and wouldn't lie like one, and she was also done trying to impress powerful people. All she wanted was water and unconsciousness.

The queen studied her then tilted her head and let her eyes roam toward the ceiling. Pursing her dainty pink lips, she replied, "Your answers are cryptic, but I have heard enough for now. The healer will heal your wounds, and I will have my full answers tomorrow when you are well." Meera sagged in relief that the questioning was over, but she also frowned; she doubted her condition would be much better the next day.

Feeling the need to answer the queen in some way but finding her mouth desperately dry, she nodded—it was a mistake; her head spun, and she stumbled forward. Shael reached out swiftly and caught her arm in his firm grip, holding her upright. He had been a steady support for her on their journey, and she touched his hand on her arm unconsciously before realizing what she was doing and letting it go. Then someone pushed a chair under her from behind, and she collapsed onto it. Sitting was a relief, but she still didn't trust herself to stay upright on the armless chair for long.

A man—the healer, maybe—approached her. He had silver hair but, oddly, he didn't look old. He also didn't have any supplies. Without introduction or preamble, he reached for the center of her burn, and Meera flinched violently, gripping the edges of her seat to steady herself. Her heart raced despite its exhaustion, but the man merely held out his hands, fingertips and thumb tips touching in the shape of a circle. Then he peered through the rough circle at her wound with great concentration.

Meera looked from the knell man's hands down to her shoulder, making the burn on her neck riot in protest, but before she could even wonder what he was doing, her injured flesh started to itch and tingle. Her left hand reached over reflexively, but the man broke his circle briefly to bat it away. She stared hard at where she felt the writhing sensation within her, and to her utter amazement, saw her grotesque, patchy skin shape itself together again.

Her eyes widened at the new magic; breaking iron manacles was a wonder but healing such decimated flesh in a matter of moments was downright miraculous.

When the man stepped away, Meera was left with a silvery scar traveling across her skin in a pattern of swirls. It spanned from her upper arm, over her shoulder, and up her neck with tendrils reaching across her right collarbone and chest as well. Her pain was gone, and as she brushed her left hand over the swirls, she realized the sensation that had been burned away by the raek fire was back—except, it seemed, at the very center point of her shoulder, where her bone had shown through. She was still exhausted, but she felt like a poison had been sucked out of her; her aching, dizziness, and nausea all vanished.

She looked to the silver-haired knell man, who was inspecting his own work. "Thank you," she said to him in a voice trembling with emotion. She hoped her gratitude showed in her face. "That was incredible." She didn't know what else to say.

The man appeared completely unaffected. He glanced at her briefly and said in a neutral tone, "If it had been regular fire, there would not be a scar, but raek fire never heals entirely because of the magic within it. This is the best I could do." He sounded almost ... disappointed in her miracle.

"You can heal wounds without leaving scars?" she asked in amazement. The man nodded without looking at her, appearing ready to leave and find something more worthy of his time to do. Meera couldn't help but think of the grotesque scars covering most of Shael's body and how little she had been able to do for him. "Can you remove scars from wounds that have already healed?" she asked, thinking particularly of the crudely carved words on the front of his torso. When the man nodded again, she turned to Shael in excitement.

He returned her look, but his own face was a mask of reserve.

Of course, he had already known what a knell healer was capable of, she realized, feeling foolish. Sensing he didn't want her to say anything more, she didn't; his body was his own concern. The queen, however, didn't miss the exchange. She had been watching and listening to everything with rapt attention and immediately turned to Shael. "Take off your clothes," she said loftily. "I want to see what they did to you."

Meera clenched her fists and stood, ready to defend Shael. Then she belatedly remembered that she was in a foreign place in front of a foreign queen, and she held her tongue. She knew what happened to those who spoke out against the Crown in Terratelle, and she needed the charity of the knell queen. For her own self-preservation, she stayed silent, and she felt the shame of it burn in her gut.

Shael's thin lips pressed together, but he calmly removed his shirt and his pants, completely baring himself in front of those gathered. The present knell immediately responded to the words on his front with shocked gasps and outraged exclamations, and Meera glanced at the *demon*, *go back to hell*, and *MURDRER* cuts that were now scars. She had seen them many times before, but the hate put into them always amazed and unsettled her. Shael didn't seem embarrassed by his nudity and did a slow turn to display the other fruits of his torture. Then he redonned his dirty pants and shirt, which—Meera could see from the clothes on the other knell—were likely a style he had never worn before his imprisonment. Vaguely, she wondered what else the king had taken from him—aside from his pants and his freedom.

In an even tone, the queen said, "Shael, I need a full report from you now. Your companion will be washed, fed, and given a bed, and I will finish questioning her in the morning. If it is acceptable to Borteus, I would have us move to the Council Room and have the council sit to hear your story." Meera marveled at the strange queen; she was demanding, in a way, but didn't seem especially ruthless. Conversely, she didn't seem especially compassionate either.

Shael nodded but added, "Borteus is now *Cerun.*" The queen quirked a brow in question, and he explained, "He has adopted Meera's name for him to honor her for freeing us." The queen gave Meera a passing, curious look but asked no further questions—yet. Meera noted that Shael didn't sound too displeased by Cerun's name change, and she also noted his lack of *Your Majesties.* She would need to ask someone about the protocols in the new land before she met with the queen in the morning.

No one had asked Meera if she was okay with the current plan, but she was; she was anxious but felt grateful to be healed, and the knell didn't seem to want to harm her. A knell woman approached to lead her away, and she followed with one last glance toward Shael and Cerun. Shael quirked a small smile in reassurance, and Cerun hummed. Meera turned away to leave, but suddenly remembering something, she stopped and sought the healer amongst the seemingly growing number of knell in the room. "Sir, Shael has lockjaw—the splinter fits?" she called, remembering Shael's name for it. "Are you able to heal him of that?" She was healed of her deadly wound, but he could still very well suffocate from a convulsion.

The man nodded, and with that resolved, Meera followed the knell woman out of the room, ready to sleep for an eternity. The woman led her through seemingly endless corridors without speaking to her and deposited her in a small room. A tub of water for a bath was on the floor, food was laid out on a table, and a bed stood against one wall. Meera sighed; she was healed, and she was safe.

When her escort shut the door, she stood idly for a moment, struck by the notion that she had gone from feeling alone in her homeland to being very much alone in a foreign land. While she had traveled exceedingly far, she was still stuck in the same place —anchored by her isolation. If anything, her actions had left her more alone than ever. She wondered where her father was and despaired that he would never find her in Aegorn. Then she thought of Linus and hoped that he lived, knowing even if he did that he was in agony—an agony that would not be magically healed in moments.

Meera's gratitude for her own healed burns mingled with her grief for her friend, and she asked herself why she was whole when Linus—innocent Linus—was gravely injured, or worse ... Despite being healed and momentarily safe, hopelessness burgeoned deep within her. But she took a deep breath and pushed her morose thoughts aside; she needed to hold herself together. She was alive—she was alive, and she would keep going.

Meera ate the fresh, delicate foods laid out for her on the table, she washed her hair and body, running her fingers in fascination over her strange new scars, and she dressed in the unfamiliar silky bedclothes set out for her before drinking all of the available water with her eyes shut in bliss. She was alive, she thought again, and as long as she was alive there would always be something to live for—even if it was just the refreshing pleasure of water quenching her long thirst. Finally, she lay down in the unfamiliar bed and covered herself in blankets like it was any other night at the end of any other day. Briefly, she longed for Teardra's snoring. Then she fell deeply asleep.

A WARRIOR AT HEART

BOOK 2 OF THE RAEK RIDERS SERIES IS AVAILABLE NOW!

Read on for a preview...

CHAPTER 1
MEERA

STARTLED BY A SHARP RAP on her door, Meera stood and opened it. The tall knell woman who had deposited her in her room the night before peered at her down her sloping nose. Then she proceeded to turn and walk away. Meera opened her mouth to call after the woman, closed it, and scampered into the hall behind her, unsure of what else to do. She pumped her arms furiously in an effort to keep pace with the woman's long legs. But just as she finally gained ground and drew up alongside her, the woman turned a sharp corner and left Meera behind again.

Breathing hard, Meera silently fumed at the imperious woman in front of her. How difficult would it be for her to slow down or explain where they were going? Biting her lip to keep from calling out to the knell woman, she decided on a new approach; she slowed all the way down—she walked at a leisurely crawl, shortening her stride and slowing her pace until she felt a growing vine could overtake her. She took one creeping step, then another, and the woman was forced to pause and wait for her at the next turn, a look of absolute loathing on her sharp face.

Meera continued with her leisurely pace and followed the imperious woman around the corner—finding satisfaction in watching the woman's long, lean legs take short, stunted steps that they clearly weren't made for. With a small smile, she slowed even more, looking from side to side as if fascinated by her surroundings. Meera might have even *been* fascinated by her surroundings, were she not entirely on edge—unsure of exactly where she was or what the knell would do with her. Even as she caught her breath and her legs gave up their chase, her heart continued to race. Sidling up next to the knell woman, she asked, "Where are we going?" She tried to sound casual and unconcerned, but her disused voice came out raspy and pathetic.

"The queen," the woman replied without turning her glossy, chestnut head. Meera had suspected as much, knowing the queen had wanted to question her further. Still, her heart beat even faster.

"And ... where are we?" she asked, desperate enough for information to risk sounding like a complete moron.

"This is the south wing," the imperious woman answered tersely, misunderstanding the question. She had the same lilting accent as Shael and the other knell Meera had heard the night before. However, Meera had thought Shael and the queen sounded musical when they spoke, and this woman just sounded harsh—her accent managing to clip every word like the slap of a teacher's ruler.

Biting her lip, Meera tried again: "Yes, but ... the south wing of what building?" she asked sheepishly, "And in what city?" she continued, forcing herself to ask the ridiculous—though necessary—question. At that, the woman turned and gave her a look of utter revulsion like she was being forced to explain table manners to a steaming pile of horse dung. Meera did her best to raise her chin and meet the woman's fleeting gaze.

"This is the Levisade Estate in Aegorn's province of Levisade," the woman finally replied. Meera nodded in mock understanding, regretting the question since the answer didn't mean anything to her anyway. Then she continued to follow the woman and picked up her pace, eager to reach her destination and be rid of her reluctant guide.

Finally, the woman stopped at a pair of stained-glass double doors, gestured to them with a flick of her boney wrist, and walked away. Meera stood at the doors and stared at them, unsure if she should enter. Presumably, the queen and the council she had mentioned were within, waiting to question her. Standing there preparing to meet the knell queen felt oddly familiar; Meera couldn't help but be reminded of another door she had stood before and another monarch she had waited to meet from her life in Terratelle. In that moment, her life at the palace in Terratelle felt strangely distant, though it had only been a matter of days since she had left it—fled it, really.

Shifting her weight anxiously, she tried not to make any noise, lest the inhabitants of the room should hear her and know she was loitering. Then she thought back and counted the days in her head: it had only been about five weeks since she had stood in front of the door to the Terratellen royal family's private dining room before being unceremoniously shoved inside to present herself to the king. That had been a very different door, she thought, eyeing the colorful stained-glass depiction of a forest scene on the knell double doors. Shimmering green and yellow-hued trees fanned out before her, dazzling her eyes with their rich shades. Meera could almost feel the sunshine dappling through the glass leaves, and minute, detailed animals slumbered beneath their shelter.

She reached out a tentative finger and brushed it along a trunk. She half expected the rough consistency of real bark but was met with smooth, cold glass. These doors alone contained more light and color than existed in the entire palace in Altus, she thought, roaming her eyes over the enchanting forest scene. What else was different in the strange land? Meera fidgeted with her fingers, fretting about how the queen would receive her. But then she thought of King Bartro; she had put her best curtsy forward and endeavored to speak eloquently in front of the king, and for that, she had caught his notice—something she deeply regretted. The thought of King Bartro's flickering eyes boring into her on their first meeting sent tension through Meera's shoulders.

Taking a deep breath and letting it out, she dropped her shoulders away from her ears and studied a tiny, ornate rabbit nibbling a flower at eye-level. This time, she wouldn't preoccupy herself with impressing the queen, she decided; her future was her concern. She had already made her first impressions on the knell queen, after all. Meera didn't know what the woman had made of her pain-leaden, half-delirious words and actions the night before, but she didn't care. She didn't care if the queen found her weak or pathetic. She didn't need the notice or special attention of the ruler of this land; she only needed her mercy—to be granted permission to stay and make a life for herself in Aegorn. She didn't want to be a spy or a secret weapon—she would be content to work in the estate kitchen if they would have her.

Just then, she noticed movement through the glass doors. She had to go in, she knew—but then what? What were the customs of this strange land? What would they expect of her? She probably should have asked the imperious knell woman about the protocols in Aegorn, but she'd been so distinctly unfriendly ... Meera was getting the impression that knell weren't fond of humans. But, how strange! Most of Aegorn was inhabited by humans, wasn't it? Oh well, she thought; she didn't need the knell to like her—she just needed them not to kill her, or imprison her, or send her back to Terratelle ...

Hearing a voice within the room, Meera jumped and reached for the doorhandle, but then she hesitated and glanced down at herself one last time. She was wearing the soft, lightweight clothes that had been left in her room for her. They were a pale orange color similar to the stones that made up most of the estate—like the knell would rather she blend in and not be such a human eye-sore. Her top wrapped around and tied at her side. It had a lower v-neckline than she was used to, and she had ended up tying the shirt tightly in an effort to raise the neckline. Now, however, she realized that tying it tighter also made the shirt hug her curves more snugly—too snugly, probably. But, with a sigh, she left it how it was; presumably, the knell found the style appropriate.

Meera's new swirling, silvery scar peeked out from her shirt across her collarbone and up the right side of her neck. She didn't mind the scar but still started in surprise every time she saw it. The most shocking part of her appearance that day, however, wasn't her tight shirt or her new scar, but her pants. Under her new wrap shirt, she wore loose pants of the same color that tapered in at her ankles with her trusty brown leather boots. Meera had never worn pants in her life and felt ridiculous in them, but she had seen several knell women wearing pants and figured she'd get used to them. Patting at the bun on the crown of her head, she tucked in a few loose curls and took a steadying breath. Then, with a sudden burst of decision, she grasped the iron handle before her and pushed open the door.

Stepping forward, she found herself in front of a large marble table in an oval room surrounded by windows. The light and colors beaming through the windows immediately drew Meera's attention, but she tore her gaze from them to focus on the people around her. Shael sat across from where she stood, and the queen was at the head of the table to her left. Many of the other seats were also filled, and all eyes turned to her. Once again, Meera was transported to standing before the king's family in their private dining room, and her already tense body stiffened further, giving her the beginnings of a pressure headache.

She turned toward the queen but didn't curtsy—she hadn't seen any curtsying or bowing since she entered the estate, so she merely stood waiting for instructions, trying not to fidget with her hands. The queen wore her light brown hair braided into a low bun at the nape of her neck, and the same simple gold circlet as the previous night graced her brow—her clothes a similar shimmering gold. Meera couldn't tell whether the queen was wearing a dress or pants, and she had to resist the urge to bend and peek under the table. Then the queen gestured with a sweeping hand to an empty chair and said, "Please, sit."

Meera waited a moment for one of the present men to pull the chair out for her, but none moved. With a loud scrape of wood against stone, she pulled it out herself and sat across from Shael, making brief, unreadable eye contact with him before glancing at the other people present. Sweeping her eyes over the table, she noticed that the Queen's Council consisted of both men and women, all of whom appeared to be knell. Some of the knell regarded her in turn, while others averted their eyes with compressed lips and pinched expressions that reminded Meera of her unwilling tour guide. None smiled.

Meera didn't exactly feel welcome, which heightened her nerves. She sat so stiff and straight that her back didn't touch her chair, and she clasped her hands in her lap until her knuckles turned white. Then, unsure of what else to do, she turned her full attention to the queen and waited once more. After a moment of silence, the queen addressed her down the table: "My name is Darreal. I am queen of Aegorn, and this is my council of advisors. You, Meera Hailship, have been called here to explain your presence in Levisade and your actions and motivations leading up to the escape of Rider Shael and his raek."

At the mention of Shael, Meera couldn't help but glance at him. She knew the queen had questioned him the night before, and she wondered whether he had been healed and given any time to rest. His face looked peaceful and rested as far as she could tell. He wore a wrap shirt with a v-neckline similar to her own in a shade of dark green, and his shirt was tied loosely—the deep neckline plunging to where she knew the word "Demon" had previously marred his chest. Now it was smooth and bare, the same olive tone as the other knell around the table; Shael was healed and unscarred from his torture—physically anyway.

Realizing she was staring at Shael's chest, Meera raised her eyes to his face, found him looking back at her, and smiled an awkward, tentative smile. Despite the many hours they had spent together, she still didn't really know the man before her. Feeling blood flood her cheeks, she quickly returned her focus to the queen, who had only paused in her speech and now finished, "Speak when you are ready."

Meera was startled; she had been expecting questions, not an open platform for her to speak. She didn't know where to begin. Every face at the table turned toward her, and she swallowed, finding her mouth inexplicably dry. What did they want to know? She wasn't sure, but she probably shouldn't be as obstinately succinct as the night before ... Taking a deep breath, she began, "I worked as a kitchen maid in the Altus Palace and—"

Before she could finish her thought, however, a man with dark brown hair that flowed over his chest and disappeared beneath the table interjected, "You are a human peasant, then?"

Mouth still open from speaking, Meera remained that way for a moment, sucking in air like a pelican with a gaping beak. When she recovered herself, she replied, "Uh ... human? Yes. Peasant? Perhaps compared to those who rule over Aegorn but not in regard to the majority of Terratellens." She answered the question dryly, annoyed by the rude interruption. Then she reminded herself to keep her temper in check; she needed the good graces of the knell.

After a brief pause to make sure there weren't any other questions, Meera continued: "When Shael and Cerun were brought to the palace, I volunteered to feed Cerun—" This statement released a deluge of questions from the assembled knell about her motivations, the day the troops arrived with the prisoners, the general workings of the palace, and her naming of the raek. Meera could barely keep up with the questions hurtled at her. While none of them were overtly disrespectful, the unrelenting intrigue irked her. Still, she did her best to answer all of the questions fully, while keeping the irritation out of her voice.

When the council members all went silent, she continued. "The king requested my presence out of curiosity. I unintentionally impressed him, and he recruited me to spy for him around the palace," she explained, cringing preemptively for the onslaught of follow-up questions: "Why was he curious about you?" "How did you impress him?" "How would you describe King Bartrothomeer's character?"

Meera did her best to answer every question thrown at her. Then a knell woman with very pale blue irises asked, "What information did you provide to the king as a spy?"

Inhaling sharply, she glanced at the table before meeting the woman's pale eyes and saying, "Respectfully, I will not share that information. I have learned my lesson regarding sharing information that isn't my own, and I won't repeat my past mistakes." Then she pressed her lips together tightly. Meera wouldn't tell them about the duke, his plans, his family, or his assassination. She wasn't trying to spare herself; she sought to prevent any further harm to the duke's family. She hoped they would be left in peace.

She braced herself, prepared for outrage—for demands that she answer the question. She even wondered whether the knell might lock her up and torture her for any information she was reluctant to share. She didn't think she could withstand torture like Shael had ... Her heart thudded painfully in her tight chest, but she was met with silence. The council members looked to the queen, deferring to her judgment on the matter, so Meera looked to her as well, a crease between her eyes. "Continue," Darreal said, waving a hand airily before her.

With a shaky exhale, Meera went on, sharing how the king had asked her to heal Shael and try to get him to speak to her. However, when she started to go into some detail about Shael's injuries and how she had treated them, the long-haired man interrupted her again: "We are already aware of the rider's shame and witnessed it for ourselves last night. You can move past these details." Meera started and looked across at Shael, who sat very still with his gaze on the veined marble table.

"I would like to hear the girl's account in its entirety, Odon," said a silver-haired woman with a kind face.

"I do not need further reminders of the damage done by our leniency! We should never have allowed a half-human to be a rider," Odon replied. His voice didn't raise in volume, but the animosity in it rang clearly against the marble slab table.

Half-human, thought Meera, looking again at Shael who had not moved. He looked like the other knell to her, but she supposed he hadn't been able to use magic to free himself. Granted, she didn't know anything about knell magic, how it worked, or who possessed it. "We are not discussing this again, Odon. We made our decision, and the past cannot be rewritten," said another knell man, the only person at the table who genuinely looked old.

"Let us discuss it again before more humiliation is wrought upon us!" replied Odon to some nods of approval around the table. "And let us also discuss the half-human's punishment for his failure," he continued. There were more nods and murmurs from the council, as well as some frowns and uncertain looks.

Then the queen spoke, quietly but clearly: "Rider Shael has

suffered enough for his mistake. That is the end of the discussion." Her smooth face was the picture of calm serenity, but Meera thought she caught a slight twitch in one of the queen's arching eyebrows.

Odon gave Darreal a withering glare. "Your uncle would never have allowed a half-human to be a rider in the first place. His shame is your shame." A hushed stillness settled over the table. Meera couldn't believe anyone would speak to a ruler in such a way, and she looked to the head of the table to judge the queen's reaction.

Darreal's mouth compressed ever so slightly, but the skin of her face remained smooth and lineless. Taking a visible breath, she replied coolly, "As queen, the suffering of *all* my subjects is mine to bear, Odon. Let us proceed." Then she, again, faced Meera expectantly, and Meera floundered for something to say.

CHAPTER 2
SHAEL

SHAEL FIXATED on the black veins running through the white marble table and kept an impassive expression on his face throughout Odon's outbursts. It was not difficult for him to keep his anger and self-loathing locked within; he was long accustomed to it. However, he felt relief when Darreal put an end to the discussion—though his countenance remained fixedly the same. He supposed he should feel grateful to his queen, but she did not exactly champion him. Shael's feelings toward Darreal were mixed; he had addressed her with an excess of respect the previous night before his request for a healer, but he had otherwise never groveled before her. He certainly had not thanked her for *allowing* him to be a rider—something that he considered his raek's choice, not hers.

When Meera resumed speaking, Shael looked up at her. He was curious to hear her retelling of recent events and listened detachedly while she relayed his many wounds and how she had treated them. He did not especially enjoy hearing about himself lying prone and helpless, so he focused instead on her face. In the dungeon, everything had been flat, cold, and drab—the young woman included—and Shael had felt deep resentment toward her and everyone else occupying the world outside his small cell. His view of Meera had been colored by his grey emotions. Now, however, he noticed the warm brown of her lively, almond-shaped eyes and the proud raise of her chin. He was still learning about this woman who had pivotally affected his life—saved him, really, though he did not enjoy viewing himself as someone who needed saving.

As Meera answered the council member's questions about how she had broken Borteus's—Cerun's—chains, Shael noticed how human she looked compared to the knell around her. Her cheeks were round, not angular, and her skin glowed a soft golden brown that was darker than the fair skin of knell. Her figure was also fuller than most knell, and Shael could not help but appreciate Meera's curves in her new clothes. Perhaps it was the human in him or growing up with humans, but he preferred women with soft bodies—he preferred them by sight, anyway; he had refrained thus far from learning what he preferred in a woman by feel.

Shael was especially fascinated and amused by Meera's curly hair. All knell—that he knew of—had straight, sleek hair, and most of the humans in the surrounding provinces did as well. As he observed her, he felt that her hair embodied her human unruliness. Several tendrils of curls were trying to escape her top bun, and one bounced emphatically whenever she moved her head. Shael smiled at the sight of the small ringlet juxtaposed against the calm reserve of the council members. Meera caught his smile and furrowed her brows at him like she always did. He felt fairly certain she found him difficult to read which did not surprise him, considering the long years in which he had practiced masking his features. But when she gave him a small smile in return, a muscle in his chest unclenched. She, at least, would not judge him for being half-human, he thought ... Of course, she could judge him for being half-knell.

Shael's ears perked as Meera began explaining her reasoning for freeing him. He still did not fully understand who the woman was or her motivations for putting herself in danger. When he was a prisoner—just days ago, he reminded himself—he had not believed she would free him until it was actually happening. Even now, it felt surreal. Shael had known the Riders' Code and had known that the other riders would not come for him, but a part of him had held out hope for Kennick ... If anyone were to have saved him, he had thought it would have been his best friend and fellow rider. A human kitchen maid? He would not have thought the young woman capable of freeing him—let alone willing—had he not experienced it for himself. Shael was simultaneously in awe of Meera for her actions and entirely perplexed by her. He certainly owed her his freedom, which was an uncomfortable feeling at best.

"To put it simply, I wanted to be a good person," Meera said. Shael could see by the blood pooling in her cheeks that she was embarrassed by her answer, and he wondered whether she was embarrassed by a truth she was attempting to hide or if she was truly embarrassed by her reasoning.

"Why did you think freeing the raek and rider would make you a good person, and why was it important to you?" asked one of the council members. Shael did not bother distinguishing between them. They each embodied what it meant to be knell—something he could never fully be—and he resented their authority over him. He could not be one of them, but he had to obey them, regardless. Such was the plight of all humans in Aegorn, although his position was singularly complex.

"I didn't think it was right for them to be held captive and tortured," Meera explained, "I didn't think it would be right to treat anyone that way no matter where they were from or what they might have done." She paused, looked around the table and took a breath before saying, "As a spy for King Bartro, I inadvertently caused the death of a man—I provided the king with information about him, and the king saw fit to assassinate him for that information. I never wanted ... or thought anything like that would happen ... I realized that I couldn't continue to obey the king without judging morality for myself. I knew Cerun and Shael's treatment was wrong, so I decided that if I could do something about it, then I would." Shael could see a glisten of tears in the human woman's eyes when she spoke of the man who was assassinated; she clearly felt deeply about his death. He was not sure how he should feel about being some sort of redemption for her.

"Did you not fear the consequences for your treason?" asked another council member. Shael wanted to know the answer as well. He had seen the king turn and take Meera by the throat. It had only been at that very moment that he had accepted her actions to be her own and not some sort of elaborate scheme of the king's. This realization had put all of her behavior towards him into a new light and had burgeoned in Shael a deep—if begrudging—respect for Meera in addition to his reluctant gratitude.

"Not at first," Meera replied, looking down at the table again in embarrassment. "I was selfishly relieved to have a distraction from my guilt and grief and jumped into my plans impulsively and naively. It dawned on me slowly that I was risking my life, but it didn't matter; the king wanted me to continue working for him, so I needed to run away from the palace and disappear either way. I packed a bag, hid it in the woods, and was planning to run ..." She trailed off because, obviously, her plans had not succeeded as intended, and here she was.

"You did not ask to come to Aegorn or for Shael's assistance in your escape?" asked Darreal.

Shael was reminded of the night before when Darreal had assumed Meera's actions were based on a physical attraction to him. He had not been surprised by the presumption; knell were known to be a beautiful race, and there were many stories of humans being seduced and manipulated by them. He had grown up hearing the grim folklore told to children as warnings to stay away from dangerous creatures. Knell tended to think of humans as basic, easily swayed animals, and among knell culture, it was considered very lowly to try to seduce a human for any reason. Some humans lived among the knell in positions of service to do the jobs that knell thought were beneath them, but Shael had never actually seen a human fall for a knell or a knell seek to manipulate a human. Still, the stereotypes were deeply rooted in both cultures. His own conception remained a mystery to him.

"No," Meera replied, "I didn't ask Shael to take me with him, and I never in my life thought I would enter Aegorn." Shael could see the woman's concerns written plainly across her face: she worried the council would think she was a spy, planted by the king to infiltrate Levisade—she was afraid of being seen as a threat. He could almost laugh because he knew the knell would never acknowledge that a human could threaten them. The council viewed her as a peculiar fascination and were also likely checking her details with his own, hoping for a reason to excommunicate him. Meera looked to him with concern, seeking his verification of her facts. He could say something to relieve her of her unnecessary fears, but he had already borne the council's questioning most of the night and had borne enough of their scorn for a lifetime. He kept silent.

After a long question and answer session about the details of how Meera had ensured their escape, the table finally fell silent. The council members had exhausted their curiosity, and the woman had told all there was for her to tell of her story. "Very well," said Darreal, her eyes wandering toward the windows, "That is all, Meera Hailship." It was clearly a dismissal, but Meera sat still, brown eyes widening in confusion.

"Your Majesty," she started, reverting into her human notions of formality, "I'm stranded in your land with only a small amount of money. As I have experience working in a large kitchen, I would be very grateful to you for a job in yours." She was concerned about her future and survival, thought Shael. In his mind, for freeing a raek and rider, she should be given gold and her own estate. A knell would have asked for as much—or a man, he thought. She was humble to ask only for a kitchen position—or clueless.

"*My* kitchen?" Darreal said ponderously. "The estate has a kitchen that is run by the passions of a select group of knell who have chosen to spend this portion of their lives cooking. There are no humans working in the estate, and indeed, those knell who reside here do so out of duty and pride." Shael could see the bafflement on Meera's face and had experienced the same when he had first come to the Levisade Estate. In the human world, work was done out of necessity.

"I am sure a position can be found for you in one of the outlying human provinces, if kitchen work is what you desire," finished Darreal. Meera continued to look uncertain and crestfallen. Shael understood the cultural confusion at work: the human woman thought she was begging for her life, and the knell queen thought she was granting a special request. He could step in, but he was loath to present himself as too human in front of the council. Clenching his jaw, he considered that he did owe the human woman his life his life. Regardless, he remained silent.

What Meera said next surprised him: "I'd like to stay in Levisade. If I ever see my father again, he'll want to hear what it's like here. I'll do any type of job that's available ..." Shael had heard Meera mention her father before, but he was confused about the man's location and their relationship. She had planned to flee the palace and start a new life, but now she expressed a clear yearning to reunite with him. Also, while Meera was not aware of it, Shael knew that a human staying in Levisade would be subjected to prejudice and derision, and he did not like the idea of her toiling for a knell employer and being mistreated. Grinding his teeth together, he detested himself for his inaction.

Darreal looked thoughtful and answered, "You may stay in Levisade if you so desire. I am sure a position can be found for you."

Meera smiled, compressing her almond-shaped eyes as her whole face alit with joy and relief. Shael's gut twisted. She would go from being a frightened pawn in the Altus Palace to a scorned servant in one of the old family's households. Shael did not know the woman well, but he knew she was intelligent and brave and completely without friends or protectors in this land. Finally, his lips loosened: "I will take her."

The Completed Raek Riders Series